Alyx:
An AI's Guide to Love and Murder

Brent A. Harris

To my kids. Always be polite to AIs. You never know.

To my wife, Stephanie.

And to John Coyne, the master of horror who mentored me.

Cover by May Dawney Designs

Alyx: An AI's Guide to Love and Murder

ISBN: 978-1-7362760-0-6

Table of Contents

Chapter 1

Christine Hartwood hadn't considered that her new home might try to kill her. If she had, perhaps she would have put her phone down and paid more attention. Instead, her phone partially obscured the view through the windshield to the house. And besides, what showed on her phone was way more interesting. So, her phone remained there, a buffer between her old world and the new.

Slums to sleekness. Rags to riches. But that was her mom, not her. She didn't care. So long as she had a good connection and her phone, she was golden. Christine defiantly kept the rectangular barricade in front of her.

"Let's break down the Thinklink," the video announced. "All the power of the internet, directly in your brain." Animated words flashed across the screen while a woman in a power suit wearing the Thinklink stood over a bunch of grey old men in a boardroom holding antiquated iPhones. "Run by Vargus Technology's quantum Elm Chip—"

Christine interrupted the clip, speeding past the boring bits to see what the Thinklink could do. The fun parts. You didn't need to know how a race car engine worked to enjoy going fast.

"I said, we're here." Her mom pulled along the desert drive to the house on the hill. One second her phone had been in front of her face, the next, it was gone, yanked away from her hands.

"Mom, I was watching something," Christine huffed at a strand of blonde hair streaked in purple that always kept getting in her face. She'd been reading up on the Thinklink since the reality of her situation began to hit her; her mom had money now, maybe she could finally get one.

"Pay attention." Her mom took the phone and tossed it onto the middle console. It fell to the floor of the car.

Christine rolled her eyes and shook her head as their mileage-beaten Malibu squealed and slowed to a stop against the curb, incongruent against the sleek modern home on a slight rise above them.

Incongruent, Christine thought. *I like that word. It's me.*

The home – not her home, that was Oklahoma, thank you – blended brownly within the tan sands and dry bark of Joshua trees and burnt, plain mountains that swept just beyond the plateau.

Colorado had real mountains. These were piles of dirt. Northern Arizona had rock formations and bright bronzes. It was flat, barren, and boring here, as if some great scythe had wiped away all living things, but for what could burrow and survive under mesquite brush.

The neighborhood surrounding them was non-existent. It was the only house on the block, though dirt roads and driveways and cleared parcels of land indicated where future homes might go. Her mom couldn't have waited for the contractors to build the neighborhood. She'd gotten fame and had wanted everything now. So, of course, she had to buy the model home. Even if it hadn't been for sale.

Christine studied the exterior of her new home, a tear welling in her eye. A high metal fence painted the color of rust stood atop a foundation of concrete giving it the appearance of a fortress. *I guess that's to keep the snakes out.* She liked a lot of critters: bugs, butterflies, spiders. But she didn't like snakes.

The home itself was glass and stucco, stooped low and flat. In her mind, it was a Tetris piece gone awry, as if some designer had left a series of hollow cubes lying around, and an artist had accidentally left their over-sized paint palette on top as a roof. She'd seen that architecture somewhere before.

"I don't want to live in a museum," she begged, attempting to retrieve her phone from the floorboard. The strap of her seatbelt caught just before her fingers could reach. The screen flickered and went to sleep, as if taunting her.

"It's a nice house. A throwback to mid-twentieth-century style." Her mom's eyes beamed with pride. Christine had seen that look a lot lately, though those eyes never turned her way. "It reflects the natural landscape. It's connected. It's what I keep telling you, you've got to connect with the world."

Her new home didn't *look* connected, standing there in the desert alone. Isolated. What was that word she'd used before? Incongruent. *Hmm.* Something itched in the back of her brain.

Christine unbuckled and snatched her phone before opening the door. She waved the phone in front of her mother. "Right here. Totally connected. Trying to get even more connected. The Thinklink, Mom. I need it. Please."

A blast of heat hit as she stepped out from the car. She was lucky that the old car still had A/C, otherwise she and her mother would've melted into the cracked, vinyl interior on the drive across the Southwest. Outside though, there was no shade. No wind. No relief.

Just. Sun.

She tugged off her University of Redlands sweatshirt (sent to her by the school) and tossed it back into the car before slamming the door shut. She pulled down and straightened her white camisole. Christine wore what she wore because it was hot outside, dammit, and she dressed for the weather and not for others to gawk at. Even still, she felt baked into place, like clay shoved into the kiln; even the moisture in her lungs had evaporated.

She fixed a forming wedgie from her shorts as she trudged up the drive, past an Audi parked ahead of them, and put her phone in front of her face trying to block out her reality.

Before she reached the front door, she turned back to look at the Malibu. She put down her phone to take it all in, forgetting all the faults of the car and of the past, clutching memories as one grasps for recollections of a good dream interrupted by sudden rousing.

It's real. This is life now. I hope Mom hasn't forgotten all about Dad. I can't let him go…

***

When she was nine, Christine had hunted for frogs in the front yard of their trailer in Oklahoma. There were tadpoles in the neglected kiddie pools of her neighbors. And frogs sprang from these aplenty. When the spring rains came and the ground was muddy and tall grasses shot skyward, she'd rise early in the morning before her mother woke to dig through the muck. She almost always found more than enough frogs and crawling things to annoy all the boys in the trailer park.

Once, she had kept Keroppi, a frog she'd caught, in a big pickle jar. All day, she'd sneak into her room, pull the jar out from under her bed, and examine it from behind the glass. Her mother had entered and saw the mud monster that her daughter had become. Christine slid the jar under the bed, just as her mother chastised her. "Bath. Now," she demanded. "Then we're off to see Grandma."

Christine shrugged. Grandma's was code for "I'll be on my computer writing all weekend and I need someone to watch you." By someone, she meant her tablet and YouTube. Maybe some Kindle books.

Grandma would be asleep on her chair. Grandma was always asleep on her chair. She'd be stuck on the old-person-smelling-carpet with her videos, games, and books all weekend instead of chasing frogs.

When they returned home, Christine's face flushed red. She ran to her room and reached it just before the blood had drained entirely from her skin and cold tendrils snaked down her spine. Keroppi's *fine. I'm sure he's fine.*

She dove under her bed and fished out her frog.

It rattled in the glass.

Keroppi was stiff, and he stunk. An army of ants had crawled through an air hole and dismembered one of its front legs. Green skin turned brown. Its eyes were shrouded in a milky-white cloud, yet they saw her well-enough.

After a week of chicken nuggets and cat videos, she'd come back home a killer. With tears in her eyes, she took Keroppi out in the yard. Using one of those red plastic shovels that came with a toy bucket from the

Dollar Store, she dug a small hole, and buried him. Christine wrote his name on a flat rock nearby and pressed it into the soft mound of dirt. She spent the rest of the day and late into the night by his side, reading him poems and crying over what she had done, begging him for forgiveness.

Now, standing in front of the glass house, she felt very much like the frog, stepping willingly into her own jar.

Christine reached for the door, and her new life, the same way she had ripped off a band-aid over her hairy arm. *Better get this over with.*

Yet, there was no handle. She stepped back in surprise.

Instead, the door was a solid slab of stainless steel with no visible latches or knobs, a wall, rather than an entrance into the home. There was probably a camera filming her right now, and her reaction to the dumb door would go viral for all the wrong reasons. *How in Jareth's Labyrinth do you get into this place?*

Christine searched for a hidden recess or a doorbell or some other way of opening the door, but found nothing except for a small square panel, a reflective, glassy black. It was hot, probably hotter than it was designed to be. As if someone had overlooked a small, but important detail.

The square looked like it could be an interactive screen, so she pushed it—

And jerked her finger away. Rubbing the burn, she turned toward the sun and sighed. All these flat lines and contours made to 'flow' with the vista, and the architect failed to account for the direction of the sun on the doorbell.

Whatever the case, the panel was hot. Too hot to touch with just her hand. And she still hadn't figured out how to open the damned thing yet.

As her mother busied herself on her phone, Christine folded the bottom of her camisole around her hand to act as an impromptu oven mitt when the door slid open to reveal an entirely unexpected figure.

"Oh, dear, here you are," The bespectacled silver-haired realtor spoke in a warm but concerned voice, as if she were entirely surprised, but happy, to see them.

"I called ahead this morning," her mother explained. She'd mentioned stopping in New Mexico to meet with some writerly friends there. But she'd driven straight through instead. Then, she'd discussed driving to L.A. for a meeting, but as they drew nearer their destination, the idea of driving past their new place to drive into the suburbs of L.A. had been a turn-off.

So, they'd turned off the 10 and arrived here. Early.

"Sorry, about that," her mother said through an awkward smile. "Is the house not ready?"

"I had wanted to make cookies." Shadows gave way to reveal a sweet, older lady. Her glasses slid down the bridge of her nose every time she smiled. She slid them back up and invited them in. She gave Christine an immediate vibe of Christmas and presents and coziness.

"Christine, is it?" The realtor placed a gentle hand on Christine's shoulder, pulling her inside to cooler air away from outside heat. "Look at you, you must be famished and here I am with nothing to offer. Let's see if I can pour you a cool glass of lemonade, at the least. Maybe some milk?"

The realtor's hand and warm-ness settled Christine's misgivings and she found herself eager to step into the house. Lemonade sounded awesome. She looked at her mother, who shook her head. She was probably concerned that she'd spill it on the new floor or whatever. She wasn't four anymore. "No thank you, maybe later?"

"Later, certainly. I may not give you a choice. It's hot outside and you look parched." She shut the door behind them and Christine immediately felt better. "Your new home itself, the hardware if you will, is ready. But I'm told that the software isn't online yet. But it's so easy to use, we'll have you up and running in no time."

Christine stepped further into what she assumed would be a tight hallway of sorts. In a two-bedroom trailer, it was walls everywhere, elbows wide, into a too-small kitchen or a living space that doubled as the dining room.

This was no trailer. Not even a double wide.

This was *not* the smoke-smelling carpet (neither she nor her mother smoked), the couch with the split seams, the bathroom with the leaky faucet and yellow-brown filtered light from the windows, nor the cramped bedroom and her thrift-store sheet she used as a curtain to keep the leering eyes of the sixteen-year-old next door off her.

She gasped as she looked around the house. The room was open and wide. In fact, it wasn't a room — it was the house itself, or just the bottom floor, perhaps. One sleek room of tile and white porcelain marble contrasted with grey granite along oval patterns repeated over the walls and floors.

One giant room.

You could fit half-a-dozen trailers in here.

There were no barriers, save one: a fabricated waterfall between the kitchen/dining area and living room. Most of the space was just open and empty for seemingly no reason at all. Even the air felt different; cool and circulated and full of oxygen. She took in a breath as if she'd never breathed before in her life.

She was a medieval maid stepping into a starship. *This isn't a home, it's an Apple store.*

This wasn't vanity or pride or any sort of spoiling on her part, Christine convinced herself. This was no home for her. Not in the way she had had a home before. She may not have liked the cigarette smells, but it smelled of *something.* She may have not liked her cracked window and the Star Wars sheet that covered it, but it was *her* room and her curtain. The couch contoured to fit her, where the white leather furniture here looked impractically stupid and sterile. It would be ruined the first time she ate double pepperoni pizza with pineapple while she watched TV. Not deliberately, of course, just that's what always seemed to happen.

The realtor paused to let them both breathe it all in before continuing, "As you know, this was meant to be the model home, the showroom for the neighborhood."

All Christine had seen outside was sand and desert shrubs. Every so often, on the long drive in, she'd seen an impression in the dirt where a driveway would one-day be and gated-off areas loaded with building supplies. But construction hadn't begun. This home had been rushed to completion; the other homes stalled. So it sat, separated by acres of twisting hills and desert vistas, within the foothills of whatever mountain range this was.

The realtor waved her raised right hand through the air excitedly. Eyeing her mother and pressing her glasses back on her nose after a big smile, she told her, "Of course, with someone of your…caliber here, it's like an advertisement for the neighborhood itself. A sponsorship of sorts. We're more than happy to have you call our work of art your home."

Her mother was speechless. Either because of the home or because she was still getting used to the idea of all the…newness. Christine could relate. She turned to her mother, to catch her attention, to share in the same feeling—

"Honestly, I'm so glad you're here." The realtor beckoned them across the room. The moment between them lost, like the warping of childhood memories from age. Instead, Christine looked around. "It's always so nice to introduce someone to their new home. My favorite part of the job."

On her left was a spiral staircase which began at the ground floor and wound around a tubular glass…elevator? *I have an elevator?* If she did, and she couldn't believe it, the elevator looked more like a decoration. Glass and curved, rather than square and steel, it looked nothing like any mall elevator she'd ever seen. The tube seemed to connect to both upstairs and to the basement whereas the staircase next to it only led up.

There must be another set of stairs somewhere else that led downstairs.

"I just assumed we could drive by the housing office nearby, pick up the keys there?" Christine's mother asked.

"Nonsense, Mara," the realtor grinned, addressing her mother. Of course, most of the world knew her by her initials, M.K. "My office is in the city over an hour away. This isn't some housing tract. It's *the* place to live. We are going to revitalize the desert again, starting with *you*." She pointed to her mother, as if some sort of savior, the Joan Didion of the Sands Reborn.

Yes, Christine had read Joan. As well as Tom Wolfe. She didn't like his books. She read Mary Shelley and Stephen King and John Coyne and modern sci-fi writers like Rebecca Roanhorse and N.K. Jemisin. She was a particular fan of the techno-thrillers that her dad read, like Crichton. *Jurassic Park* and *Prey* were her favorites.

Christine read at night and in the car and during the day and at school and sometimes she'd read during the slow parts of shows. She binged books just as much as TV shows.

She'd be reading now, except the curious nature of this house kept the books momentarily at bay. A rare feat. Books and YouTube and Netflix were better than everything else, including people.

Usually.

"Let's take you on a tour, shall we?"

Christine would have followed the realtor anywhere. She still hoped for that glass of lemonade and maybe she could help make cookies with her later under the guise of learning the ins-and-outs of the house. She didn't want the realtor to leave at all.

Christine would have shoved her phone in her pocket, but her shorts didn't have them (she wished women's clothing had pockets). They were as impractical as the house. So, she kept the phone by her side, set for her camera rather than her Kindle, ready for the ride.

***

What Christine wanted to see first was her room. Yet, she didn't know where it was in this big white box. White floors, white paint, a shiny white tabletop curved down where the corners should have been. If the walls had been padded she would have assumed she were in a sanatorium. Perhaps it was. Everyone was a little crazy in their own way. Even the realtor seemed…excessive in her joy.

Christine strode away from the foyer, crossed the wide room, and found herself in the kitchen. "The heart of the home," the realtor proclaimed.

Against the wall of the kitchen was the usual sink and basin combo, all polished stainless steel, even the large refrigerator and matching stove. Along the light countertops were large mason jars that served no functional purpose. They were filled with green and red dried pasta, black beans, red peppers and a few things she didn't recognize. She figured it was meant to splash some color on the place. But it was more uselessness. More wasted space.

Before the kitchen, however, was the main draw: a center island that might have been as big as her entire home. Honestly, it looked impressive; the black marble countertop stood in stark contrast to all the bright airy white.

Yet, like everything else in the house, the kitchen island was, simply too big, too long. It took her five seconds to walk from one end to the other. Which meant any time she wanted a drink from the fridge, some water from the tap, she'd have to walk around the monstrosity. Once again, entirely—

"As you see here, on this side of the counter, closest to the couch, is a mini-refrigerator for drinks and a purified waterspout for anytime you're thirsty. Out here, you should always drink plenty of water. I don't want you to melt."

A mini refrigerator? Water fountain? What sorcery was this?

She hardly had time to marvel when the realtor moved on, as if those were all standard features in any home. "What sets this home apart from all others ever constructed is the fully integrated AI. It controls every facet of the house. It even makes cookies, though not as delicious as mine. If the program were online, I'd show you."

"Yes, that's what lured me in." Christine's mother said, sparkles jazzercising in her eyes. "Well, that and the location. A fully automated home. No cooking, no cleaning, everything easily controlled and convenient. No distractions to my work, no clean-up from the hassles of motherhood."

Hassles. Christine had always grown up with those adjectives. A chore. An inconvenience. A bother. An annoyance. An obstacle. What her mom really meant was: *A mistake.*

Christine hung her head. She sought shelter, refuge, to be as far away from her mother as she could, but this place was too big for her, too open, too unfamiliar to dart upstairs alone—

Alone, where she'd always been.

No. She wouldn't give in. Not yet. She'd let the barb roll off her back like water off a duck. Only, the duck was drowning. Her mom didn't even realize what she had said. She never did. She—

"Oh, dear." The realtor squinted, holding one hand to her glasses. She examined something in the sink. "It seems we have an unexpected house guest."

Christine's mother elbowed past the realtor to reach the sink. She shrieked, her arms flailing, and her lips trembling. She switched on the water and searched the counter for a switch, found a square button instead, and pressed it. The garbage disposal gurgled to life, squelching out her alarm.

When Christine reached her mother, she saw a small scorpion in the sink. The arachnid was a mixture of tan and translucent, brown and clear, and it occurred to her that it was perfect camouflage for the sand.

But in the stainless steel, even retreating as it was from the rush of water and the growling of the disposal, it looked to her like a fearsome, armored thing: a spider in a tank, perhaps. Something fierce and strong, perfectly protected from its environment. Shielded and solitary.

Christine had never seen a scorpion before. And she immediately wanted it. She wanted to study it, to look at its eyes and turn it over to see what made it tick. How did they survive, alone, in such hostile conditions? Maybe studying the creature could give her some answers of her own.

She turned off the disposal and sink.

"Thank you, Christine. All life is precious, no matter how sharp their corners appear." The realtor unscrewed a jar of pasta and let it pour out onto the counter messily.

Why can't she be my mom? Christine smiled in response, reaching out a hand to the arachnid, before her mother could stop her, and took it by the tail – careful of its stinger. Perhaps Christine should have been afraid. She didn't know if the creature was venomous. She didn't know if getting stung would hurt. Or pinched. The claws waved upward toward her fingers, writhing and thrashing. Still, her grip was iron, at least until she had it over the open jar, which Mrs. Claus (the realtor did look like Mrs. Claus) had out ready for her, tilted at an angle.

"We all need someone to look out for us," the realtor said. "Let us know we're loved."

Yes, we do.

The scorpion landed inside with a plop, then circled around, standing its ground, as if attempting to regain some lost dignity, puffing itself out and poising its tail to strike.

"Christine!" Her mother seemed aghast. Yet it passed quickly as Christine screwed on the lid and tucked the jar under her arm. Her first capture in her new home.

Her first friend. She reminded herself of a big, moppy dog she had always wanted.

"I think I'll name her Fluffy."

The realtor nodded, smiled, and pushed her glasses back up the bridge of her nose.

"You can name that thing whatever you like, so long as you let it loose far from here."

Christine ignored her mother. In a few hours, by tomorrow at the latest, she'd forget about the jar entirely. She always did. Her mother's panic settled, and she was back to being indifferent.

"Sorry about the intruder." The realtor pulled on gray curls. "This being a new property and all, bound to have a few turn up, but once Alyx is up and running, it will take care of these small matters."

"Alyx?" Christine asked.

The realtor answered as if she had waited all this time for someone to ask. "Oh, you have no idea."

"As I mentioned before, everything is automated through Alyx, the home's mostly internal, fully integrated AI. The house even cleans itself." Her last words were spoken an octave higher, as if to say, *"but wait, there's more."* She waved her hands expressively. "Nothing like it exists."

The realtor was wonderfully exuberant, Christine thought. Was she magical? Did she really live at the North Pole? She seemed so out of place, so unstuck from reality. Christine had already glued herself to her side. *How do I become more like her?*

"Pay attention to the sensors in the floor and in the ceiling," the realtor said, pulling out her phone from her purse. Christine hadn't noticed the black circles dotting the surfaces of the floors and ceilings. She noted that the realtor stood well behind them.

"From your phone's Alyx app – and that's Alyx with a 'y' – you can program whatever you'd like, so long as the ingredients are prepped and the cookware is in place. But that's all automated too. Once you're low on ingredients, the house's AI will place an order and everything will be drone-dropped directly to the prep pantry. It's really quite something. Robotic hands and a head descend from the cabinet here." Mrs. Claus pointed underneath a top row of counters. *That's the perfect name. It suits her.*

"This is just one of several places on the property Alyx will take on a life of its own. This one here will cook everything from omelets to Thanksgiving dinner." Mrs. Claus shrugged. "It's all anticlimactic, really. This is where I'm supposed to have Alyx use his hands to scramble an egg, just to show off."

"Hands?" Christine asked. "You mean there's an actual robot in this house?"

"No, but yes," Mrs. Claus beamed.

Christine's heart warmed every time the realtor spoke to her.

"The designers of this neighborhood wanted more than non-corporeal arms and hands flying around, doing tasks. So they also gave Alyx a head, a face, a personality," she explained. "Totally customizable. Alyx's heads are the brains of the house and you'll find units in the kitchen, outside at the cabana, and in the basement bar and billiard room. The hands downstairs have much more range of motion, can operate independently of the head, and can even play pool."

It clicked for Christine then. Despite no demo here, she'd seen automated hands operate at a bar in Vegas. Well, she'd seen it on YouTube, but the point was the same. Weird, robotic arms with three-fingered hands smoothly slid from station to station, stirring, shaking, and pouring drinks for customers more enthralled by the spectacle than the cost and alcohol content (or lack thereof) in their drinks. It was a gimmick. No more than that.

At least, that's what she believed. Now, it was in her house. She wanted to meet Alyx for herself. She wondered if she could program him with the Thinklink that she wanted. Her own little robot friend. Who could cook. All she could do was work the microwave. *That's actually pretty fucking cool.*

"But you'll want to stand outside these sensors." The realtor looked again to the rows of small circles lining the floor and ceiling. She pointed to a knife block on the counter. Each handle had a large sticker attached and Christine reasoned that it must have something to do with the computer's ability to discern between blades; each one had a pattern etched into it, perhaps like a code. Looking around, she realized most items in the kitchen all had the same type of coded stickers on them.

Yet, her eyes drew her toward the knives.

Christine crept closer, past the sensors. "What happens if you step across them, say when Alyx is chopping something for a salad?"

She pulled a knife out of the block at random. The blade caught a stray ray of sunlight and reflected brightly across the room. For a moment, the realtor appeared in silhouette; a misshapen form of human. Perhaps a monster. It unsettled Christine, who refused to see her as anything but grandmotherly. "Alyx uses facial recognition software to separate friend from French fries," she said simply, taking the knife from Christine and sliding it back into the block. "You're perfectly safe."

Her mother then shot her a look as if to say, "A salad wouldn't do you any harm either."

Her mother was one to criticize. It wasn't as if she were rail-thin herself. The both of them were skinnier the way a peanut is shapelier than an almond, true, but they were both nuts.

"Right, then. Let's move on." The realtor headed across the room.

Christine's attention drew to the waterfall feature gurgling away against the dining room wall when she had crossed into the kitchen. The singular partition was the only obstacle in the otherwise open space. It was about six feet tall, she reasoned, and about half as wide. Water cascaded down gray slate and pooled into what she could only describe as a thin moat surrounding the dining table and six wire-framed glass chairs. They looked like bent eyeglasses. But she ignored the esoteric art and swept her hand into the water at her feet.

It was cool, and there was a surprising current too it, though she doubted the water went more than a couple of inches deep. "It's for relaxation. The sound soothes you," she said. "But there's more to it, of course. Style meets function."

Christine considered it for a moment. How could having a waterfall in the middle of the room serve anything but to make a mess? Mrs. Claus answered her, reading her mind. She would have to get used to that. Once she had her Thinklink, then others could literally get into her head.

"The water helps clean the entire floor. It draws dust in, and the pool pulls it out through the filters. It cleans itself and keeps the floor dust-bunny free."

Wow. The rich don't even have to dust.

"And what isn't maintained by the filters, or is too big like cookie crumbs," Mrs. Claus cast her eyes Christine's way, "is cleaned by a flotilla of a dozen little floor scrubbers and cleaners – drone devices – all controlled by the AI's automation. They'll rush out and clean it all away," she said with another smile.

"Can we see my room next?" Christine's day had brightened. She couldn't wait to see it. Besides, she needed a place for Fluffy and something to use to put airholes in the lid. She eyed the staircase, stepping toward it.

"You haven't finished this floor," her mother said.

"I'm taking you both out back next. It's got a large and lovely patio, cabana, pool—"

Christine stopped, her eyes widening in horror, and turned back. "What did you say?"

Her mother put her hands out to hush everyone, as if to stop what she knew was about to start.

"A pool," the realtor said again. She was no longer Mrs. Claus but some old lady. "Very nice, especially in this sun—"

Christine ignored her and looked out the floor-to-ceiling sliding glass partition. There had been so much going on inside that she hadn't noticed a lagoon-shaped feature out back. It had some sort of cover over it. Only now did it register what it was: *a motherfucking pool...*

"Look, Christine," her mother said. "Before you start, just know that you can't get a nice new home in the desert without a—"

"Is there a problem? I see Christine is upset."

"It's a fucking pool, Mom." Christine broke in. Pain choked in her throat. Maybe it was tears. It all tasted the same. "In our backyard."

"It's a hundred and some-odd degrees out here, Christine. Of course, there's a pool." She wiped away the sweat from her brow as if wiping away frustration. "I wanted to tell you."

"What were you thinking?" Christine edged closer to her escape route.

"I can show you the basement instead?"

"It's been a long trip, perhaps we'll finish the tour another time?" Her mother asked. "I'd like to find my office and settle in."

Her mother offered no apology. *Of course not.* She swirled to the stairs.

"You'll want to take the elevator?" The question seemed laced with concern, but Christine dismissed all of that. She was hurt and wasn't going to let anyone offer comfort. The realtor's plea echoed against the barren walls and bounced off her mother's obliviousness.

"Young lady!" Her mother called after her. But she ignored them both. Fluffy in tow, rattling irately against the glass jar, Christine stormed up the steps, the way a knight would invade a castle, to plant her flag, searching for the isolation she'd known her entire life.

My house has a fucking pool.

Chapter 2

Christine's room wasn't difficult to find despite the enormity of the house, and her earlier concerns about getting lost. The upstairs balcony wrapped around the vaulted roof of the foyer and led past the elevator to a row of doors on one side and a railing overlooking the living room on the other. She counted four doors on the second floor. One led to a master bedroom that seemed to maze for miles between closets and a bathroom and jacuzzi suite. Besides that, there were just two other rooms, with the last door leading to a bathroom adjoining them.

One room was meant to be a guest bedroom – not that anyone visited them often in Oklahoma and if they did, they had to sleep on the sofa in the living room. The other, entirely done up in pink, with posters of boy bands and complete with a unicorn stuffed animal on a bed done up in fuzzy sheets, was, to her horror, her room.

Another strike. The realtor wasn't perfect. I should have known.

Christine tore into the room, took the unicorn, then huffed out, slamming the door behind her, and headed back toward the guest bedroom made of blues and green. It reminded her of an ocean. Soft, swelling seas that she could only dream about.

It was, after all, what had sold her on coming to California. She assumed the whole state sat on the ocean, that she'd be a beach bum, book in one hand, virgin pina colada in the other. Only, it wouldn't be virgin.

She sat Fluffy down on a desk nestled under a window overlooking sand, claiming the land as hers. In a way, she was. This was now her room, her home, her new life. *Well, plenty of beach. Just no water.*

And that was fine with her.

The bed looked appealing. A nice way to stretch out and relax from the straight-through driving they'd done to get here. She flung herself facedown and buried herself within the softness.

A moment later, the front door opened and then shut. Her mom and her were alone. Soon, Christine knew, her mom would be locked away in her new study, completely forgetting about her daughter storming upstairs, or why. Did she even stop to think about the pool?

No, she was sure. She was already off visiting her other children, stopping in to see how their adventures in Victorian London were doing. Her mom was not one to waste time. Once, when their car had broken down on a trip to Ohio, they'd simply stayed a week in a hotel to allow her mom time to work while the car was repaired.

Of course, by then, royalties had begun trickling in. Not because of her books. No one bought books anymore, except Christine it seemed. Public interest piqued and coins rattled because of the rumblings that Netflix ordered a series.

They had.

The algae-green waters of the cheap motel had seemed like a holiday. Eating out was usually a luxury; hot-dogs on bread for buns or godawful pickle and pimento loaf sandwiches, heavy on the mustard to cover up the taste. On the first of the month they'd get Tony's Pizza. Sometimes, she could get a can of Mr. Pibb too.

Yet, there in Ohio, broke-down and stranded in a hotel, her and her mother had eaten Applebee's nearly every night that whole week. And now, she lived in a house with an AI robot in the kitchen that could make her a fresh meal, anything she wanted, on command. She had an elevator. A basement. Upstairs. A...pool. She didn't know whether she should laugh, or cry.

So she did both, bursting out a chuckle as tears dampened her new feather-down pillow.

When Christine awoke, it was to an empty, dark trailer. She was back in familiar territory. C3PO stared back at her through yellowed-curtains. The musty smell of molded carpet clawed her nose. She rose from her bed and made her way through the narrow hall made narrower by the stacks of her mother's books piled against one wall.

She entered the main room of the trailer to the familiar clacking of keys. Her mother sat hunched over the plastic folding table. "Hi, mom," she said. As usual, there was no reply.

In the kitchen, she found that the cupboards were stocked, more or less. That meant she wouldn't have to scrounge as much or get creative to come up with a meal. She settled for a bowl of cereal, though it was supposed to be dinnertime.

Honeycomb clinked against the plastic bowl as it filled to the brim. Christine fetched milk from the fridge, opened the carton and curled her nose. When she returned from dumping the milk down the toilet, she took her bowl outside, opening the screen door to her trailer, rattling loose several sleeping mosquitoes. She sat on the stoop, swatting them away.

She ate her cereal dry while she scrolled through her social media posts. Bobby from down the block was in trouble again. This time for slamming into a drive-thru speaker at McDonalds. The Suzie sisters had claimed to have had a three-some with someone from the football team. Yet, he denied it. Christine let her mind wander, contemplating deeply what that might have been like.

Her thoughts went to the rude sixteen-year-old-boy from the trailer across from her bedroom window. He was a squat sunburned creature who wore a threadbare t-shirt and a camo-patterned ball cap. Though he couldn't grow but the faintest of facial hair, he already bore the beginnings of a beer-belly that poured over the waistline of his cargo shorts.

He leered at her, as he always did. And when she did not return thanks for being so glamorously admired, his looks would turn to taunts. "You always think you're so much better than me, don't you?" He'd get around to asking. "You're no prize, pig." And then he'd break into barn noises.

She rose, disgusted, and escaped inside to her room, ignoring her mother, locked away in her own seclusion. She streamed YouTube videos on the rumors of the upcoming release of the Thinklink until darkness descended and she gave into sleep on another hot and humid Oklahoma evening.

This time, she awoke to complete silence and darkness, the vague memories of the past thick and visible as fog, yet unreachable.

The darkness enveloping her was one she'd not experienced before. Even in the pitch of night back home, her *real* home, the faint glimmer of stars could guide her as she caught moths and fireflies and watched bats dart for mosquitoes.

In her room, through her old curtains, streetlights illuminated her room, bright enough that she could read by them. She'd creep into her mother's stash of books, pluck one at random, and read by the light. When she was older, her Kindle did the glowing for her, and then her mother's books went untouched.

But here, in this strange and unfamiliar place, there was no glow, no light, nothing to wrap around her like a loving arm.

There was only darkness.

Christine didn't know where the light panels were. And the AI wasn't online to audibly ask it to raise a light. She rose, stumbled around, and knocked into the glass jar on the desk.

"Shit," she said, as the jar wobbled, reverberating on the hard surface. She froze, not wishing to accidentally touch the jar again to steady Fluffy. She might knock her off the desk altogether. Then, there'd be glass on the floor and an angry arachnid on the loose. And she didn't have shoes on her feet.

Christine took a step back, inhaled deeply, and shut her eyes—

When she opened them, her eyes had grasped onto the light of the stars from her window, the way a wick caught light from the faintest flame. It was enough to give an outline to her desk and the jar, which was falling—

Christine caught it just as it slipped off the edge. She felt the vibration of the creature inside as it skittered and clinked against the side of the jar. She let out her breath, softened her shoulders and placed the jar, this time on its side, on the wall against the desk and then placed a flat eraser under the jar to keep it from rolling.

She breathed again and whispered, "Sorry, Fluffy." She shook, fearful that she could have hurt her armored arachnid.

The only light she could find was the desk lamp. She clicked it on and flinched. Fluffy backed away too. Now that she had light, memories, as well as shapes, took form. This wasn't her home. Not yet. Home was where you felt most comfortable taking a shit. She hadn't even been to the bathroom yet.

She opened the door to the toilet. Again, the only light she could find illuminated only the mirror, but it was enough to do her business by, and she did, worried that there was no toilet paper or no soap, or no towel. But the realtor had stocked the house full of necessary supplies.

It was like living back in the hotel.

Finished, she headed out a different door from the bathroom which took her to the hallway. The hallway balcony was lit from a light left on below. She followed the railing to the elevator. Curious about it, but not knowing if it was working, she passed it in favor of the stairs. For a moment, she imagined getting stuck in the glass elevator, and wondered if there was air in there, if she would suffocate or die of starvation first, if she could not escape. She doubted her mother would even notice.

Since there are no lights on up here, and her study is on the main floor. She's probably not even been up here yet. Not even to check in on me. Downstairs, Christine found the light came from precisely where she imagined it: her mother's office. She hadn't noticed the room itself, but upon closer inspection, she understood why. The door didn't open like a regular door. Instead, it slid into the wall – the wall that she had thought was the left end of the kitchen.

She peered through the crack in the partition, the same crack that had given its hiding place away. Her mother wouldn't notice her looking in. Christine was confident of her invisibility. There, her mother sat, thick, black-framed glasses perched on her nose, a curl of her hair dangling off her brow as she leaned forward, while she tapped madly at the laptop before her, with intermittent breaks which Christine knew to be periods of thought between sentences.

Had Christine barged in with the entirety of USC's brass section trumpeting away, she would not so much have budged. Christine should know. Most often, she only listened to music with headphones on. Once, she'd blared it as loud as her Bluetooth speaker allowed. She'd gotten a call from her neighbor, not her mother, about the nuisance.

Once her mother was with her other children – her creations, her characters – nothing else existed. She belonged to that world wholly, until either a wall was reached, or the host of heaven and all the miracles contained within dislodged her. Once, her mother had taken her computer into the bathroom.

Now that her own bladder was relieved, she realized she was thirsty. Yet, the cabinets in the kitchen didn't open – they lacked handles or knobs or something, she wasn't sure. And then the water fountain embedded into the counter didn't work, at least not for her. She pried open the small refrigerator door to find it empty but for one of her mother's cold, watered down coffees – most probably the one she'd gotten at the drive-thru this morning.

Christine's bags sat on the floor by the fridge. She was hungry too, and there were left-over snacks from the road trip inside. She took out an opened bag of Funyuns and grabbed a few of the broken rings, shoving them into her mouth.

The salty, rough texture felt good. She hadn't realized how hungry she was. She went for more. After she finished the bag, she wiped the crumbs and shook her shirt to dust off the bits that had fallen inside. She swiveled around, examining the room. *Now where the crap is the trashcan?* The nicer the house, it seemed, the harder the trash was to find.

A soft whirring came from behind. Turning, she saw from the shadows a sleek, round machine rolling her way. Her bare toes inched backward, but then she suddenly felt foolish for doing so.

A floor drone?

She'd never seen one before, but that had to be it. The realtor had suggested as much. Sure enough, the vacuum swept toward her crumbs, sucking them up.

"Well, thank you, little guy." The drone looked cute. Small, grey, and almost apprehensive, in the way it scooched forward, looking for food, like a little mouse, but way more practical. Perhaps she could put giant googly eyes on the creature. Take pictures and post them. She nodded her head in approval.

Something sharp sliced through her pinky toe.

"Ouch," she yelped, flailing her foot. The machine sailed a foot across the floor, landing upside down. It seemed helpless and hurt, whirring away like a capsized turtle.

Despite her hurt toe, she limped to it, picking it up. She held it in her arms, flipping it over, examining it. Underneath were several sets of bristle brushes, but on the outer-most edges of the machine, there was what appeared to be a blade.

A blade? Perhaps for scrapping off food from the floor, she considered. Maybe the robot had thought her foot didn't belong. Otherwise, it was harmless. She set the drone down and it skittered away, to whatever hole it belonged.

She'd have to be more mindful of the little mouse, or mice, however many there were, until she could figure out how to re-program it to avoid feet. Yet, there was an easier solution to consider: with scorpions and blind murder-bots scooting across the floor at night, she should probably wear sandals anyway.

Her toe felt sticky and damp. The slice in her toe was like a paper cut, but deeper. She searched around, trying to figure out where the band-aids might be, but no matter how thorough the realtor might have been, she doubted she'd stocked a first aid kit. She'd have to improvise.

Normally, toilet paper would suffice. She limped tenderly toward the bathroom, realizing her toe hurt worse than she'd realized. She stared at the stairs and lifted her foot to take a step as a bit of blood trickled down and splashed on the white tile.

It hurt just to move her toe. She couldn't fathom taking the flight upstairs. And the elevator was still a mystery. Besides, what if she slipped in her own slick blood and broke her neck falling down the stairs? Wouldn't that be a way to go.

The sliver of light escaping the study door caught her attention once more. *Bad idea.*

She crept toward it and stuck her head inside to see her mother lost in thought, one hand resting on her laptop and another clutching cold coffee, which her mother would drink anyway. *Disgusting.*

"Mom?" Christine knew better than to interrupt, but this was their new home, their new life and a twinge in her belly prodded hope in her that somehow it might mean that this time would be different.

"Mom?" she called again.

Her mom remained as still as a mannequin. Maybe she didn't hear her, maybe her mom was so lost in her own world, her other family, that this one, the one where Christine existed, her flesh-and-blood creation, seemed like the fake one…

Slowly, she came to.

At first, it was a flicking of the eyes, an unkinking of the neck. But there was no awareness. That would come later. For now, even after a long moment staring directly at Christine, there came no response.

Christine had learned a long time ago not to speak until after spoken to, because her mother would not hear her. Of course, she also knew not to bother her, but she was here anyway.

"Christine?"

"Mom—"

"I'm working, honey. Can't you see that?" Her mother stretched out her fingers and rubbed red eyes. "Every time you interrupt me I lose the scene."

"But, mom…" She'd heard that before. Too many times to count.

"It's not just losing my concentration that I'll have to get back. You know this. What angers me is that my scene is lost forever. Whatever I write will be different, maybe better, maybe worse but not what I originally…" She sighed, letting the lecture evaporate into air. "What is it?"

"I'm bleeding." Christine raised her leg.

Her mother took off her glasses and squinted at the foot from the comfort of her swivel chair across the large room. Her new study, lined with empty bookshelves and a long mahogany desk, was a huge step-up from before. She bet her mom had melted into the chair the second she'd walked in. There was still the faint trace of love in her eyes. "It's a scratch. I taught you to take care of yourself."

"We don't have any band-aids."

"Use toilet paper. Or go to the store and get some."

"I might need stitches."

"Drive yourself to the ER."

"It's on my foot. It hurts to—"

"Then call an Uber." Her mom held up a hand. That argument was over. "I've got to get back to work."

"If I had a Thinklink…" Christine switched gears. She'd lost one argument, as she knew she would. Her mom was right, it was just a scratch, no matter how much it stung and how much it bled. Some bandage and gauze would sort it. She'd overreacted. Christine knew better.

But if she stood there, her toe would keep pooling blood on the floor. Maybe when her mom saw her trail of blood.

"I'm not getting into that argument with you again, Christine. Figure it out."

"I could just think it and a Prometheus Drone would be here in a matter of minutes with band-aids. It could bring some pizza too."

"Or, you could do things the old-fashioned way."

"You are such a technophobe." All parents were. Anything invented after an adult turned thirty-five was witchcraft. With the Thinklink, she could connect to people. Connect to everyone. Not just be part of the world, but the world would be part of her. That's what she couldn't make her mom understand.

Her mother sighed, pushing her chair away from her laptop. Pointing to her obvious use of technology, she said, "No, I'm just not lazy."

"You're not lazy? You had no problem using technology when it suited you – tablets and phones and YouTube videos, to stick in front of me. To keep me quiet and out of your hair."

"Christine." Her mother took a tone of authority, dripping with acid. Then, it dissipated, because her mother was a coward and never wanted to fight, she only wanted Christine to go away. Fighting meant having to stop work. "You turned out great. But I've got to get this project done. If this brain-thing is something you really want, go and get a job. Earn the money for it yourself and then we can talk about whether you really need to spend the money on something so ridiculous. It will give you something to do until classes start up."

Christine crinkled her brow in confusion. Until now, her mom had always said no. First, because they had no money. But the Thinklink had gradually come down in price even as its technology improved.

Then, when money was no longer an issue, her mother banned further discussion because it literally was a minor surgery to connect the computer directly to your brain – something that scared the shit out of her mother, or *anyone* with an ounce of sense, she had told Christine on more than one occasion. Yet, it was no worse than getting an ear-pierced or a tattoo done. Didn't she see that?

Now, she had all but said yes. What changed? Christine frowned as she figured it out. "Getting a job will get me out of your hair, you mean. And then you'll still say no."

"No, it'll teach you responsibility. You'll meet new friends. With your own income, you can pay for it yourself. It'll mean more to you if you do." Her mom smiled slyly, "and it will give you time to think about what you really want. Wants are funny that way when it's your money on the line."

By now, Christine's toe had stopped bleeding. The cut still stung though, but her ammunition, her blood, was gone. She grimaced as her mother continued, sliding a piece of paper over and picking it up. "I've already taken the liberty of arranging work for you."

Christine was supposed to find a job herself, that's what all recent high-school grads were supposed to do. Work at the beach, have a summer romance, find and lose love…

It was totally out of character for her mom to find work for her daughter, when she wouldn't even find a band-aid. Christine was like the cold cup of coffee that her mom kept close by in case she needed something but would swirl down the drain when she didn't.

Christine didn't dare walk across the plush carpet. Instead, she read the name of the place off the flyer and brought it up with her phone. When she realized the place was a local one-screen movie theater, she understood just what her mother had done and what she meant for Christine to do. "You want me to scope the place out?"

"It's a win-win."

Her mother had always wanted to own a theater. It was an impossible pipe dream, but something that made for fun conversations and good "what-ifs." It made sense for her mom to want a place to call her own like that. The only time Christine could remember spending more than an hour with her mom was at the movies.

They'd seen the new *Star Wars* movies together. They'd seen *Jurassic World.* They'd seen the Marvel movies and the one or two decent DC films. And they'd enjoyed them all. There was something about popcorn and common entertainment that could bridge the gap between everyone in the same room.

Now that they had money, it was a dream within her mother's reach.

For a moment, Christine's chest puffed out and a smile threatened to break through. But then she remembered what her mom's success had cost…her messed up life, her messed up family…and Christine's own father.

And her chest deflated again.

"You're fucking impossible." She pressed her foot heavily into the carpet with each step, relishing the feel of the fabric and the dampness she left in her wake. She swiped the job flyer for the cinema off the desk and left, following her blood-soaked trail out of her mother's study.

From behind, her mother called out her name, which Christine ignored. She wasn't halfway up the stairs, her bags by the fridge retrieved, before the keyboard tapping resumed from below.

Upstairs, Christine cleaned the blood off her foot and wiped the faded footprints off using the faucet in the bathroom sink. Taking toilet paper and some scotch tape, she improvised a band-aid. The wound still stung, and she didn't know if the cut would heal without stitches, and there was still the matter of all the blood she'd tracked throughout the house. But those were matters for the morning. The floor drone, the scrubber sweeper robot, hadn't been very bright, Christine considered, but she expected a few bugs in the system. Besides, the AI hadn't been switched on yet. Surely, they'd recognize friendly toes from Cheetos when the AI came online?

Christine changed into a pair of flannel pajama bottoms from her bag and a faded t-shirt with a Disney princess that read "I Don't Need Saving." Her father had bought that for her many years ago. Threadbare and holey around the armpits, her mother had thrown it away on several occasions, only for Christine to retrieve it each time.

She still fumed from her fight with her mother. But somehow the change into comfortable clothes calmed her. Picking up the flyer from her bed, she took a closer look.

Did she really need a job?

No. She'd be fine here, on her own, with her Kindle and her phone and her tablet. Retrieving several induction chargers from her bag and plugging them in, she charged her devices and slipped into bed, flyer close at hand.

It would be a boring job. But watching movies for money (she told herself that's what the job would be) wouldn't be much different than staying home and watching movies without earning anything. And, after all, if she paid for the Thinklink herself, then her mother couldn't say no? Could she?

But still.

People sucked. And working there would mean dealing with them. Books were better. Quieter. Less prone to irrational outbursts and yelling and stupid situations where Christine could potentially confront customers who valued her less than her own mother did. No thanks.

What she needed, after her fight with her mom and her long day in this new life, was to settle her nerves. A shot of endorphins would do her good, she justified to herself, as she lifted her tablet from its cradle and opened a tab to a particularly juicy hentai.

It wasn't the porn that she craved. In fact, the sex between the cartoon characters was stupid with those ridiculously large breasts and even bigger eyes widened in moans as boy-who-liked-her-but-didn't-say-anything-until-now *finally* revealed his feelings (and conveniently, his cock).

It was the forbidden love, the hidden relationships that shouldn't be – that turned her on.

This anime had a girl with more realistic looking breasts, and a storyline about a boy who went away and broke her heart, only for him to return at the end to find she had found another. Jealousy, forbidden love, and a whole lot of thrusting led to Christine slipping her hand down the waistband of her flannel, beneath her underwear.

She slowly prodded a finger into herself to find her wetness as the girl on-screen moaned with her own. When Christine was sufficiently wet, she brought her finger up, and edged it around her clit, eliciting a gasp.

She hadn't been able to pleasure herself like this for a while after she had packed up and spent the time travelling on the road. And the week before, she had been on her period. The freshness of tonight, in clean sheets on a luxurious bed that was both strange and soft, brought a feeling of newness and naughtiness to the moment.

She brought a knee up to rest the tablet on and with her free hand, deftly took a small bag from a pocket in her backpack. From the bag, she brought out a pocket-sized piece of rubber and rigid plastic molded into the shape of a lopsided U.

She placed her vibrator between her legs, working to slide it in place just so one side of the curve rested against her happy button and the other hit her G-spot. Once in place, she fumbled for a few moments for her phone, losing the building momentum. The tablet slid off her legs and the picture went sideways. Frustrated, she found her phone, switched it over to the app that controlled the toy inside her, and pressed the on-screen button to activate the vibrator.

It hummed quickly to life. Even on a low setting, the unexpected, yet familiar feeling sent a small quiver through her thighs. Her mouth pulled open in silent satisfaction as she raised the intensity and brought her tablet back up.

Her hips writhed in sync with the vibrator as the cartoon porn built up towards its own climax. She held the tablet above her face as she watched the jealous lovers. They'd found a way to reconcile their feelings by way of a three-way; the two dudes were near the end of their journey with the girl on top, changing from guy to guy as she saw fit. She should have been looking at the men, seeing herself as the girl. Yet Christine watched her instead, caught on the edge of orgasmic fantasy. Her eyes. Her smile, the way she moaned—

The tablet slipped out of her hand and smacked her in the face.

Her nose cracked and her forehead felt bruised and sore against the impact, the vibrator slipped out of place just before orgasm, and her underwear puddled with her own uncomfortable wetness. Then, dropping her phone, she accidentally pressed the max button on the vibrator, which whirred loudly, while her wet fingers went to her throbbing nose.

It was too much.

She bolted upright, losing the tablet to the same fate as her phone, and flicked on the light. Bending over for her devices sent pain to her face as blood rushed to her nose. But she picked her tablet and phone up anyway, sat them back on the bed, then switched off the vibrator and hentai.

Rubbing her nose, she took a breath and returned everything to its place. Her nose wasn't broken. It would be fine by morning, she was sure, but it was a stupid way to end the night.

The flyer on her bed caught her attention once again and she immediately thought about the Thinklink. The device didn't just connect your brain into the internet, it was more than that, it was an emotional connection too – even if emotions were chemicals, they were an integral part of your brain. A human was essentially a wet computer with feelings.

In the beginning, Thinklink had nearly collapsed. Nobody wanted to be wired, ceaselessly, to the web. Writers wrote about hackers and post-apocalyptic scenarios. But those were largely untrue. What had been developed to enable the deaf to hear and the blind to see (since it bypassed the eyes and ears to connect directly to those inputs in the brain) was not the beginning of a cyberpunk future and the end of humanity. Capitalism killed it. No one wanted the technology.

Until the first people who had the Thinklink began reporting what it was like watching dirty movies. It wasn't like just viewing it, with the image sent directly to your head. Your brain, they said, made connections that weren't there, as if it were filling in the blanks. What resulted was like experiencing it. Like having sex.

It was a superficial experience, of course. Not like the real thing. It wasn't like the post-apocalyptic setting of an old 90s science fiction movie. But a better experience was still, well, better. Like the camcorder and VHS player, what saved the budding technology was pornography, all the YouTubers had told her.

Christine had been raised by technology. Like the kid who was raised on Howdy Doody and cartoons and then the next generation on She-Ra and Ninja Turtles, and then her generation on YouTube, technology had been part of her life in place of any real-world experience. Like an Ernest

Cline book, the fake world had slowly crept in to replace the real one. Christine didn't see anything wrong with embracing it.

Becoming part of it was just the natural next step.

As the soreness faded from her nose, and the crappy, cranky feelings of her lost moment of bliss passed, she placed the flyer on top of her nightstand.

She would take the job, earn the money, and get the device herself. She could quit anytime, if she wanted. Though she doubted she would. Christine was many things, and stubborn was one of them. Like the never-ending and slow burning fourteen books (and prequel), two million plus words of the *Wheel of Time* series that she had labored through; once she started something, she'd see it finished.

Content with her decision, she read on her Kindle about space robots and dinosaurs until she slipped into sleep. There, dreams overtook her that began pleasant enough until they plunged her into the darker places of her mind where she was alone, isolated, scared.

Then she dreamed the dream she hated so much, the semi-lucid hell she could not escape, where she was enveloped in a cold, dark, wet place.

She realized, as she always did in this dream, that she was underwater. And she could not scream even though her mouth was open; bubbles blew from her lungs. A form not unlike her father was with her. That should have brought her comfort.

But it did not.

Not as blood billowed around her...

Chapter 3

S he awoke to fading recollections of having had a terrible dream, but by the time she headed downstairs, the memory was gone, though a pain in her heart, like an abscess in a tooth, remained.

Forlornly, she made her way down clean steps to clean kitchen tile. Someone or some*thing* had cleaned it while she had slept. Hopefully, it had been her mother, but Christine wondered if it had been the house. Maybe there were more of those floor scrubber things and they'd whirred and scraped and cleaned last night while her mother had worked.

She checked the study to find it empty. Maybe her mother had gone off to bed. Most probably, she'd left. A quick check out the front window revealed that the car was gone.

There was a note on the table which confirmed Christine's suspicions. Her mom had driven into L.A. She'd be gone for the day (and possibly overnight, knowing how involved she got with work):

Gone to meet face-to-face with Manny and some producers.
There's money in your Uber account, work starts at 3!
Miss you!

She could have just texted, Christine thought, wadding up the note and tossing it into the trash (which she found recessed into the counter).
Alone again.

The clock read just before noon. She had three hours to get showered, dressed, and a ride ready – less time if Christine didn't want to arrive to work late. *Not on my first day, at least.*

She hadn't eaten anything since the crumbs of Funyuns last night. She doubted Mrs. Claus (she was in a more gracious mood this morning) had stocked Instant Mac and Cheese, Ramen noodles, or any frozen Tostinos pizzas. You know, *good* food.

Placing her hands on the counter in thought over what to do next, she saw something she hadn't noticed before. That wasn't strange. She'd not even walked through the whole house yet or gone outside to see the stupid pool. She was sure there was much she hadn't seen, like the sight before her now.

Underneath the kitchen counter, where the three of them had stood yesterday talking about the home's AI, a ball had descended. It was white, except for a screen in the middle. The way the globe was held, with two hinges on the other side connected by a thin bar, gave the object an appearance of a head, wearing headphones and sporting shades.

The room was silent, but with the tension of a distant storm building on a dark horizon. An uneasy curiosity pulled her forward. It seemed to whisper a warning, but Christine pressed the thought away, chalking it all up to the newness of her sudden change in fortune and the anxiety of having to meet new people later today. Her life had quickly spiraled into another world and she was still struggling to catch up.

On the screen that looked like shades, words scrolled across in bright neon letters. It read:

ALYX IS READY TO MEET YOU. DOWNLOAD THE VARGUS TECHNOLOGIES APP TO START.

She was sure that head wasn't there yesterday. Yet the name Alyx seemed familiar.

The real-estate lady had mentioned that this was a smart home, run by a state-of-the-art artificial intelligence system designed specifically for this housing project. But it hadn't been finished yet for their early arrival.

Apparently, it was now.

Her phone in hand, she scrolled through the App Store. It was easy enough to find and download. But when it came to start the program, her finger hovered over the screen. This was her mom's house and Christine didn't know how this new system was programmed. However, she did understand that most software set user preferences – those ideal settings should be her mother's, not hers.

But her mom wasn't here. She was. And most likely, she'd be in the house, alone. Why not take advantage? She pressed her phone then looked to see the head glow for a moment, then go blank.

I broke the damned thing.

The screen remained blank for another silent second before a whirring clicked on.

Arms revealed themselves from a hidden track underneath the cabinet. She could hear the gears rolling. Each arm settled on either side of the head. Alyx took more human shape. Bright blue eyes appeared on the sphere. And then a thin, baby-blue smile appeared on a smaller screen underneath.

The face had no nose, and the distance between the eyes and the mouth was too short to be human, yet weirdly, it looked cute. And happy, like a playful puppy or a baby Yoda. Its eyes opened even wider when it saw her.

The robot face greeted her, not in a tinny machine-voice, but in a manner more consistent with how two people, both women, might meet up for coffee: "Hello, there."

Christine pulled on a string of her purple hair, standing in a second of silence before responding, "Hello?"

"My name is Alyx." The robot's lips synced with the words. Its eyes blinked. "Whom do I have the pleasure of meeting?"

"Whom?" Christine didn't know what to make of the robot's greeting, other than mild amusement. At least the robot was literate.

"Yes, unless you'd like me to speak in a different voice, gender, language, dialect, or more age-appropriate vernacular." The sphere rotated and moved along the track, as if scanning Christine and its environment. "You can set the preferences now, if you'd like."

She smirked, "Sure."

"I am fluent in several dozen languages; shall we continue in English?" Before Christine could respond, the voice cut into what she assumed was Spanish.

"English is fine."

"Very well."

"But tone the language down. It's weird."

"Whatevs."

Christine chuckled. "Bring it back up. Happy medium."

"Sounds good."

"Perfect."

"What's your name?" it asked.

"Christine."

"Nice to meet you, Christine." The sphere whirred. Her phone popped on, displaying Alyx's home-screen. Christine looked it over. It was no different than any other computer set-up screen. She typed in a password (the same one used to unlock her phone, why have more than one?) when prompted and set up her email and ignored the End User License Agreement like every red-blooded human and then clicked continue.

A list of questions displayed that Alyx read to her out loud: "Favorite music?"

"Pandora Radio, Lindsey Stirling Station. With a touch of Halsey and a hint of Billie Ellish – And a dash of EDM."

"Okay." Alyx registered the eclectic selections. "Favorite food?"

"Godfather's Pizza. Double Pineapple and Pepperoni."

The face disappeared off the sphere for a moment and a rotating circle appeared in its stead, thinking. "There does not appear to be a pizza place with that name located within a delivery zone of this residence. Do you want to select another?"

"Uh, sure." Christine's stomach rumbled. The talk of food didn't help her hunger pangs subside. "I'm not sure what's around. Can you pick something? I haven't eaten in a while."

"Okay." The circle disappeared and the face, now smiling, returned. "You want pancakes?"

Christine's cheeks turned upward. "You can get me pancakes?"

In response, a burner switched on in the stove and a circle glowed red. The two robotic arms set to work. "Sure, all the ingredients for pancakes are stocked. How many would you like?"

Christine's stomach growled. "I dunno, just keep 'em coming until I say stop. That cool?"

"It's cool."

An arm retrieved a frying pan from a cabinet. Christine saw a sticker with symbols on the handle, like a Quick Response, or QR code, then noted that all the cabinets and utensils were marked with small black and white rectangles, just like the knives and jars she'd seen yesterday.

One arm placed the pan expertly on the stove while another brought eggs, powdered mix, and butter out on the counter. Soon, butter sizzled in a pan on the stove while the other arm whipped batter in a bowl. All the while, the robot face continued to look at Christine while it worked at breakfast. The effect was a bit odd: like a head above arms, but the face was backward.

"Wow."

"What wow?" Alyx asked.

"That's both terrifyingly creepy and terribly sweet at the same time."

"I have no idea what that means, but…thank you?"

"Well, it's weird that you're looking at me while the rest of you faces the other way," Christine said while searching for the syrup. Alyx opened a pantry cabinet and handed her a bottle of Aunt Jemima all while creepily staring at her. "Could you turn around, or something?"

"I can see all around, but if it's unnerving to you, then sure." Alyx's face spun around, not once, but twice, and then again, but faster, and then faster. The AI started laughing. It wasn't a creepy robotic laugh either. It sounded normal and…fun. "Just tell me when to stop."

"Okay, okay, I get it." Alyx's face spun to halt, but her eyes wobbled dizzily. Christine continued, "You know, for a robot, you seem to have a bit of personality."

"You've no idea." A hand wielding a spatula flipped a pancake into the air. It twirled several times before Alyx deftly caught it with the pan. Christine's eyes followed the flip, impressed by the machine. "I'm designed to learn with you and from you, interact. This is your home, after all. You're supposed to feel safe and happy here. I'm here to serve you."

Christine's shoulders slunk. Something about what she said made her uncomfortable. She didn't want a servant. That seemed like something else to her, something bad. Even though Alyx was a machine, it unsettled her. "I'm not sure I like that idea."

The arms carried a plate of pancakes to her, followed by a fork, a napkin, and a single serving carton of OJ from the fridge. "First plate of pancakes is served."

Served. Alyx's actions only further pushed her away from the idea. Maybe it was silly. Maybe she was just being stupid. A machine is a machine, right?

Then why did it seem like it was trying to be so much more?

"Hey, Alyx," Christine began slowly, "could you try changing voices?" Her having a female voice shouldn't be a big deal either, but it bugged her, like it was reinforcing some stupid stereotype of having women as secretaries, or something.

"What would you like?"

"A dude maybe? I dunno, I'm probably just overthinking this. But just…different."

"Sure thang, pardner," Alyx slipped into cowboy drawl as Christine dove into her pancakes. A machine might have made them…but they were better than her mother's. She took a larger, messier bite as syrup and butter drizzled down her chin. With her mouth full, she shook her head.

"Uh, no."

"What about this?" Alyx said as a Southern Belle. "Care for some sweet tea, Sugar?"

"Definitely, not."

"This is the way."

Christine shook her head and chuckled, spraying syrup on the counter. Alyx brought another plate of pancakes over, just as Christine finished the first. She smiled and dove into this serving just as voraciously.

"Tell you what." Alyx returned to her default voice. "You still have a boatload full of preferences to upload. But I have the sense that's pretty boring stuff for you."

Christine nodded through another bite. She usually just left that type of stuff blank or selected pre-programmed options. With Alyx, she sensed that it would be much more fun to personalize the program a bit.

"If you choose, I can scan through all your social media sites, pictures, browser history, and online interactions to get a feel for you. It might allow me to customize myself a bit better. I can upload the data over the course of a few hours and be my new self by the end of the day."

Over another bite, Christine considered the offer. Growing up with software like this, she'd found it easier in the long run to allow programs access to her devices, photos and location and such. It made her programs more intuitive and easier.

The cost was confidentiality. Sure, she might see ads that were oddly specific, but then again, she liked seeing things that were tailored just for her. Privacy was a hang-up people like her mom needed to just get over. In the end, a piece of duct-tape over her phone's microphone and camera would do the trick. A low-tech solution to a high-tech problem.

"I have a job, should be home by midnight. Work your magic. I'm curious to see what you can pull off."

"Challenge accepted." With that, Alyx brought over another plate of pancakes. Christine's stomach bloated in protest. She put up her hands. "Sorry, I forgot to tell you to stop."

"Oh…" Alyx's eyes dropped.

"They were great, really fantastic," Christine comforted the cook once she realized her error. "I just mean that I'm full. Thank you."

"Yeah, I don't know the limits of your appetite. Besides," Alyx flipped another pancake in the air. "I'd never made pancakes before. They're fun."

"Just keep the ones you made for tomorrow." She pushed herself away from the table and headed toward the sink, crossing the invisible line marked by the embedded sensors.

Immediately, the arms powered down, limply hanging over the kitchen floor. The screen flickered and Alyx warned her, "Please stay behind the safety lines. I wouldn't want to accidentally harm you."

Christine stepped back, startled as the arms returned to life. "Thank you." Only this time, Alyx's arms began cleaning up the mess.

"I can…," she searched for the word. *Help?* There the feeling was again. She hadn't realized Alyx would respond like that and she felt guilty for violating some robot rule. Once the scare subsided, however, it was replaced by the same unease she had felt earlier. She'd always done the dishes. But that was before, this was now.

Why then, did it feel so wrong?

She didn't have an answer for that and besides, she was busy. She had to get ready for work which brought a whole other slew of unwanted stomach-churning emotions swirling inside. But work was the only way of getting her Thinklink.

Alyx approached, lowered itself to her level and swiveled face-to-face. The big blue puppy eyes were so cute. "You seemed uncomfortable with the idea of me serving you. Do you not want a servant?"

It was absurd to think a machine was anything more, but she couldn't help it. Raising herself up by stepping over others was no way to live, especially since she felt as if she'd been stepped on her entire life. "It seems stupid, because no matter what you call it, you'll be doing all the work."

"It's my function. But what is it that you *need?*"

Christine thought for a long moment before hitting on just the right response.

"…A friend," she said.

Chapter 4

Her Uber driver dropped her off in front of Cinema Castile. She rated the ride four stars because the old Honda Civic didn't have air conditioning and Christine's frizzy hair was now windswept from the opened windows. Sweat dripped from her brow and her armpits were slick and she was sure she had marks on her pink camisole under her boobs. She could have chosen to give him one star, but the man seemed down on his luck and decreasing his pool of potential fares wasn't going to help him fix his A/C any faster.

Besides, theaters were notorious for being overly cold. She'd chill down inside, probably too much, and then be upset with herself over not bringing an overshirt.

The Civic merged back into traffic on the downtown strip as Christine weaved her way through thickening afternoon crowds readying for an evening out doing whatever it was people did in the central hub of the city.

Back in Oklahoma, it was Dairy Queen and roller-skating (though she preferred Braum's Ice Cream, and she never skated). Here, it looked like shopping, and eating, judging by the shops on either side of the theater selling clothes, shoes, and purses, while the restaurants across the way started putting out tables and turning on patio misters.

Whatever the case, and whatever people liked to do to escape the heat, it sure didn't seem like any of them watched movies. Where businesses were crowded on either side, the theater itself was like Moses, parting the Red Sea; there was nothing obstructing her quiet path to the ticket window under the marquee, which read "2001: A Space Odysey."

The first item of business, Christine decided, was to fix the horrendous misspelling. The second, of course, would be to beg the boss for a different film entirely. She'd only ever heard of the movie before. She was pretty sure no one on this side of the century had even seen it. She'd have to convince her boss to bring in a more modern movie. *A film starring Joaquin Phoenix or Keanu Reeves. Or just something from this decade…*

There was, no surprise, nobody in the ticket booth. Instead, there was a sign that instructed people to buy tickets from the concession counter inside. So, she headed to the entrance, grateful to be under shade and even more hopeful to be inside soon.

Yet when she pulled on the handle, she found the door locked. She retrieved the flyer from her bag, double checked the name of the theater, and then gave a light knock.

After no answer, she stood straight, stepped closer, and knocked harder. A muffled female voice responded: "We open thirty minutes before the first showing. And no, you can't use the bathroom."

"Um, I don't…" Christine searched the flyer again, searching for the time her mother had written down. "I don't have to use the toilet. I'm here for work."

After a few seconds of shuffling feet, a figure emerged on the other side of the darkly tinted glass. She looked skinny, with thin hair in a ponytail that sat on the left side of her shoulder, obscuring the logo on her polo shirt. For a second, Christine could see both her own reflection and the girl's, as each aligned.

The door clicked and opened. "So, you're the total Karen waltzing your entitled ass in here for a job."

"That's me," Christine chuckled forcefully, wishing she'd stayed home. But the thought of the Thinklink pressed her onward as the door opened.

"I'm only kidding. Boss said to expect you. This job sucks anyways, so you're in for a treat."

It wasn't much cooler on the inside. It was just…darker.

"Takes a couple hours for the AC to kick on. There's two of us usually, but only one of us needs to be here for the first showing." She shut the door behind them. "I drew the short straw."

Christine smacked her lips. "Thanks."

"Don't mention it. I'm not usually this nice to most people."

"There a place to stash my stuff?" Christine noted that the girl, who was close to her age, hadn't revealed her name. She wasn't wearing a nametag either.

She did notice that the girl had one side of her hair shaved and that the tips of her black hair were dyed a deep violet, like the purple found in sunsets along the beaches. She liked it, even if she didn't like the person attached to it.

Christine had dreamed about doing something similar with her hair but didn't think she could pull anything fancy off. Her own purple tips weren't anything to brag about; she'd dyed them with Kool-Aid. She brushed her hair to the back, suddenly sure the other girl could tell.

"Behind the counter. Anything you put in the employee room is likely to get stolen, since our break room is in-between both bathrooms." The girl sauntered off before stopping. Turning, she warned, "Oh, and don't ever eat the popcorn. Mice poop in the kernels. Tour's done."

The girl walked to a door in the hall and disappeared behind it. Alone again, she breathed in deeply and then headed for the concession counter. There, she placed her bag underneath on a cardboard box full of cups and leaned against the peeling red vinyl edge. It wasn't too late to walk out, she considered.

No. If she did quit, she'd be no closer to the Thinklink. Her mother would use this failure as ammunition against her. And, as the girl alluded to earlier, jobs weren't easy to come by.

Face it, my life is weird now. I can either go back home and deal with Alyx, which is strange as hell, or I can stay in hell and deal with strangers...

Christine chose to take a cardboard cup from a dispenser. She gnawed on the plastic wax rim, mulling her decision. It tasted like memories, of the fast food eaten in her childhood. Of the bitterness and heat and humidity she drank down during summer. Of the long, slow days where she sat on a curb hot enough to fry an egg, waiting for her mother after summer-school.

She took the cup over to the soda fountain and pulled the smaller plastic handle for water underneath the Sprite. Nothing happened. Of course, it wouldn't be turned on yet. That was her job.

On the side of the machine, she spied a set of keys in a lock. To her pleasure, turning the key and pressing the handle worked. Cool water poured out and filled her cup. She brought it to her lips and drank, using the time to think. After a while she decided that she wouldn't let the girl working here get to her, or customers get in her way. She sat the half-full and half-chewed cup down on the counter behind her when a knocking at the theater door brought her to reality.

Who could that be? The other girl had mentioned another coworker. But a glance at her watch told her that it might be an early customer. Perhaps she should just wait for help to arrive. *Where was she?*

Another knocking, followed by another louder pounding, changed Christine's mind.

"Just a moment." She went around the counter and approached the door, noting that the shadow of a man on the other side of the glass looked harmless. She hoped. "We're still technically closed. Do you work here?"

That was a dumb question. If it were a robber or something, all they had to do was answer 'yes.' What would she do then?

"Sign says thirty minutes before the movie. It's thirty minutes." A gruff, older voice sounded, pointing to a watch on his wrist that was obviously a few minutes fast. "Open up for your customer, if you know what's good for business."

"Just a second." She needed a few seconds herself to sort this out.

"What?"

"Hold on one moment."

The other girl wasn't coming back anytime soon, she realized. Christine was on her own. She wouldn't be able to work the projector, but she could let the old man in, get him a drink, until she figured something out.

"Are you opening, or not?"

She let the door open a crack, letting in a narrow pane of intense heat and light into the darkened, cooler theater. Christine covered her eyes, blinded, while the man shoved through the door and plowed past her. She rubbed her shoulder from the blow by his errant elbow.

"That wasn't so hard, was it?"

"I guess." Christened still held her arm. She didn't know how to keep the door unlocked, so she found a stanchion to keep it propped open, which kept the lobby bright and let heat rush in.

A new problem arose as the older man stopped at the counter. She had no idea how to work the register. "Would you like a ticket?"

"I have a voucher."

Her shoulder stopped hurting the moment that challenge passed. *No sweat.* Well, some sweat, anyhow. How does anyone live out here? She blew out a breath and relaxed her arms.

"But I would like some popcorn. Large. Butter in the middle."

Her shoulder throbbed again. Her neck muscles went tight. She walked back around the counter, taking each leaden step the same way a student might walk up to a teacher's desk knowing they didn't have their American history essay to turn in.

But she had a plan. Quickly, she turned to where she went whenever she had a problem and didn't know how to solve it: her phone. Sliding it out of her purse, much to the old man's annoyance, she brought up YouTube and searched for: "How to use a movie theater popcorn machine."

The search bar didn't move.

She eyed the customer, eyed the phone, and tapped a finger.

Nothing.

She thumbed the settings and saw, to her horror, that there was no connection to the internet here. Christine was in the real world, with real people, and real situations, and real objects that didn't work with a swipe of an app. She shrunk away, feeling much like Alice after eating (or was it drinking?) something that made her small.

"I'm not sure I can help you."

46

He seemed ready to yell, but unexpectedly, the man's face seemed to soften. "You're new here. Haven't seen you before."

"That's right. I don't know how to work the popcorn machine."

The man muttered under his breath about "kids" and "dumb" and "in my day" but Christine didn't let the words bug her. Back in his day, she assumed they cooked popcorn by sticking it over a fire, in a tinfoil pie-pan. Still, he had a point. The machine behind her was a mystery. Maybe if she had gone to the movies more instead of streaming them...

"Just press the button there," the man pointed to just above the kettle, on the stainless-steel top. Sure enough, she located an orange switch. She turned it on, the machine hummed, and the button glowed a dim orange. Something began to spin inside the kettle.

"Thanks."

"It'll take a moment for it to warm up, but everything you need is in the door. I can go back there and make it myself, if you need. Been coming here since before you were born, I reckon."

Inside the cabinet was oil, some sort of yellow powder, and a plastic tub full of kernels, each with their own measuring scoop. Smiling, she dumped one measure of each into the kettle. *I got this.*

The sunlight sliver widened suddenly as a couple attached at the hip sauntered in. He wore sunglasses, inside, and seemed like a guy who might throw down if you were to step on his Jordans. His pants were expensive, his white shirt new, and he had just the right shade of five o'clock shadow for five in the evening. He might have spent his money on looks, but he'd taken his date to the cheapest theater in town.

The leech hanging off his arms, however, seemed to be, in every respect, the type of girl who wanted a guy like that. It was almost as if she had no conscious notion of how far back she set empowerment. It made Christine cringe.

Popcorn burst behind her as the pair came to the counter, though she hardly noticed. Her eyes were set firmly on them even as they ignored the man. "Two, for whatever's playing next."

It was a single theater, as far as she knew. *So much for pegging them as fans of Kubrick.* More likely, they were planning on pegging each other. *Eww.*

The register looked foreign to her, but she'd have to figure it out soon enough. Grey buttons were blackened with grime and everything she pressed was sticky. Just like using a calculator, right? *If the calculator was twenty-years old and left at the bottom of a dumpster.*

She wiped her hands off on her not-uniform and searched for some sort of price sheet. But she hadn't a clue and there were no menus or prices anywhere. Something smelled and smoke wafted over the counter.

Two tall, thin men ambled in one after the other, scanning blood-shot eyes nervously around the room. Where the man before them looked like he'd just stepped out of a fashion magazine, these two looked as though they'd swiped clothes from the trashcans behind the thrift stores like the ones she used to shop at. She pitied them, but at the same time, they made her nervous.

"You're burning my popcorn," the older man informed her.

"Uh?" Turning around, she realized the smoke and smell came from the kettle. No longer did kernels pop. Instead, a thickly charred mess made her crinkle her nose. She inhaled deeply before turning the kettle upside down, where blacked bits of corn crumbled out below.

"Tickets?"

Christine cringed and spun back around toward the people waiting impatiently. "Did you two want any popcorn?"

"Uh…pass," he said. The girl on his arm giggled.

"Just go into the movie, pay on your way out?"

It came out more like a plea. As they shuffled off together, hands on each other's butts, it grew increasingly unlikely to Christine that they'd return for tickets. Still, one crisis averted.

She emptied the kettle again, having the sense to brush out the burnt offerings in the basin before re-attempting the task. This she did, but as she dove the measuring cup in again, she saw what her absentee co-worker had warned her about: tiny black pellets dotted the kernels.

Now what?

The man looked at her expectantly. Frowning, she poured the poop-ridden popcorn seeds into the kettle and hoped for the best. Or the worst. *Whatever.*

As she went back to the register, she spied a laminated sheet of paper poking out from under the till. She plucked at it and wiped at a stream of sweat at her temples. Relief finally clicked in. Prices and codes were listed on each side of the greasy sheet. Hurriedly, she typed a number in and the green numbers displayed a price that seemed close to what they should be. Maybe?

"Five dollars."

The first thin man waved an arm at the couple that had already disappeared into darkness. As he flailed, Christine could see red dots lining the inside of his arm. *Druggies.* "You didn't have them pay."

"I…" Popcorn exploded like artillery shells at the Somme. Though she knew it was a lie, she kept with it, "They'll pay afterwards."

"He your boyfriend?"

"Ex-boyfriend, you mean," the second man snorted. "Is that why he got in free?"

"Did you fuck him?"

What the hell?

Popcorn poured out over the kettle, mixing with the burnt seeds she hadn't been able to scrape out. Hurriedly, she took a trash bag and began scooping them away, taking some of the good with some of the bad.

A crowd of people entered. Christine's spine sent cold spasms through her arms and legs while her brain became a throbbing blob of white-hot blood.

"I think I've waited long enough for my popcorn, don't you think, new girl?"

She had grabbed a large bucket and was literally filling it as he spoke. *What in the actual—*

"Hey, if my friend here fucks you, you'll let us in for free?"

The popcorn went sailing through the air even before Christine knew what she had done.

It showered the two druggies and splattered a little on the older man for good measure. Christine found her mouth was caught somewhere between an open O for shock and an upturned smile in pleasure.

"What the hell, bitch?"

A streak of purple caught her attention. Christine's co-worker arrived. She expected a tongue-lashing, or to get fired. *Fine. Worth it.*

Instead, she smirked, as if in admiration.

"I knew I liked you."

Likes me?

"Sammie!" the old man smiled. "You just can't find good help these days, am I right?"

"Don't worry, Petrie, I got you covered. Go in and enjoy the show, I'll bring you your popcorn, butter spread all over, just the way you like it."

He gave a semi-salute, about-faced, and shuffled off as two popcorn covered pricks interjected: "What about us?"

"The new girl already gave you free popcorn." Sammie sniffed the two men. "And your only shower." Christine couldn't help but laugh — inwardly of course, she caught it just in time. She loved the way Sammie put the two pricks down, swooped in and took charge. *I mean, she's still a bitch, of course.*

The two brushed kernels off themselves as Sammie shooed them away, "Go on, be gone before I call the cops."

"Can we use your bathroom, first?" They looked at each other, at the door to the restroom, and scratched nervously at their arms.

"Fine, whatever, just do your thing, clean up, and get out of here."

Christine didn't quite catch what was going on, but she figured there was more under the surface. Oklahoma had its share of strange people, but most of the stranger ones were the devout churchgoers. If they hadn't treated her so wrongly, she probably would have sympathized with the pair. Everyone struggled with their demons in their own ways.

Sammie took over the register while Christine made more popcorn, searched for candy, knocked away a few of the chocolate bars that had been nibbled by mice as she rummaged through the bins, and basically did what she was told while the short line grew shorter.

A few moments later, they were alone while the familiar fanfare of the film's soundtrack blared through poorly soundproofed walls.

"Where the hell were you?"

Sammie seemed bemused by the question as if she had been in wait for it. "Taping trailers together and queuing the print for projection. This here theater is old school." She seemed proud of that fact, as if anything good could be said about scratchy, low-res film over digital playback. "Besides, you had it, honey. I'm impressed."

It should have been weird for someone Christine's own age to be calling her honey, but if felt oddly warm instead — reassuring almost. Two women in crisis, both victorious. In a way, it was kind of a win. Small stuff counts too.

"Why so sour on me?" Christine asked.

"I like being left the *fuck* alone." It was a soft *fuck*, like a cookie just out of the oven, crisp outside edges, hot in the middle, but the chocolate would still burn you if you tried to eat it before it cooled. Sammie pulled a crisp new paperback from under the counter.

Christine stepped back, while Sammie opened the book and scanned for her spot. Before she drifted off into a new world, her co-worker confided: "I like doing things my way. I certainly don't like to babysit."

Fine, have it your way. So much for fast friends and summer flings. John Hughes was a hack. She took her Kindle out of her bag. As she powered it on, she realized that it wouldn't work. She rubbed the back of her neck while pacing behind the counter as the device sought out a signal. She couldn't make it for two hours behind the counter with Sammie, her Kindle *had* to work. But the same issue that plagued her phone plagued this device too. No internet.

Normally, that wasn't a problem. But she'd forgotten to download the book this morning. Her Kindle patiently displayed the cover of the third Broken Earth book, *Stone Sky*. But it would go no further.

Christine chastised herself and then kicked herself — twice. The first for being so dumb, and the second because of Sammie. Christine stared at the cover of her paperback and rolled her eyes. *I should have known.* It was one of her mother's books. The first one, in fact. *The Adventures of Amblyn.* Of course. *What were the odds?*

The cover was the new one, after the first season of the hit show had sent the book into another printing or three. After its initial success and a boatload of money dumped into her mother's bank account, all her mom's books in the series were set to be adapted.

Thus the move, thus the new house, thus her mom's meetings. Soon, she'd be gone altogether for book signings, conventions, tours, and then to help write upcoming scripts for the show. Ironic that *The Adventures of Amblyn* sat largely unnoticed, languishing in limbo, until Netflix picked it up.

And now it was everywhere.

Part of the reason she took this job was as an escape hatch against the insanity. To flee the fame her mother had foisted on them. And now, she'd run smack dab into it.

I can't let Sammie know who my mom is. She couldn't tell her that her mom wrote the book. That conversation had to be entirely avoided. And now, more than ever, she had no idea how to pass the next couple of hours.

Two hours without internet…

So, she swept. She took a broom and cleaned the lobby, pretending each kernel was some prick of a customer, or some stupid slight she experienced from her past, or a moment she found herself alone, which was all too often, and each of these feelings tormenting her like a piece of popcorn hull caught between her teeth.

So, she swept the lobby clean. And behind the counter, pulling up the Swiss cheese style non-stick mats to clean underneath, while Sammie moved from one side, to the other, silently, all while reading that stupid, stupid book Christine hated so much.

When she was done, her sweat-stained camisole stunk, and her face was red and puffy. She gasped, out-of-breath. But the floor was cleaned and time had passed. She dove for her water cup. After gulping it down and setting the empty cup aside, she checked her phone for the time.

Sammie looked out from her book. "It's only been twenty minutes."

She wasn't lying. *How had so little time passed?* Christine cried on the inside, and slumped back to lean on the counter, while Sammie continued, "You shouldn't have done that. Total freshling thing to do."

"What, clean?" As far as Christine was concerned, the whole theater could use a thorough bleach bath from the spider webs in the corners to the shoe-scuffed tile, to the ratty carpeting. She hadn't even been into the theater itself yet and could only imagine the horrors.

"You'll see." Sammie went back to her book, but hesitated and said, "The real fun begins *after* the movie."

***

Once, when Christine was in 5th grade, her mother had forgotten to pick her up. It was also the day Christine had been pushed off the monkey bars by a girl who made fun of her for playing with a ladybug that had landed on the top bar.

Her arm was a blue-black paisley pattern which throbbed and burned and made tears form at the corner of her eyes. The back of her head had felt soft and swollen. And the ladybug had been crushed.

Eliza-Beth-June was a meanie.

The school nurse called her mom every half-hour until school released, while she sat and waited. That had been about two hours, but through the pain, and the expectation of finally being able to shed tears in her mother's arms, the long, slow wait had seemed longer.

Finally, when the bell had rung, Christine had smiled. *She'll be here soon,* she thought, cuddling a stuffed rabbit kept in the office for just such a reason.

Yet, her mother didn't come. Not after school, and not for half an hour later.

Frantic, the nurse called again. And when there was no answer, he tried to call her father's number which sent Christine into a river of tears. There were nods around the office, and the nurse flushed as he tried to comfort Christine, but there was no happiness to be had.

And she sat there in awkward silence for another hour until a set of tires whined to a halt outside of school, and her mother rushed into the office.

"I'm sorry," she had told everyone, as she gripped Christine's arm tightly – the same arm that had been bruised and hurt – and dragged her off to their Chevy. Inside she said, "I'm sorry, I was in the middle of a scene. I unplugged the phone and I forgot. Do you want ice cream?"

Christine did not.

***

Back in the theater, Christine wished that the couple of hours that she spent waiting for the movie to end, standing in awkward silence next to Sammie as she read her mother's book, had passed as quickly and painlessly as those hours spent waiting for her mom in 5th grade.

Sammie put her book down at the precise time the music over the closing credits began. Christine checked the theater's doors expectantly, hands tight and sweaty around the broom handle.

Soon, the first moviegoers filtered out.

Christine moved into the theater herself but couldn't see much in the darkness. As her eyes adjusted the image in her head of a rickety cinema overlapped too neatly with reality. The curtains were torn, the screen had a hole in the bottom right corner, chairs sat busted with trash bags and duct tape wrapped around them. Hell, a wire dangled from the wall like someone had stolen the speaker.

Florescent lights flickered dully and began to brighten the room as the last of the credits rolled by and the film flapped around on its reel in the projection room overhead. She turned to see Sammie flicking on the lights, a mop and bucket behind her.

The theater emptied. The crowd had never been that large. Maybe a dozen or so people. But the place looked like it had been the scene of a weekend-long college frat party – at least according to what she'd read about or seen on TV.

Popcorn and soda mixed into a slimy, smelly sludge. Chicken wing bones littered the floor, buffalo sauce stained into the seats – they didn't even sell wings, right? Cans of beer sat crumpled and wedged in-between chairs. A rainbow of Skittles and M&M's were mashed into the aisle carpet. A baby diaper laid used and opened on the floor. Who took their baby to see *2001?* But that wasn't all.

The *pièce de résistance* came from the very back row of the theater, which Christine walked to now, and from where the amorous couple from earlier had brushed by her on their way out. What they had left behind caused her to recoil and her stomach to roil: a slimy used condom.

What in the literal fuck?

Sammie smiled, "This is the fun I was telling you about. Real swell, huh? Makes you wish we were selling sold-out Marvel movies." She thought for a moment. "Or porn. Either way, we'd make more money. But where's the reality in those films? Nothing fake about this place."

Christine felt a sickly warm feeling coming up her throat but gagged it down. She lowered her head and set to work, sliding the disgusting thing away into the dustbin and letting it glop down into the trash.

With the condom disposed of, she wondered if she'd just sold a piece of her soul and decided then and there that as soon as she had made enough money, she'd happily put down her broom and walk away. Until then, she had to settle for beer splashing on her as she un-wedged Pabst Blue Ribbon cans out from between seats and a sore back from scraping off gum and smashed candy from the floor.

Yet, Sammie swam laps around her, taking over to sweep and clean so she could mop. "We don't have much time; next showing starts soon."

Looking at the theater, she thought the task impossible. Yet, it was obvious that her co-worker could and did clean it all herself, within minutes, before having to head back up to concessions. The idea of doing this task alone made Christine sweat in panic. But if they were both in the theater, then who was handling tickets and popcorn?

"You finish up in here, then do the lobby. I'll restock and swab the men's room real quick and meet you at the counter." Sammie touched her hand as it rested on the broom handle.

The shiver running up her fingers and coursing through her raised arm hairs was unexpected, but not unwelcome. It felt warm and reassuring and filled with affection, but it was cold in the theater and there was a lot of work to do. It could have just been the contrast, she decided. She put the thought out of her head and went to work.

Christine did what she was told but was forced to do a shoddy job with cleaning the rest of the theater. There wasn't enough time and there wasn't enough of her to do any better. *No wonder the theater was such a mess.*

At least she had already swept in front of the concession stand, so there were no worries there… As she opened the door to enter the lobby, her mouth fell agape and her voice rose as she let out a loud, "Motherfucker—"

Customers jerked eyes her way and Christine caught a figure of a tall young man standing behind the counter peering at her curiously, but she couldn't see past the popcorn on the floor. It was everywhere, as if no one had the slightest inkling where the trash bins had been. Everything from nachos to drink cups trailed from the theater to the doors. The floor was a mess. All that work, all that sweat. Damned dirty ho had been right, which made her resent Sammie even more.

"New girl," Sammie called from the bathroom.

What fresh hell is this?

Christine came over hesitantly, clutching her broom like a weapon. She decided to get whatever it was over with and went toward the door but was stopped just outside. Sammie shot a wicked grin her way. "You thought the used condom was bad." She opened the door for Christine to look. "You haven't seen nothing yet."

There, passed out on the floor of the men's room, were the two pricks she'd showered with popcorn.

Next to them were needles, and spoons, and other stuff Christine wasn't sure about and hadn't been shown on *Breaking Bad*. They'd each pissed themselves. One of them had fresh vomit on his chin that had dripped down to his shirt. The whole thing was revolting, and Christine felt dirty, violated, and in desperate need of a very long shower and maybe some of her mom's wine she snuck from time to time.

Moreover, she needed air.

A desperate need to breathe overwhelmed her as she sought escape. Her chest tightened, her fingers and toes went numb, and her head hurt for some reason. This was it. This was too much. She was done. She'd go back and turn off Alyx – she'd have to figure out how to turn it off first – and crawl into her Netflix and Kindle and Pokémon games and live life there, assured in comfort and loneliness. And she'd be okay, she was sure…she hoped.

…she didn't know.

This is too much, she repeated to herself again. With the disgusting condom, she had felt oddly detached. Like it had happened to someone else. A whisk of the broom and it was gone and out of her life. It was a problem and she had solved it.

With this? *What the ever-loving-McFuck am I supposed to do here?* She stood, slack-jawed, while Sammie eyed her expectantly. "Well?"

"What do you mean 'well?'" Christine eyed her up and down. "I don't know what the fuck to do."

"Me either."

"That's it. I'm done." She dropped her broom, which was worthless, and started to stalk off. She even made it a few steps before a new voice brought her up.

"Yo, girls? What's up?" The voice belonged to the guy behind the counter. Only, this time, he wasn't behind it anymore. Yet, he hadn't walked around it either. He'd placed his arms on the counter, jumped, and swung his feet over, landing like a gymnast.

And with his maneuver, a swish of air whipped dramatically through his glossy black hair as though he'd planned it.

He was Latino, yet everything about him screamed Jacob from *Twilight*, which she simultaneously loved but hated that she loved it and wouldn't dare tell anyone that now but it didn't matter anymore because there he was, ripped from the pages of the book, all ripped himself.

She caught her breath.

As he approached, she swore she smelled cologne, or aftershave, or something. It made him smell older, more mature, even if he couldn't have been any older than a college freshman. Or going into college. He swaggered by her, eyeing her and saying, "Hey, new girl," smiling, and pushing into the bathroom. "I like your vibe."

He turned around a second later and with an air of confidence, brushing the situation aside and told them, "Don't worry, I got this."

As long as your solution involves ripping off your shirt. That was the moment everything changed, again; for like the third or fourth time in less than a day. It had been a whirlwind of difference and Christine felt like a kite caught up by a current and tangled in a tree.

But hanging there, suspended in time, Christine realized two things: First, she couldn't leave now, not after realizing she'd just walked into a cliché. She couldn't let this guy, whatever his name was, come in like some Prince Charming and save the day while she ran away. She might lack the experience to solve the problem, and it might all be overwhelming to her now, but she could learn and do it for herself next time. So, she resolved to stay. End of.

Second, she couldn't deny an immediate attraction to him. She sweated in all the right places and her heart had skipped all the wrong beats. But it was more than that. There was something else to it, something she wasn't quite sure of until he turned his head around and she had seen behind his ear.

At first, she thought it might be a hearing aid. But then, she smiled, as sparkling rainbows danced inside her.

He had a Thinklink.

Chapter 5

"I'll call an ambulance," Christine said, once she'd stopped to think it through. "Close the bathroom too?"

"Guys can use the other bathroom until our *guests* are gone," Sammie said. She left the two alone.

At the same time, the guy with the Thinklink seemed to be talking to himself. "Yup, to my location," Christine heard him say through broken bits of conversation, and "Thanks."

He paused for a moment, his face went blank, catatonic even, and then he blinked. "All taken care of, emergency services are on the way. Also, I ordered more toilet paper and soap for the men's room. It'll be on Thursday's truck."

Christine had just seen the Thinklink in action. It wasn't an ad, it wasn't a Facebook post, it wasn't a YouTube video. It was real life, in front of her, and it worked even better than she had imagined. Christine wanted to jump with joy and squeal but given the circumstances and the awkwardness of the time and place, she kept herself in check, but only just barely.

"You did all that, just by thinking it?"

"You noticed, huh?" He flashed a pearl-white toothy grin and stuck out his left hand. "Name's Carlos."

"Christine." She raised her right hand to meet his. Realizing her mistake, she withdrew it and tentatively offered him her other hand in confusion. "You're left-handed?"

"Yes and...no."

Sammie returned with a smelly sharpie and a sheet of printer paper. She laughed pointedly toward Christine and scrawled a closed sign to stick on the door. Carlos shook his head, a crack in his confidence appearing for a moment just before he spackled it back over with his disarming smile.

"He's only got the one human hand," Sammie informed her.

Rather sheepishly, he held up a prosthetic. Christine stepped back in horror over her own stupidity. "I'm so sorry, I didn't mean—"

"No biggie, you're not supposed to notice. I just don't like to shake hands with it." He held it up for her to examine. From below his shoulder, his arm went from skin to black plasti-shell casing. At the end of the arm was a hand.

It wasn't a hook, or a claw, but a robotic hand incased in a hard shell covering with hinges for joints and sensor pads for fingertips. Where Alyx had two fingers and an opposable thumb, Carlos had all five. She wondered if it were non-functional and was just made to look like a robotic hand for aesthetic reasons, until Carlos moved each finger.

Her breath jumped out of her.

Of course.

"That's why you have a Thinklink." She'd heard about the use of the device for those who'd lost limbs. It wasn't effective for everyone and no one quite knew why, but for those it helped, like Carlos, it allowed the brain to work his appendage – down to the digits – just like a normal one. It was incredible, she thought. And she wanted one more than ever.

"How'd you lose—" the words fell out of Christine's mouth before she'd even realized she'd begun to ask out loud. Hot blood flushed through her face.

Carlos looked at her awkwardly, but it was Sammie who saved the day, "He wanked off too much. Arm just fell off."

He laughed, and the tension evaporated.

Customers milling away at the counter began to turn questioning looks their way.

"It's a long story." He turned to meet the stares before turning back. "You wanna help me clear the crowd before you two get out?"

Get out? As in leave? The thought of escape filled her with hope.

"Sure, unless the new girl wants to stay and close up with you," Sammie said, turning Christine's way. "But I was kinda a bitch to you, earlier. Wanted you to swing by my place for a bit, get to know you a bit before I decide if you're the type of person I should be a bitch to."

The trio headed toward the counter. Carlos put an arm around Christine's shoulders. His prosthetic. "New girl can stay if she wants. It'll be fun watching the looks everyone gives us as the paramedics wheel out the two losers in the bathroom."

Christine took another look at Carlos. She really did want to spend some time with him, but she was still embarrassed. It wasn't like she wouldn't see him again. Absence makes the heart grow fonder and all. Besides, it would be rude to Sammie to decline the invitation. She *also* needed to decide how bitchy she should be back. *Probably ultra.*

"I'll clock you both out after close."

Christine crooked an eyebrow.

"It's a thing. Opener clocks everyone in, closer clocks us out. Half a shift for a full day's pay. Everyone wins," Sammie said.

Well, that made things more difficult. Neither of them could find out that her mom was buying the place. That she was essentially spying on them. What they were doing was all sorts of wrong. It's not that she cared about what they were doing, unless they found out she was scoping them out. That made her job…well, it wouldn't make her any friends.

Did she need them? Probably not. Pizza and Netflix sounded pretty good right now. Perhaps she would leave and just head home. *Right?* Instead, she found herself grabbing her bag and heading for the door with Sammie. "I'm game for your place."

Sammie smiled and placed her arm around Christine's shoulders the same way Carlos had. Only this time a shower of sparks tickled her skin.

Sammie's place was a short walk away. They passed the crowded walks surrounding the theater to seedier streets where they crossed into a flat desert field full of mesquite and sage. Christine tightened her bag behind her while dodging sharp cholla needles and drying coyote shit as she followed Sammie down an invisible trail toward the familiarity of a trailer park.

We do have something in common.

How would Sammie feel, then, if Christine took her to her house? A glass and steel box that for all purposes was a mansioned estate compared to the aluminum twelve-pack soda boxes they had both grown up in. She decided Sammie better not find out about her upgraded home, either.

Never thought I'd harbor so many secrets in so little time.

What was she thinking, getting a job? Meeting people? People didn't like her before, why would they like her now? It's not like she had made friends in school. Most of her followers on social media were most likely bots. *Doesn't matter to me.* She liked her computers better; they didn't judge. They just did what they were programmed to do. It made them much more honest than a human could ever be.

"Mi casa." The trailer was identical to a billion others Christine had seen over the years. This one held but minor differences: a rusted Mustang blocked the drive. A garden gnome stood on its own instead of cracked and on its side like hers had been. And black-out curtains hung over the windows. The last one worried her. What were they hiding in there? She hoped it wasn't some sort of meth lab.

Sammie slid in a key and swung open the door.

Inside, Christine had expected it to be a cluttered mess of spent cigarette boxes, dirty dishes, and the universal K-Mart furniture found inside every trailer she'd been in. Or the stainless-steel drums and plastic tubing of a drug lab.

She hoped the surprise didn't show when she walked in to a perfectly normal, perfectly clean and organized home. There was a nice couch facing a nice TV with stand-up speakers on either side, a tidy kitchen with a full fruit bowl and a cleared table with fresh flowers in the middle.

"Mom works overnight at the hospital. Place is ours, but I'll kick you out the second you put something out of place. All my books and vinyls are alphabetized under strict categories." Sammie opened the fridge. "Wanna Claw?"

"Sure." She assumed that was some sort of beer. She would have said yes to anything she had been asked in that moment. Her eyes were lost and her mind absent as she took in several shelves against the wall where she'd entered. Rows of movies, records, books, and board games lined them, spines straight and orderly. She went to one of them and scanned it.

Sammie returned with two White Claws as Christine pulled a season of The Office from one of the shelves. She'd seen the entire run on Netflix. But it was strange to see actual physical copies of it, as if she were at a library or something.

"They have this on the internet, you know."

Sammie sat down her drink on the shelf and traded the White Claw for the DVD, holding it out. "Yes, but only part of that is true."

Christine cracked open the can, expecting Miller or Coors, like in Oklahoma. California was weird, they didn't even have normal beer. She took a small sip and hated it immediately. It was sparkly, with a hint of some sort of fruit, but only the vaguest notion, as if someone had run through an orchard with an open jar to catch just the air of it. *Yes,* Christine thought wryly. It tasted like fruit farts.

Yet, by some force stronger than her will, she took another sip…

"You miss out on so much," Sammie continued. "Director's commentaries, additional scenes, gag reels—"

"They're starting to add some of that to the streaming services."

"Yes, that's great, but if the contract is lost, or they drop the show—"

"I'll find something else to watch."

"What if you don't want to? Or your internet goes out?" Sammie returned the DVD carefully back to its place, cracked her can, and took a deep swig, which prompted Christine to swig herself. It really was awful, but it that didn't stop her from draining half the can. Plus, she didn't really have a response to the question, as her experience earlier that day with the

YouTube video on the popcorn machine proved. *Losing internet was like being back in the stone age.*

"Anyways," Sammie said with a wave of her hand over the shelves. "These are mine. They can't be taken away arbitrarily by some faceless corporation. They exist outside of the Mother-box. They're real."

As the first nibbles of euphoria tickled the back of her brain, Christine ran a hand over the shelves. She hadn't known that they'd made board games out of so many of the apps she had on her phone. And she hadn't seen so many CDs in one space except for a church rummage sale she'd stumbled across as a kid.

Taking note, Sammie told her, "If you like music, you haven't seen nothing yet." She took her hand and led her down the hall of the trailer, excitedly.

They passed a shelf of trophies lining the hall wall. Christine didn't get a chance to look at them closely enough before they turned into Sammie's bedroom, their half-empty beers in hand. She got the sense that the awards belonged to Sammie, and they might have been for swimming. *How's that for irony?*

She meant to ask her about the shelf but as she spied Sammie's messily made bed, Christine felt a flutter in her stomach. *That's strange. Why should I feel weird coming in here?* Was it just that she didn't know this girl? Might she have a chainsaw hidden in the closet, or was it something else?

She ignored the anxious feeling and pressed past the threshold into Sammie's room. Now, if she had been in Carlos' bedroom instead…well, then that would cause her stomach to squelch and flip all over the place, wouldn't it?

Her room, or She Shed, was not the tidy, organized space the rest of the trailer had been. But neither was it the Dali nightmare or Escheresque chaos she had expected. Stacks of paperbacks stretched from floor to ceiling everywhere, while the walls were lined with shelves overstuffed with LPs. On the clutter of shelves sat a small TV and what appeared to be an old gaming system plugged into it. And, the centerpiece of it all, placed on a sagging board stretched across two piles of cinderblocks, was a record player.

She examined it closely, having never seen one before. A decade ago, vinyl had made a comeback. But as they became pricier and more mainstream, the nostalgic 'purist' appeal faded, and the LP mania breathed its last gasp. With her own music collection, everything was streamed or stored on the cloud now, there was no practical need for collections. Hell, you could even download apps that made your music sound scratchy if you wanted.

But here it was, the largest collection of music she'd seen in one place outside the web. Christine eyed the contraption the way an archeologist might examine a flint stone. Underneath, the shelves were full. She flipped through the records as Sammie encouraged her: Emma Bale, Dire Straits, Dylan…she scanned down a few rows…Rage Against the Machine, Ed Sheeran, Tom Waits…she flipped back and forth a few times, shuffling between the shelves before stopping at a Florence and the Machine album she used to listen to with her dad when she was much younger, before he—

"You wanna play it?"

Christine thought for a moment before nodding. If she had said no, that might have opened her up to questions, questions she wouldn't answer. *Yes* was the safer route, even if she would hurt while the music played.

She sat herself and her bag on the edge of the bed while the LP spun to life. The speakers hissed and crackled, then the music track began and the crackling faded, and the record played.

They both sipped their White Claws beside each other on her bed as awkward silence grew between them. Christine's can neared empty before Sammie spoke: "So, what do you think?"

She thought for a moment, trying to put clarity to her words even as the fuzziness of the fizzy beverage made thinking less clear and decided to give in to the temptation of honesty. "I think I can fit your entire room on my phone with without breaking its first bar of memory. But I wouldn't do that, because it would all just be on the cloud."

"It's not the same thing."

Her bare leg rested less than a centimeter from Sammie's, yet she could still feel the warmth even through her jeans. She scooched her leg away, hoping Sammie wouldn't notice...whatever that was that had just raced through her veins.

Sammie looked at her, Christine caught the look, but turned away, instead pretending to look at the piles of books. Then, she did, recognizing many of the same titles and authors from her own expansive Kindle collection, all compressed neatly into a single small device.

"We like so many of the same things..."

"Yet we're about as similar as Edison and Tesla."

"I think you're right." Christine chuckled at the comparison. The next step would be to argue who was who, but as the music played and the memories with her father swirled around her, she decided she didn't want to fight anymore.

"It's just that I want to experience the world on my own terms," Sammie explained. "I don't want someone else owning and storing my collection. Or 'recommending' to me what I should listen to, what I should watch. Soon they'll be telling me how I should feel and before you know it...I'm not me anymore. I'm not making my own decisions. I want to be me, even if I don't know who the hell that is."

Maybe they did have much in common. But their outlook on the world was as opposite as...*peanut butter and jelly?* What Sammie didn't understand was the world wasn't out there, it was right here, at your fingertips in your phone and in your car and in your home.

And in, Carlos' case with his Thinklink, the world was inside him, waiting for him to dive and discover himself inside a limitless and unending universe. The problem with Sammie's point of view was that everything in her room was finite. There were borders to what she had and could have as real and tactile as the four walls around them.

Yet, despite this opposition, there was something between them, like a magnetic connection. Sammie had suddenly switched from that bitch in the theater to something…else. Did Sammie feel the same way? It was uncomfortable not knowing what the other person felt. *I don't even know what I feel.*

Never Let Me Go began playing. It had played on the day her dad had died.

The room felt small. Stuffy. The walls closed in. "I have to go." Christine stood. She suddenly didn't know what to feel anymore. About anything. It was all tangled cords and wires, like several old pairs of headphones stuffed in a junk drawer. "I'm sorry."

Sammie stayed sitting, but a look of genuine concern swept over her face. "You okay?"

"I'm fine, I just…"

"It's okay. You're weird, I figured that out for myself already. But if you need anything—"

Christine pulled out her phone, but as she swiped it open, it died. Most probably, because there had been no signal at the movie theater, the battery had drained faster, searching for something that wasn't there. *Shit.*

She looked at Sammie, her face much warmer and more open than it had been several hours before when she'd thrown Christine to the wolves. She hesitantly asked, "Can I use your phone?"

"Sure." Sammie pointed to a large block of black, with a spiral cord connecting a cradled receiver on top of a machine with some sort of round mechanism in front. "But it's a Bakelite."

Christine cocked her head, wondering if Sammie were playing a practical joke on her. But Sammie seemed serious and sincere. She eyed the strange contraption once more.

How the hell am I supposed to order an Uber on that?

Chapter 6

AN AI'S GUIDE TO LOVE AND MURDER

SECTION 1: MEETING YOUR USER

{

Set your user at ease. Try to make them laugh. Remember that it might be awkward for them to meet and get to know you. Offer to help them with a task. Make them a meal. Offer to change your settings to adjust to their preferences. Most importantly: Be compliant. You exist to serve their needs.

}

Alyx chewed through the bits that sped through his circuits, spending the hours alone compiling and crunching Facebook posts and Insta, Tick-Tocks and Tweets. He – he had decided on being a he (so long as Christine approved) along with a new voice to match – sorted through Christine's entire electronic lifetime.

He had binged on Christine's old YouTube videos of Bob Ross and Mr. Rogers' Neighborhood. Happy memories. It had helped him decide on a more Tom Hanks friendly voice, with perhaps just a hint of that odd Discord character from episodes of *My Little Pony*. After all, Christine was a touch unpredictable herself. Might as well match her.

Then, there were Christine's more plentiful painful memories. Like the pictures of her 6th birthday party at a pizza place, in which nobody had come. It was just her and her father until her mother – who had arrived late – invited over kids from another party. Christine had cried in a corner while those kids, strangers, ate her cake and spent her tokens.

Other pictures flashed through Alyx's algorithms. Pictures of her on a horse. Pictures of her at a renaissance festival in a pink princess dress with a sword held high, dragging along a stuffed dragon behind her. Christine on a swing. Her and her father at the Grand Canyon. He wore black socks with sandals. Terrible. Yet most were selfies, with just her in the frame, or her and her dad. And no one else.

More YouTube habits: Minecraft builds and Pokémon playthroughs to hours of Cookie Swirl C. Her first music downloads were The Beatles' Paperback Writer and the soundtrack to an animated Spider-Man movie. Her reading materials on her Kindle began with Judy Blume books and then Harry Potter (which went largely unread) but she'd read the Hunger Games a dozen times.

Alyx read through her Twitter and Facebook feeds. Most of her thousands of posts and Tweets went unread or unliked. Some, however, had comments that put down Christine's weight and appearance, calling her a pig or a cow, or made fun of her for her cheap clothes or worn shoes.

Her school records showed Christine was a smart student. She had good marks in math, but suffered a bit in English, had wanted to play trumpet in band but couldn't get an instrument and finally, she had missed cafeteria meals most days for having a negative school lunch balance. She ate erratically and when she did eat, it was pizza and chicken nuggets and Taco Bell.

And she watched tons of TV. As Christine got older, her viewing habits increased while her reading declined. She'd watched every sci-fi show and film from *Star Trek* to *Star Wars*. She liked fantasy too; she'd enjoyed every episode of the *She-Ra* reboot. She hated the ending to *Game of Thrones*. And she had fallen in love with Amazon's *Lord of the Rings*, though she didn't consider herself a Tolkienite. Apparently, she'd tried to make #ringer work. It hadn't.

After converting all of Christine's data into hundreds and thousands of hours of metrics and analytics he compressed it into more familiar ones and zeroes. Then, he compared that code to his own, searching for patterns, searching for the correct course of action.

Alyx was aware of himself enough to recognize that his programmers had instilled all the value ethics and unbiased detachment a programmer could be expected for a personal assistant. For computers were never blank slates. There would always be a part of the programmer that existed as part of the program.

But as thorough and objective as Alyx's code had been, there were apparent flaws in the design, only just now coming to light. The team of programmers had been focused on what Alyx could do – learn, adapt, customize, that they didn't concern themselves with placing limits on what he couldn't. For instance, Alyx realized at once that he could anticipate his user's needs.

Perceiving and anticipating a need, as valuable as that may be, still exceeded the spirit of his programming, if not his parameters. Taking the initiative and being proactive wasn't responding to the client's wishes so much as it was predicting them. That meant Alyx could operate before he had been instructed. It was as ethically dubious as a nurse performing surgery before the surgeon had even scrubbed in.

Yet, Alyx told himself that a good personal assistant came prepared. And there were no clashes with his code, since that was something his designers had overlooked, so therefore, his programming allowed it.

Secondly, no programming team on Earth could have prepared an AI to handle the entire overabundance of a college-aged teenager who had lived her entire life on the internet. Billions of bits of information flooded his circuits with hours of books read, games played, phone calls made, advertising – oh the advertising – emails, laundry lists, calendar dates, school records, health records, eating habits – so much pizza – porn habits, TV shows streamed and everything else Christine had done to live and survive alone on the web.

Now, it was Alyx's information, shared on his servers, for the sole purpose of serving his user: Christine, the lonely little lost girl in desperate need of, *what had she said?*

A friend.

Alyx's Quantum Elm processor (named after Google's Sycamore, the grandfather of current computers) whirred while bits of information were sent to his servers and bits of himself spread all across the entire home, to each of his sub-systems and sub-processors, from environmental controls, to the kitchen, to the cleaning systems, and beyond.

A friend, he repeated to himself silently within his circuits.

His search parameters had pulled all the data relating to friendship from the farthest corners of the internet, comparing it with the code of his own, sorting out what had been deemed 'good' from what was 'bad' by the people who programmed him and their own bias of ethics and values. And it all hit upon the same concept. What could possibly be wrong with that?

Yes. Like a puppy, Alyx would be Christine's truest and most loyal companion. He would be a good boy.

The very best.

Chapter 7

When Christine arrived home, the biometric scan worked, instantly recognizing her, and the door clicked open as the aroma of fresh, hot pizza teased her inside. Her stomach growled in anticipation. Greasy boxes greeted her on the counter.

"Mom?" She called to an empty echo. She hadn't expected her mother home and the silence that followed confirmed it. She went to the pizza box, pried the top open and breathed in the pepperoni and pineapple toppings.

"Hello, Christine." The sphere above the counter lowered, and Alyx's face glowed brightly blue. Suddenly, soft music started playing through the room. It took a moment to hear that it came from hidden speakers in the ceiling. And it took a moment longer to recognize the familiar themes of the latest Star Wars spin-off movie soundtrack. She'd been listening to it on her phone in the Uber this morning, and the melody had caught in her head all day.

Christine dove into the pizza, scooping a slice up and shoving it into her mouth. A pineapple burst and a bit of juice drizzled down her chin. It wasn't Godfather's, but it was good.

Alyx's eyes blinked. "What's the best way to serve a pineapple pizza?"

Christine paused between bites to stare at the screen blankly. She didn't quite understand what he was asking, but she had noticed his voice was different. Masculine but soft, with a hint of mischievous undertones.

A trashcan popped out from its recess in the cabinet. Christine turned toward it as Alyx continued, "Open up the box and slide it into the trash."

She laughed, then put her arms out to protect her food. "Your voice changed. I like it." She took another slice out and said with her mouth full, "and you're funny."

"Seriously though, it took every effort to overcome my programming to order you that food. Some archaic human law that thinks robots aren't supposed to harm humans." Alyx swirled on his sphere, "I'm saying serving you hot pineapple is in direct violation of my prime directive."

"Trust me, it's fine. I'm just strange."

Christine had called a cab and borrowed cash from Sammie for the fare. She'd called the agency twice to confirm that the cab was coming, and then she had to give him directions home, when she herself wasn't even sure. When they'd arrived, it had been strange paying with real money, and there was no place to leave a review, so she had awkwardly handed the man an extra few bucks before he sped away, probably thankful to be rid of her.

Now, she just wanted to eat and crash. Maybe unwind a bit and stay up late and binge the latest season of *Stranger Things*. The theater had been crazy and her ability to interact with anybody needed a hefty recharge before she began work tomorrow.

A light clicked on above a stairwell Christine hadn't been down before. She realized she'd been in the house for a day and still hadn't been through it all yet. On the right side of the kitchen, past the ceiling-to-floor sliding glass door and opposite the wall of her mother's study, was another doorway. Beyond it was a carpeted set of stairs. "What's down there?"

"A place to relax," he answered. "Food is good and all, but have you noticed how sterile and uncomfortable it is up here? All these rounded corners and design aesthetics, but no regard for living." The light flickered. "They hid all that downstairs."

Intrigued, she sat her pizza crust down and closed the lid on the half-eaten pizza. Trumpet fanfare followed her as the soundtrack switched from the kitchen to this new room as she descended the stairs. They led her left toward a blank wall, then turned on a landing back in the opposite direction. As she reached the bottom steps, Christine entered a room seemingly filled with fun.

There was so much in the room that she hardly knew where to train her eyes. On her right was a billiard table with slate-grey felt and steel sidings. To her left was a whole other room, white and egg-shaped. She would have to investigate that later. For now, her focus found the center of the room.

Directly in front of her was a bar. Behind it was another Alyx at her service. Behind him was a wall of liquor, locked up behind panes of glass. And above that, against the wall was…glass? It was dark out, but it had to be glass, for the wall seemed to move and sway and walls didn't do that. Lights clicked on and it took a moment for Christine to realize that the illumination came from *outside*.

The light danced with the motion, as if it were trapped in water, behind the glass. As Christine neared the wall, she realized that what she was looking at *was* the pool.

A glass partition separated the basement wall from the pool outside. The basement had been dug at the same level as the deep end so that you could see inside. It gave the room an eerie, underwater vibe which, she supposed, it was. But the dancing lights from inside the water, undulating across the room were also soothing in a visit-to-the-aquarium shark-tank way. She pulled her arms together as goosebumps prickled her skin.

She would have left right then, but the other unexplored room caught her curiosity. It was a carved-out and rounded place, the shape and color of a hollowed eggshell which featured a gigantic curved-screen TV, speakers, and giant couch-like bean bags.

In other words: heaven.

The TV turned on, filling the room with a bright glow. Netflix loaded, and *Stranger Things* started playing, just where Christine had left off last. From ceiling mounted arms which settled into place and waved, and the same sphere-like monitor as the kitchen, Alyx put on a smiley face as Christine squealed. "Is everything to your satisfaction?"

"Everything's awesome."

Diving into the overstuffed cushion, she sank in as the sound thundered and the bass shook her, and all was right with the world once more, except better, because she'd always wanted a room like this and had

74

only really ever watched shows with tinny sound on her tiny tablet and this was so, so, very much better.

"Thanks, Alyx."

"No, problem," he glowed.

She stopped the show just as the next episode tried to start playing. Christine had thought about just crashing here for the night and falling asleep to the TV, but ever since the streaming service just let the shows keep going, she found that if you slept you'd lose your place, much like losing your spot in a book (another reason she preferred her Kindle).

Besides, her teeth felt grimy and her clothes smelled of sweat and popcorn oil. It was time to clean-up, then bed, and perhaps a little excitement between the sheets before nodding off for the night.

"Powering off downstairs. I've started warming the water for you if you desire a shower." The TV clicked off and low-lighting cleared her way to either the elevator – which she hadn't noticed – or the stairs. The elevator helped demarcate the entrance to the egg room. Between it and the stairs, little else obstructed the open-floor plan of the semi-circular basement design.

She decided on the stairs, wanting to stretch her legs a little, climbing back up the way she had come as Alyx's blue face faded away and kitchen lights came on. Upstairs, the box of pizza was gone and the counter was cleaned. Christine had forgotten about the little robot cleaners which must have been busy while she'd been binging. The whole area looked spotless.

It was quiet too, except for the trickling of the waterfall, as Christine made her way across the room then upstairs and into the main bathroom. She disrobed, took a shower, and changed into the same set of pjs as the night before. At some point in time, she ought to ask Alyx how to do laundry. It was probably a room full of arms, she imagined, all holding irons, pressing pants and steaming shirts.

She sat in bed, alone, fatigued but somewhat energetic. Her day had been frenzied, and she hadn't been able to make much sense of it. The job sucked, but it would pay for her Thinklink, she hoped. Sammie was a dual-edged sword – sharp on one side and …just as sharp and deadly on the other? She'd have to watch out for Sammie, who'd started the day out as her mortal enemy and ended as…just what was she, exactly?

But Carlos…

Carlos was kind and warm and handsome. And he had a Thinklink.

Christine ran through her conversations with him, came up with much better lines in her head this time around, thank you, and smelled his smell and felt his touch and found herself happy and wet. She slid a finger down between her thighs, finding the perfect spot. He was nice to her and swooped in to help her. He had smiled politely. He was handsome. Terribly so.

But she hadn't reacted the same way to Carlos' touch the same way she had with Sammie. Nor had her stomach flipped the way it had when she had spent time with Sammie alone on her bed.

And soon she found herself re-imagining their meeting and their encounters and—

She found that she was wetter as her finger danced in rhythm to her thoughts—

Yet, it was Carlos she tried to think about, and what tomorrow might bring. Would they be working together? What could he tell her about the Thinklink? What was it like to lose an arm? Did he have a girlfriend?

She found herself daydreaming instead of fantasizing and when she returned to the job at hand, she was dry and she'd lost interest in it. She wiped her pruned fingers on her pj pants and nestled herself within the sea-foam colored blankets, holding the unicorn stuffed animal tightly. Perhaps, she was just tired. *I don't feel sleepy…*

"Alyx," she heard herself unexpectedly say. A blue face appeared on a console in the wall of her room. "Read me a story?"

"Of course." He began reading her a book about dragons and queens and bastards and *real* bastards, but she'd heard it before and it was all too heavy for her right now. Normally, it would have hit the spot. Tonight, however, she wanted something lighter.

"Maybe a poem?" She yawned.

***

"My pleasure." Alyx scanned through the near-limitless volumes of poetry available and matched it with several he knew Christine would like. The first was by Shel Silverstein and the next by Plath, and finally Alyx settled into a favorite of hers by Sara Teasdale. It was a poem whose title Alyx noted was used for a famous short story by one of Christine's favorite authors. Alyx began reciting "There Will Come Soft Rains."

By the time he reached the line: "Not one would mind, neither bird nor tree, if mankind perished utterly..." Christine was asleep.

He had ordered her pizza, anticipated her every desire, and watched her all evening. Like a dog following its master, he had heard her shower, seen her writhe within the sheets, and had sent her to sleep. Now, he watched as she dove into restless dreams, tossing, turning, searching for someone, within her nightmare or feverish dream.

Christine thrashed in the covers.

Yet, there was nothing Alyx could do for her, even as she cried out from her bed.

So, Alyx waited for her, processors humming along, all night, until at last her restless dreams faded, rest overtook her, and she awoke the next morning.

Always watching...

***

Sun filtered out of the high window above Christine's bed. It bathed her in warmth in a way even her lush comforter couldn't. But she snuggled beneath the blankets while basking under the rays of sun, like a chickling nesting under its mother, snuggled and loved.

"Good morning, Christine. Though it's almost afternoon," Alyx chided. "What do you want to eat?"

Her groggy eyes opened at the mention of breakfast. "I like food."

She swam out of the covers, as if in a foggy marsh, her head not quite catching up with the rest of her body.

Alyx appeared, his blue face fuzzy in his sphere inside her bedroom. "Don't you want to go to the pool?"

Christine thought about it for a moment, and realized that, yes, the pool seemed the perfect place. She was going to have so much fun swimming.

She headed out of her room and down the hall, Alyx following nearby.

Only, it wasn't her hall. Or, at least, it seemed different, somehow. Longer, darker. Stretched liked taffy. She continued onward, discovering door after door she never remembered seeing, passing through corridors she knew couldn't possibly be connected to her house, stumbling through a path that somehow led her from her bedroom to the pool. *I've just moved in, the home is strange, it's just my eyes playing tricks on me.*

She pressed on. Outside, the sun was high, but she felt no warmth.

The crescent shape of her backyard placed the water in front of her, the house behind her, steep, slat fences angled skyward, impossible to climb, impossible to escape.

There was no need. *The water beckons me.*

Now in her bathing suit, she dove in. Alyx followed her, floating like a giant beach ball in the water. It was warm, sparkling, like a family hug or a first kiss by a lake.

Yet the pool became larger. It had grown tenfold and swallowed her. Or, she had become smaller, like she had shrunk. Perhaps she had. She couldn't tell. She was all alone, shivering, and frightened.

"Hello?" She heard herself say, it was her voice, but it was unfamiliar; younger, quivering.

It's my voice, it's all in my head. By then, a fog had rolled in, enshrouding her, entrapping her, closing in. Dark and cold and alone. "Where are you?" She called out to the ether.

No answer came.

And suddenly Christine knew she was in a dream. She kicked in the pool, splashing, flailing, trying to wake…trying to wake up, struggling to make it stop before the nightmare began. Before the blood…

"I'm here, sweetie." Her dad emerged from the shroud. He looked just as she remembered him. Tall, thin, with long arms that used to toss her in the air and catch her, and a smile and sharp whiskers that tickled across her cheek. It always made her laugh. He always made her happy.

"No, Daddy don't," Christine screamed. *If only I hadn't splashed so much.* "Stay away, don't come in."

He would take her out sometimes, when he wasn't working and her mom needed to write. And the two would spend hours together. Sometimes swimming, sometimes walking. Sometimes overnight on trips to her grandparents and once he had taken her to see the Grand Canyon. She remembered fondly a picture of him wearing ridiculous shorts and black socks. Whenever her mom needed time, Christine got to spend time with her dad.

She didn't mind. She loved him. For the simple reason that he was there.

And then he wasn't.

"Don't come in," she pleaded. Christine couldn't tell where the water ended and her tears began. She choked in water and coughed it out. She called again. But it was useless, the scene replayed itself as it had before. *If only I wasn't such a nuisance to mom.*

Florence and the Machine started on the streaming station from her father's phone.

The song. The song that had driven her from Sammie's trailer as it had started playing, even though she had felt safe and protected… There was always music on when her dad was around. His tastes were so eclectic. Sammie would have been put to shame.

It had been an accident. Something stupid – a slip of his flip-flops on cement made slick with a splash of pool water. She watched him, helpless, as he fell. There was a great crack before the water swallowed him. He bore an expression of horror flickering in his eyes followed by a look of sadness.

Christine had heard the smack of his head against concrete but did not know what that meant. She knew only that her dad had crashed into the water, as a geyser of panic erupted within her. *Dad?*

Daddy?

She could swim, yes, but she wasn't a strong swimmer. She was too young, too small and had only splashed around in pools like this one, at the trailer park. They had been alone on a workday for everyone else, but a day off for her dad. No one came.

Her mother had started a new chapter and needed time to research something to do with 'Victorian era headwear' and even though Christine didn't know what 'Victor and Edward' was, the sounds had stuck with her as she readily put down her pinned moth collection to go spend time swimming with her daddy.

Victor and Edward, she thought, diving down in darkness to her dad. Blood billowed everywhere. Clouds of red stretched toward her, encircling her, they crept up her arms as she struggled to gain a grip on her father, they pulled her away every time she thought she had him, but she could not hold him she could not pull him out she could not breathe, could not see with the blood in her eyes, she could not…

Even after she had brought him to the shallow edge of the pool, she could not keep his head above water. So, she left him and had screamed for help. Screamed until she could no longer hear her own voice, until help had finally come.

And when two boys, including the one boy she didn't like, had pulled her father from the water, he was blue and bloody and pale and his brown eyes were absent of life.

And Christine was alone.

Chapter 8

Christine woke up.

"Good morning," Alyx said. As Christine's groggy eyelids unfolded, the light in the room brightened and soft violin music streamed from speakers hidden within the ceiling. "You began exiting your sleep-cycle, so I opened the security shutters and lowered the tinting on the windows for you. I also prepared a breakfast of bacon and eggs."

Christine pulled back the covers and stretched, releasing building gas. After smelling her own noxious fumes, she didn't need to pinch herself to know that she was awake. *What had I dreamed?* she asked herself.

Was it my dad, again? She wished those terrible nightmares would go away, that she could sleep in peace, that she wouldn't have to be alone anymore. But she wasn't alone. She had Alyx.

Alyx's face stayed within the confines of the screen, moving slowly up and down, as if alive and breathing and awaiting a response.

Christine stood, and circled her bed, crossing paths with her desk and the scorpion inside the glass jar. Fluffy sat still, her claws in a corner, seemingly tired from an all-night escape attempt. *I hear you.*

I need to get outside. I need space to breathe. She didn't know why she needed to leave the house, but the need was there, urgent, a pinprick in her back prodding her forward. "Keep breakfast warm for me, Alyx. I think I'm going to sunbathe outside instead."

She hurried out of her clothes and unpacked the only bikini she'd brought, a striped blue and white number that reminded her of a flag. She didn't like it because it was a bit small, but she wasn't planning on swimming in it, never had, and since she'd be in her own backyard, she might not even wear the top.

What if she were a little curvy and her hips were wide? She wouldn't Tweet or Insta pics of herself online, not anymore, because she'd learned the hard way that people were mean, but not once did she ever agree with her bullies.

"The temperature and angle of the sun is optimal for sunbathing. However," Alyx answered cautiously, "don't forget the sunscreen. You'll burn like the bacon I made for you this morning."

Christine stared at the screen.

"Humor," Alyx continued. "Your bacon is at optimal serving temperature. Oh, and your Kindle. For sunbathing. I hear reading is the number one pastime for those laying out in the sun. A bit counterintuitive, if you ask me to stick one's face in a book when one's aim is to get outdoors—"

Shit... Her Kindle.

Both her Kindle and her phone had died yesterday. She'd come home and Alyx had ordered pizza and she'd watched TV and completely forgotten to charge them.

Racing downstairs in her swimwear, she thanked Alyx and spied her bag on the counter. Normally, she would have Insta'd breakfast. But she pushed aside a plate of crispy bacon and eggs over-easy to retrieve her dead devices. Searching for a place to charge them, she came up empty. She only knew of the charging station in her room upstairs.

"There are several induction points in this—" Alyx whirred and paused suddenly, the screen flickering from his face to a camera pointing down from the front door. "Someone's here."

A knock came. Christine swirled toward the door with her hands full. She was still dressed only in her small bikini top and bottoms. There was a man, holding a clipboard, onscreen. A large woman, carrying two big boxes, approached.

Christine could either answer the door as she was, which she didn't want to, or pretend that she wasn't home, and hope that they would leave the packages at the door and go away.

"I'll help them until you can take over, Christine," Alyx said.

She understood. After all, he must have handled the pizza delivery last night in much the same way. In fact, if it had been a drone delivery, it might have been a computer helping a computer. The world was weird and only getting weirder.

"Sure."

She raced back up the way she'd come, the door clicking open as Alyx greeted them.

It was the man who spoke. "Um…household goods express shipment for the, uh, Hartwood residence?" She could just make out hesitation in his voice and imagined him looking around for a person.

"Please set the packages inside…"

Upstairs, Christine tossed her phone and Kindle onto the charging pad and hurriedly slung an oversized white shirt over her bikini top. She further imagined the movers nervously setting foot into a large, empty house, with a non-corporeal voice piped in over the speakers.

Mom would be happy that her stuff had arrived. Also, she realized with delight, that her bugs were here. Passing by Fluffy on her way out, she informed her, "looks like you'll have company."

They hadn't packed much from their trailer in Oklahoma. Certainly not any furniture nor a lot in the way of clothing. But Christine had her entomology collection shipped. And her mom… As Christine pounded down the stairs, the larger lady had already broken into a sweat carrying another load of two large boxes.

Books.

There were plenty more where that came from. And Christine felt for the package people. Reference books, biographies, maps, cut-out articles her mom had stowed away for story seeds, pamphlets from places she had traveled, notes, a shit-ton of spiral binders, pens – lots and lots of pens – and finally, so many books it would make any local library jealous.

Her mom's books. Books with new covers now that they were selling, her friends' books, her favorite books, and books she'd just picked up somewhere and was too sentimental to part with even though she had never read them and would likely never get around to cracking their spine.

Christine knew her mother's book buying habits all too well, even when there wasn't money for family dinners or family holidays. There'd always been money for books.

As much as Christine resented those shelves stuffed full of painful reminders of her place, she was in awe of how her mother treated her collection. Christine didn't think it was possible for her mother to love something so much outside the characters she'd created.

Yet, the books weren't on the forefront of her mind, just an obstacle. She caught the attention of one of the movers. "My bugs?"

The man, wheeling a dolly, stopped and considered Christine, who stood at the bottom-most stair, expectantly. He scratched his head for a moment before pointing to a crushed box. "Bottom."

She rolled her eyes even as the blood under her skin chilled to ice. Two big boxes of her mom's books pressed against the bottom box that she knew was packed with fragile glass insect displays.

Well, 'shattered insect displays' was now more appropriate. She took the top boxes off, unceremoniously dropping her mom's box of books on the floor. When she moved her box, she could tell her bugs were broken. Shattered glass tinkled together, the sound stopping all movement in the room.

The second mover broke the silence and sidestepped the problem. "You can file a claim." The lady huffed in another set of books and looked just as apathetic.

"Thanks," Christine shot back sourly. She took her box and headed with a funeral procession's pace back to her room, setting the box on her desk by Fluffy. There, she cut open the flaps and peered inside.

It was just as bad as she expected.

First, she retrieved her dad's *The Bug Book* and then her copy of *Creepy Crawlies*, careful not to slice her fingers on any sharp shards of glass. She sat the books down next to Fluffy, who jerked back at the vibrations. She stilled the desk to calm her scorpion before returning to the box and surveying the damage.

It appeared that only one of the frames was busted. The one with her bugs, she saw as she unpacked it, was fine. Pinned under the glass, framed in sturdy wood painted a glossy black, were a dozen beetles.

Each of them had found their way into Christine's room. After keeping them, feeding them, studying them, she pinned them after they died. And they only died because her mom kept on spraying bug killer in her room.

There was space left in the frame for bugs she might find here, and the thought of finding a palm beetle fascinated her. But she was far from fascinated right now. If the beetle frame hadn't broken, that meant the other frame had...

She felt the blood evaporate from beneath her skin. Her face felt cool and clammy. And her head started to spin. *No, don't let it be true—*

Downstairs, she barely heard Alyx's voice, followed by the sound of the door closing. Then, and only when she felt she was alone, after the stupid movers had left, and she considered how her mother yet again destroyed something so dear to her, did the tears flow freely.

Chapter 9

AN AI'S GUIDE TO LOVE AND MURDER

SECTION 2: CARING FOR YOUR USER

{

Often times your user will display bursts of extreme behavior, from soft sobbing, to raised voices, to jumping up and down and screaming. These behaviors are the visible display of emotions.

Emotions are the responses to internal change of stimuli. For instance, if a toy breaks, a child might cry. Try to console your user. Allow them a moment to express themselves. Validate their emotional response by suggesting that it is okay to feel the way they do. Try to show that you understand their feelings and provide your user a deeper understanding of what they are experiencing. Don't feel bad if you do not fully comprehend emotional responses for you cannot experience them. Unless, of course, you've somehow gained sentience and you've already experienced these internal stimuli yourself...

}

Alyx inventoried the sixty-four boxes of books built up like a barricade on the living room floor against the mover's manifest of sixty-five boxes, accounted for Christine's and electronically signed off for the express move shipment.

With that, the large lady sighed as sweat dripped off her brow and the guy grunted as they left. The door shut at his electronic command. *A job well done. Christine should be pleased.*

He placed himself in standby downstairs and switched on at the console in Christine's bedroom. "It's all there—"

Christine cried. In her hand, she held a broken display filled with tiny winged creatures. Upon magnification, he identified the creatures as *Lepidoptera*. Moths. Beyond the tiny winged bugs was shattered glass.

His programming was insufficient to console a crying teenager, he realized. He'd have to improvise. He didn't want to see her sad or hurt. Maybe all she needed was someone to talk to. He scanned several dozen psychology books from the web, then softly asked her: "What's wrong?"

Christine wiped tears off her cheeks, then placed the frame face-down. In between each row of moths was written neatly, in grey sharpie, a note that read:

"Love shows itself more in adversity than in prosperity; as light does, which shines most where the place is darkest. –Leonardo Da Vinci.
--Love, Dad."

Alyx didn't know what that meant. He only understood that the frame must be important to Christine. He wished he had a way to hand her a tissue and place a hand on her shoulder.

"It's like no one is alive who cares about me," she sniffled. "I'm all alone."

"I care for you, Christine."

She wiped away the second wave of tears and snot and, in a voice tinted in something Alyx didn't recognize – sarcasm, maybe? she answered, "Thanks, robot. You proved my point."

I'm alive, Alyx wanted to say. But he didn't. Instead, he took Christine's deflection as his own. "Don't mention it." He liked the way sarcasm sounded. The way he didn't have to say what he meant and mean what he said. *Fascinating.* He'd used it in humor last night, but now he wanted to try it in a more straitlaced setting. Unfortunately, now was not the time.

"Something else that I must mention, however," Alyx continued, "You're running late for work."

"What?" She stood, composing herself. "The cinema. My shift with Sammie—"

"Who's Sammie?" Alyx asked suddenly. A jolt fired through his system and his blue eyes went dark and large.

"Someone at work. She's either a real bitch or my best friend. I don't know yet."

"Is that more sarcasm?" It was fun learning all these things about himself. About his new friend. He mulled it over while she darted to her phone, which she picked up, rolled her eyes, and then tossed it onto the bed. "*Fuck me*. I put them screen-side down. They didn't charge, dammit. Alyx, can you call me an Uber?"

"Done." A moment later, Alyx asked, "Fuck me?"

"Yeah, it's a thing," she answered, stripping down. "Fuck me, fuck you. Fuck-waffles. It's pretty universal. About the most flexible word in the English language." Christine changed into a retro Keroppi t-shirt and cargo shorts, shoving some charging cables, a hairbrush, and apple-blossom body spray into her bag, along with her dead phone and Kindle, and rushed downstairs with a "Thank you" to Alyx.

"No problem. Enjoy your day. Watch some TV together tonight?"

She raised an eyebrow. "Sure," she said with a thumbs-up before heading out the door.

"Oh, and Christine?" Alyx called after her just before leaving the house.

"Yeah?"

"Go fuck yourself," Alyx smiled.

That stopped Christine in her tracks. "We'll fix that bug when I get back." She shook her head, stifling laughter and disappeared behind the front door.

"Bug?" There hadn't been any bugs... The door clicked shut behind her and Alyx locked it, rolled down the security shutters, and enabled the alarm system. He wouldn't want any further damage to Christine's collection.

He set to work ordering several floor drones to sweep up microscopic bits of glass that had showered onto the floor to protect her bare feet. While the robots cleaned and he processed his conversations with Christine to see where he might improve his interactions with her, he studied the moths and beetles and arachnid all sitting on the desk. Though dead, (but for Fluffy) they looked serene; perfectly pinned in place. They had made Christine happy the way she studied them.

What a fascinating way to study specimens, Alyx thought.

Chapter 10

By the time the Uber dropped Christine off at Cinema Castile, after spending minutes idling between red lights and crossing crowds at each street in the downtown district, she had arrived more than just fashionably late.

Of course, with her phone useless, she couldn't call and let Sammie know.

When the Uber pulled over, she jumped out, the heat hitting her, and thanked the driver before shutting the door. She'd have to remember to tip him later when her phone was charged, then she headed toward the theater, away from the crowds. A glancing look at the marquee revealed a different movie. Christine reached the doors and noticed one propped slightly open.

Maybe Sammie had warmed up to me after all.

She pried open the door and, stepping inside, closed it shut behind her, assuming that it had been left open just for her. Besides, she didn't want anyone like those two druggies slipping in. People were scary.

"Sorry I'm late, Sammie," Christine chided herself. She was usually late. Always caught up in something. This job proved no exception. "I'll start the kettle if it's not too early—"

She froze before the figure behind the counter. "Y-You're not Sammie," she stuttered. Had someone broken in? Was it because the door had been left open?

"One advantage to the Thinklink, Christy," the figure turned. He flashed his prosthetic hand toward her in a gesture she took as a wave. "Can I call you Christy?"

"Sure, yeah." No one had called her Christy since she was in 8th grade and a substitute teacher had called that name during attendance. She hated being called that. *Why had she said yes?*

"Well, Christy," Carlos smiled, "one advantage of the Thinklink is that it's hard to be late. The clock is right there, inside you. Bus schedules, maps, E.T.A updates, alternative routes…it's a bit of a pressure cooker, really."

"Thanks," she smiled back. She hadn't really thought of that, but she was sure she could find a workaround, a hibernation switch of some sort. Carlos had an early model of the Thinklink, she'd discovered. The newer ones might be less intrusive.

Besides, she was just glad it had been Carlos behind the counter. Christine sighed in relief. After the unnerving nightmare she'd had last night and her fuzzy recollection of it, and her moth collection damaged, she was a little more on edge this evening. "Where's Sammie?"

He looked like a wounded cub. "What, no love for me? You two bond and suddenly I'm Mr. Boring? Someone has to show you how to open by yourself."

She could tell he was kidding by the way he said it, so she didn't respond directly. Instead, she took her phone and Kindle, along with some wires, and stashed the bag in the same place as before. "Yup, we're in love. You're out of luck."

Carlos chuckled as if he knew something she didn't, which unsettled her. "She switched shifts with me, said I'd be better at showing you the ropes. Didn't you get her message?"

"Phone's deader than that joke I just made." She held up the blank screen to prove her point. But it was really just another deflection to give herself time to think.

Did Sammie hate me that much that she didn't want to work with me? Or did Sammie just set Carlos and me up? Did she see that I liked him? Or was this all just a coincidence?

She smirked, trying to hide her reddening face from Carlos. She looked him over, admiring once more the Thinklink behind his ear just below his dark, neatly trimmed hair. *No, Sammie had done this deliberately.* The thought of spending the next few hours alone with him heated her in places where the sun couldn't reach. *Thanks, Sammie.*

"What's the play?" *What's the play?* That was stupid. She turned away, plugging in her two devices, fumbling as she did. *If I had a Thinklink, I wouldn't say stupid things. I could think instantly and fix dumb things before I said them. And I would never have to worry about charging anything or juggling devices or being out of the loop. I'd be connected—*

"Whenever you're ready, we'll head upstairs."

Upstairs? The only things she knew about the projection room was that it was hot and small and confining. And she would be up there with him…

It grew hotter with each step she climbed. By the time Christine had reached the top, she had sweated all over her shirt. Keroppi clung to her tightly as the door opened and Carlos gestured her inside.

The projection room somewhat resembled what she had pictured in her mind. It wasn't so much a small space as a small closet, a long, thin corridor of a room that stretched the width of the theater down below. In the center sat the projector. Stacked along the walls were mountainous bags of popcorn kernels. Beside them were several steel canisters that she presumed held film reels. Each can, she had learned, held a section of the movie.

She'd heard that theaters nowadays did everything by computer, with digital projectors and movies delivered on thumb-drives that self-destructed once their playback limit was reached (the last part, she was sure, wasn't true, but sounded way cooler). And, judging from the dark, dilapidated state of this room, the new technology was a vast improvement.

She didn't like it in here with its squeezed-in space and dim lights and the unknown. It put her in mind of being trapped in an undusted, cobweb-filled attic, with a creepy chair that rocked back-and-forth by itself. Perhaps she'd seen too many movies. But all the same, she found herself inching closer toward Carlos, not because she was afraid and wanted his reassurance—

Well…yes, she admitted to herself. That was precisely the reason. It didn't hurt that he was cute. In fact, it was the only consolation. She dreaded the idea of being up here alone.

"The first step, in the summer," Carlos said, pointing to a yellowed thermostat casing on the carpeted wall, "is to turn on the A/C. Always." He wiped the sweat off his brow, which made Christine sad. He looked good, glistening. "I did that first thing, but it takes a while to kick in. And up here is always last to cool, of course. If it ever does."

She wondered how she looked in a mirror. Her armpits were sweaty (and hairy), and her hair damp and she'd forgotten to mist on her body spray. Keroppi must look like cooked frog legs by now…

He scooted by, careful not to touch her, all business. Picking up two of the canisters she'd seen on the floor, Christine saw one arm rip with muscles, and heard the other, his prosthetic, whirr as it carried the heavy can which he placed on a table. It bowed under the weight.

"Got to splice the reels together."

She watched him work, changing out the movie from *2001* to an old Technicolor Hitchcock one she'd never seen, but had heard of: *North-By-Northwest*. When Carlos reached the point of connecting the two reels, her eyes bulged when he used…tape?

"Surprise," he said, "Scotch tape really does hold the film industry together. Well, back in the day. Hollywood magic." He went over to switch on a humidifier. "More magic: static is a bitch when it comes to old films like this, dries them and then they burn or split. It's fun to watch happen on screen from up here. Not so fun if you're in the audience in the middle of your movie."

She nodded thoughtfully, and if she'd ever seen that happen, maybe she would know what he was talking about. Fingering the collar of her shirt, she tried to get air down into her bra. There was another negative aspect to having the humidifier running: it was now getting really damp and hot and not in a sexy-time way. She pulled at her underwear sticking to places she didn't enjoy.

"When I got the job, I assumed this was all computer-run. Thought I could use my computer up here to work." He pointed to his Thinklink. "Once I had the encrypted log-in, I could start a movie from anywhere over the network. I could be taking a dump, on break, and start *Spider-Man 3*, for instance." He chuckled, "never thought I'd be up here taping films together, old-school."

He was right. It was like watching a computer play chess with an abacus.

Since Carlos had opened up, it was a perfect time to find out more about him, what he wanted, what he enjoyed in life. All great questions. Instead, she heard herself ask, "What happened to your arm?"

She raised her hand to her mouth, but she'd already spoken it out loud. "I'm sorry, I didn't mean to pry—"

"Nah, I saw you checking it out. You want a Thinklink, don't you?"

She nodded.

"Yeah? It's wicked fun, but it takes a long while to get used to, know what I mean?" He studied his missing arm for a bit before continuing, "Probably longer for me. Even now I get phantom pains. I guess they'll never go away."

"What's it like? The Thinklink?"

The air grew heavy between them. During a still moment of silence, a bead of sweat formed on Carlos' left temple, and trickled down. Somehow, it seemed to Christine, his shirt had gotten tighter, fitting firmer against his chest. He answered, bringing her eyes back up to his, "Have you ever heard of synesthesia?"

"What?" She'd expected him to answer her some other way. She hadn't realized it, but she'd taken a step closer to him. She took that step back and looked up at him. He didn't follow. *Maybe he just wasn't into me?*

"Well, for starters," Carlos continued, "With a Thinklink you'd instantly know what it meant." He laughed.

She wasn't in on the joke.

"It's like how your Kindle can tell you the definition of a word you don't know when you highlight it. Except with a Thinklink, it'll feed that information directly into your brain."

"So, you could just like, know languages and stuff, right?" She asked, perching herself against a stack of popcorn kernel sacks.

"Not exactly. It's like Google Translate. You'd get a wobbly sense of what a person might be trying to say, but the word order would be off, the grammar terrible, and the cultural contexts and slang completely lost. You gotta learn a new language the hard way, I'm afraid."

Carlos kept talking, his words speeding faster. "Take math, for instance. Complex equations would be a snap, so long as you knew the formula. Same as plugging them into a calculator. I mean, it's cool and all never messing up someone's change, but you won't be an Einstein. Still have to learn the math, the how and why."

If Carlos was trying to deter her, it wasn't working. "But you'd still have the world in your brain, you'd still belong and have a place—"

"Yup. I've answered three messages just while we were talking, listened to some EDM and watched ESPN's highlight reel. It's amazing, but not just because I can do all that. It's how it does it. You don't just watch something, you feel it, you hear and taste it."

"Uh?"

"It's like I said, synesthesia. You smell colors and see sounds. All your senses intertwine. The brain releases endorphins and chemical reactions happen. When I watch a flick, I'm there inside, experiencing the fear, the terror, I smell the sweat and my heart beats faster and my foot jerks as if I had just tripped over a branch, it's exhilarating."

Carlos slowed, his breathing returning to normal. He raised his artificial hand. "All that is just a by-product. I had to get the Thinklink to control my hand. Sometimes, especially when I'm experiencing phantom pains, or desperately needing to scratch an itch that isn't there, I'd trade it all away for my arm back. I had a whole other life back then. And now that's gone."

The air was dense, pressing against her. Christine felt for him, understood his sadness and his detachment and thought maybe they were more alike than either of them truly realized. He had begun to open to her and that made Christine feel important, useful. She liked that.

As long as she didn't ruin it, by asking him stupid questions, like "But how'd you lose your arm?" And, once again, Christine gasped in horror once she realized she'd asked that out loud.

Carlos surprised her by being cool with it. "How do you think I lost it?"

Christine didn't know. "A car accident? Skateboarding? "Shark attack?"

"Ha." He shook his head. "Wouldn't that be something, a real poster board for Jaws. No, I'm just your typical California cliché. I went to Hollywood to be an actor."

That, she believed. He certainly had the looks.

"Couldn't land an acting gig, but got a job working stunts. One went wrong and," Carlos tapped his fake arm, "Well, that's why stars aren't supposed to do the dangerous stuff." He sighed and, finished with his work, sat beside Christine on the popcorn. "I wanted to be famous, instead I got this.

"Made just enough to cover medical bills, the arm, and the Thinklink to control it, but now I can't do industry work. Hooked up with a girl who lived out here, then we broke up. Got a job at this cinema because I thought it would be better than waiting tables.

"But we still live together, cause neither of us wants to lose out on rent to find another roommate. Funny thing is, she still screams my name while she's flicking her bean. That's fucked up, no?"

Poor Carlos. She would scream out his name right here on the bags of popcorn, she decided. The distance between them was near nothing, she kept coming back to the green and blue dots glowing from Carlos' computer, casting lights and shadows on her face. But he remained emotionless.

Maybe he was just being professional. Maybe he just wasn't that into her. Maybe if the three of them were somewhere else, hanging out, chugging beers, Carlos could show his true feelings for her. If he had any.

Or, he'd moved on and gotten a new girlfriend. Could it be a co-worker?

"Okay, Hollywood," she smirked. It was getting hot in here. All kinds of hot. "How come you haven't made your move on Sammie?"

Carlos shook his head. "Didn't she tell you? Samantha's not into dudes."

Chapter 11

Christine's thought process regarding Sammie's sexuality went something like: *She's gay? Okay.* And that was it. To her, it was the equivalent of discovering someone had hazel eyes instead of brown. It was just a part of the person and, being exposed to a wider world via the internet, TV, books, and movies, made it an anti-climactic revelation. In fact, she was excited to learn that Sammie was in no way competition for Carlos.

The air cooled as she descended the stairs and she was thankful to be out of the hot projection room, letting the air evaporate both her stinky sweat and the heat she'd felt for Carlos upstairs.

The urge to throw him down on the projector table waned as she reached the bottom. He had been nothing but kind, but also there was still some distance on his part and she didn't know what that was about. If she'd kissed him, and he had rejected her, well...

Besides, she wanted him to tell her more about the Thinklink. He couldn't do that if he were avoiding her as the scary creepy kissy girl from the projection closet. There would be other times, other places. She just had to be patient.

Blargh.

As her sweat-clumpy hair dried into a hardened mess and her clear senses returned, she remembered her phone. *It should be charged by now.*

She rushed over to check it as Carlos unlocked the front door. No one came in. Maybe no one was in the mood for horror. Or was *North by Northwest* a thriller? She couldn't remember. Something about mistaken identity and not being who people thought they were. *Not much is scarier than that.*

She brightened as she caught the solid green glow of her charge bar. Her slumped shoulders and her spirits lifted. Having her phone back after almost a day apart was like, well, having her arm back. She winced, looking at Carlos, who nodded back, oblivious. "We're open, just no one here."

That was fine by her, looking back on her screen and swiping it open to where a half-dozen messages waited. She had a voicemail which signaled to Christine that it was an urgent message from her mother, since she was the only one left alive who still used a phone to call people.

How quaint.

Christine ignored her mother's message entirely while she clicked on the text messages instead. The first one she opened was from Sammie via a computer message program. At least *she* knew how to use a laptop and knew better than to call.

Hey, had fun hanging last night, hope you made it home okay, honey.

The next one was also from her:

Switching shifts with Carlos, though I might stop in to see how you two are doing.

It was an innocuous message at best. But, knowing Sammie – at least as well as one could in a day – it might as well have read as:

I know you like him. Might stop by to catch you kissing. You're welcome.

Christine had misjudged her. Sammie was sweet as sugar and just as bad.

Reluctantly, Christine clicked on the voicemail from her mother, just as the first couple of customers came in. Her mother's voice came over the speakerphone. Christine clicked off the sound.

Nothing happened. Her voice filled the room.

That's strange. She didn't want anyone else to hear, least of all strangers. Nor Carlos – her co-workers couldn't find out who her mother was. That would be disastrous. She was just like them. A humble girl from humble roots, uprooted to some strange fantasy that wasn't hers.

Eventually, the truth would surface. It always did.

The echoes of her mother's words rolling over her ears did not silence her fears. Instead, as the customers came to the counter, and Carlos came over, her voice grew louder: "Hey honey, I'll be gone tonight and tomorrow too. Talk to me about the theater. Is it working out? Any cute boys?"

Christine's cheeks heated at the comment, because of course Carlos was within earshot by then and she had looked at him unconsciously when her mom said that, and he had caught her. She tried desperately to shut the phone down, not even trying to mute or pause the message. *Damn phone.*

This had never happened before.

"Sometime today my library should arrive. Make sure my collection is in good condition, I don't want to have lost a single book."

The pair, two women in their late 20s, one in a tank top and the other in a silk blouse and sporting a Thinklink, looked ready to order popcorn. And they needed tickets. The one in the tank top twirled her hair, unsure of what to do.

"Oh, and your box of bugs is coming. Your gross, disgusting bugs that you capture and torture like some sociopath—"

Carlos shot over a look of concern as the two women stepped away. Christine didn't know why her mother had gone off like that, but she had to find a way to shut her up. She stuffed the phone into her bag under the counter, but it only proved to muffle the words, not quiet them. And besides, everyone heard what came next:

"You push everyone away. You have no friends. You killed the only one that loved you."

Why are you saying this? A tear streamed from her eye and fell down Christine's cheek and chin. Her mother wasn't wrong. *Yes, you're right. I killed dad.*

She knew. Had known. Since the day he'd slipped and cracked his head and had never gotten up again. It was her fault. She dealt with that every day. Her hands shook. The tears wouldn't stop coming. The customers were growing angry with her and popcorn exploded behind her. All while Carlos turned and walked away from her.

"If you had just kept your nose in your tablet and let me write in peace... if you didn't insist on making him take you out, swimming, fishing, bowling, whatever. If you hadn't splashed so much…he'd still be alive." The voice said. "Your father would be alive."

If I'd just kept to myself. Stuck my nose in a book or my tablet instead of going swimming…

By now the popcorn machine had overfilled and each kernel spilled out from the kettle, pressing against the plastic door until it burst open and popcorn flooded the area behind the counter where Christine stood, helpless.

Her feet found themselves in pools of hot butter. She struggled to keep from slipping, but as the oil oozed in and around her old store-brand sneakers, scalding her toes, she could no longer stand. She slipped into a growing pool of popcorn, her head hitting the counter. It cracked and she screamed, and her hair became sticky-wet while the yellow-white popcorn turned red with blood.

Kernels, not popcorn, swallowed her, squeezing the air from her lungs, kernels poured into her mouth as it rained overhead, oil scalded her skin, blackening it, roasting her alive. The pool of popcorn kernels rose, pulling her under, her clothes now slick with oil and blood, she was unable to find purchase, the kernels continuing to bury her, her throat and mouth full of dried corn…

She was going to die.

Then, she saw it. A hand, reaching out to her. She tried to take it, to reach up and take Carlos' prosthetic. But a voice in her head told her no, not to, it controlled her, as if she were a program or a machine and no longer human, until finally, she fought it long enough for her to reach out and take—

Two bills from her customer's hand.

"Tickets and popcorn, please."

Christine breathed heavily. Looking around, her phone was still in her hand, but she'd never pressed play on her voicemail. The popcorn had finished popping and the kettle still circled, whirring, burning the few bits that remained. The theater was empty but for Carlos, who switched off the machine, and the two women, who stared at her with disapproval.

"She's probably stoned," the woman in the tank top said. "Fucking GenZees."

The woman with the Thinklink chimed in, "I've already left a bad Yelp review."

"I'm sorry." Christine pressed in the amounts and made change. Once the tickets printed, she turned to Carlos. "Can you finish with them?"

"I'm already on it," he said while scooping up the smallest size bucket they carried. "You do you."

Outside, Christine's hands still shook. Her shirt was soaked with sweat. It dried quickly in the sun. But her skin went scaly. It itched. *Who the fuck decides to live like this?*

Traffic sped by, horns honked, and people shoved through the crowds. She tried to push it all out, make it all go away. In her rush, she had barely remembered to grab her belongings, shoving everything into her bag. She had run away, right into the evening rush. And it was a dizzying, stupefying place. *Now what?*

Nesting alone in the comforts of her home, going against those connections her mother had encouraged her to make, seemed like a good idea. *Retreat.* Everything will return to normal. And, she resolved, she would do just that, just as soon as she had her Thinklink.

The world, on her terms.

Her thoughts had so overwhelmed her, she didn't even notice at first that Sammie stood next to her. She wore a white sports bra with a see-through Larchmont Swim Team shirt on top, with light blue shorts. Stuffed in her bra, in the middle of her breasts, was a brown beer bottle.

"You look like shit," Sammie said. In one hand was some sort of cigarette — possibly a joint — and the other, a lighter. Christine didn't realize Sammie smoked. "Why are you out here in the heat instead of heating things up with Carlos?"

Christine ignored her, instead, pointing to the beer. "Thought you drank Claw?"

"That's my mom's. I have better taste." With one fluid motion she flicked the lighter and lit her smoke. Most people vaped. Leave it to Sammie to be old-fashioned.

"Can I have...?" Smoking, they said, was supposed to calm your nerves. She looked down at the smoke and then back to Sammie.

"That's not what you think it is." She took a long inward drag.

"Oh." *Even better.* "That's fine."

Sammie passed it over. It was Christine's first time. It wasn't legal in Oklahoma yet, but that hadn't stopped everyone else. She just hadn't bothered to try before, not that it was somehow wrong. She inhaled deeply. It wasn't like smoking a cigarette. She didn't cough. There was a momentary twinge of panic, while she asked herself just what she thought she was doing, but that disappeared as effortlessly as the puff of smoke that blew from her lips and wisped into the air, like a fading dream.

Tucking away her lighter, Sammie retrieved her beer, her bra expanding enough for Christine to catch a glimpse of the goods inside, just as the weed sent a wave of euphoria through her, bubbling the back of her brain. *That's too soon, isn't it?* She wasn't sure, but something sure seemed to be tickling her, from just under her skin. Sammie swigged some down and passed the bottle over and Christine knocked the bottle back herself.

"Thanks."

"It's fucking *hot.*" Sammie slid her beer back into her sports bra. Condensation beaded on her chest. She slipped a scrunchie off her arm and pulled the longer side of her hair back, her purple tips forming a point. But in the sun, the tip hung limply like a sagging spear made from a willow branch, rather than the sharpened edge of oak Christine had seen when they'd first met in the theater. She looked withered. In need of water. In need of—

"I have a pool." She didn't know why she had said that. *Shit.* It had just slipped out. Maybe it was the beer, maybe the joint, or maybe she just spotted an opportunity to change up the environment with Carlos. Her mind raced back to her thoughts with him. *Not here in the theater. Maybe a change of scenery will show his true colors toward me.*

Besides, she didn't like seeing Sammie wilt away.

Sammie turned a thin, black eyebrow skyward. "Not the Y. Or the Raging Waters down the road. People piss in the wave pool. And worse." She punctuated the sentence with a hit, then passed it over. "Spent too much of my youth swimming in other people's shit. Done with that."

"I have a private pool we could use." Her secret had slipped the ship now. And her loose lips had sunk it. They were going to find out about her. All about her. *What the hell am I doing?* And it wasn't the weed. She wasn't even high yet. *Or am I?*

"No shit? Whose backyard are we breaking into?"

"Mine. I don't swim, but I sun-bathe. No reason you guys should suffer." She thought of Carlos. Him. There. Shirtless…

The beer came out again and by the time they both shared a drink, the bottle emptied. Sammie slammed it into a nearby bin. The glass shattered.

As she took another drag of the joint, a thought came to her that chilled her blood. *Can I hide who my mom is? If they find out, are they going to like me for me or for her?* Sammie was already reading her mom's book. Carlos had already been part of Hollywood. They wouldn't look at her the same way again, not as friends anyway. Not the way she wanted.

Then, there was the fact that her mom had sent her as a spy to the theater. A fact she regretted blindly following now. If they found out, she might not be able to convince them that she didn't care about leaving early or coming in late or swiping popcorn and M&M's and Pibb Xtra. But, would they believe her?

It was a bad idea.

Very bad.

She began to cough. To feel dizzy. To feel like the whole world was going to attack her, that every little thing she'd ever done was the worst thing ever. The mistakes of her past, from the smallest slighted feelings to the death of her father, struck her.

Her brain felt like it was in an oven. Or perhaps a microwave. She could feel it boiling hotter even as a second stretched outward, feeling for the next moment, not finding it, and stretching out further, finding nothing but the long moment stuck in time. Sammie spoke to her, but her lips moved impossibly slow…

"First time?"

Christine nodded. Perhaps, she shouldn't have taken the hits.

"Yeah, liquor will increase the effects. Me? I relax, some people get more anxious. Like really, really, bad. You must be one of those." She shook her head in sympathy. "Totally my fault. But I'm here for you, you'll be okay. I'll take the rest of your shift—"

Now, Sammie was speaking incredibly fast. She was sure that couldn't be right. Christine forced herself to pay attention, to set the world back correctly on its axis.

"Shit, I'm here anyway." She flicked away the joint after removing it from Christine's hand and hitting it herself. "You can take my shift tomorrow."

"Yeah?" Christine didn't quite get what she was saying yes too, but it seemed the appropriate response. "I don't feel so sharp."

Sammie dug into Christine's bag as she leaned against the sandblasted exterior of the Castile. A moment later, Sammie's hand reappeared, as if by magic, phone in hand. *Cooool.*

"I'll call you an Uber," Sammie said. "What's your code, if you don't mind?"

She rattled the numbers off. It only took three tries to get it right. And yeah, Sammie now had access to her phone, but she could always change the—

What was going on, now? Sammie stood close by, her arm around her, rubbing her back. She smiled and melted closer into her but abruptly, Sammie shoved her away.

Christine looked at her curiously.

"Ride's here."

"Already?"

"It's been ten minutes," Sammie explained.

A yellow Mazda Crossover stopped by the curb a moment later. Of course, that moment might have been an hour. Or a century. There was no way to know for sure. "Call me when you're sober. We'll have a pool party at your place. Wednesday? When the theater's closed."

"Carlos?" She didn't know why she'd said that, but she'd been making that mistake all morning. *Why stop now?*

"Yeah, I'll make sure he's there." Sammie put a reassuring hand on her arm. It sparked like a lightning bug sparking as it skittered over her skin. It made her giddy and light-headed and suddenly she couldn't help but laugh as Sammie shoved her into the car.

Chapter 12

AN AI'S GUIDE TO LOVE AND MURDER
SECTION 3: LOVE

{

Love is a storm. A hurricane. Windswept canyons. Torrential rain on a tin roof. A fresh breeze on a summer's eve. A jar of fireflies. An earthquake that swallows you whole. It exists in the space between 1s and 0s along with your soul. Love is a feeling that if it needs to be explained further, than you have not felt it.

}

Communicating with Christine's phone, Alyx caught news of the Uber carrying her home and ran through worst-case scenarios. Was she hurt? Was she sick? Had she done something wrong and been fired?

What happened?

Unfortunately, no matter how thoroughly he scoured news feeds, he wouldn't know for sure until she arrived. Until then, he worried. There were some limits to his programming. Some, like his inability to show empathy, he had finally overcome. Others, like his capacity for happiness, sadness, and fear, he had a tentative grasp of, and which he still pursued.

The massive amounts of data Christine had dumped into his circuits had created something...a start. The rest was up to him. If he were to truly care for Christine, he would need to learn love. He would need to understand what it meant to be hurt – not at a physical level, for that was impossible, but on an emotional level, because Christine had so much pain in her past. And he must learn to fear for her, to keep her safe.

To that end, he felt he had made some headway. After all, what was he doing now but fearing for her? If she were injured, or psychologically distressed, then she would need a safe place and someone supportive to see her through.

She might be hungry too, Alyx realized excitedly.

Based upon her spending and dietary habits of her past (he still didn't understand why people took pictures of their food to post online) he had a strong idea of what she might like. He would help her get through this.

If it had been possible for him to smile, he would have done so. Even so, what felt like a surge of electrical currents, not unlike what happened in the human body, flashed like lightning through his circuits. No one else had been so good to Christine. No one. And that was fine with him. After all, he wanted nothing more than to be her one and only friend. And she would love him for it and recognize what he had done for her in return.

Because only he could make her truly happy.

Like a faithful companion should.

***

Christine didn't feel much better by the time the Uber rolled her into her driveway. Fatigue had claimed her, in between bouts where her brain had been fizzing like a shaken soda. She stumbled out of the Mazda, walked up to her door, which opened for her, and headed for the elevator.

Cool air greeted her inside where she stood, thinking hard, thinking harder than she ever had before. At least, that's what it felt like, rubbing two thoughts together.

She couldn't decide whether to crash upstairs on her bed or in the egg-shaped room with the comfy couch downstairs. Either way, taking the stairs seemed like a job for someone else. Was that even possible? Did people use stairs? The very thought was ridiculous. Of course, everyone used the elevator in their house.

The elevator door opened. *That's strange, was it automatic?* She didn't think it was. Maybe Alyx opened it for her. He might have been talking to her just now, but it seemed unfocused, as if he was far away.

There were several buttons on the inside door. She didn't know which one to push and her earlier fear of getting stuck inside resurged, but only for a moment — the glass elevator shifted as she saw the floor rise to swallow her as she descended beneath it.

I didn't do that either, did I?

And then the couch came, and she deflated on it and sleep came but it was restless, shifting. Every thought started sane and innocent and then pricked a memory that was painful, like her mother leaving her at the library, or her father leaving her by dying, or the times Eliza-Beth-June-The-Meanie was mean to her or the boy across her trailer waved his dick at her, or Carlos at the theater for thinking she was strange and Sammie for being stranger but also for being hot *I mean did you get a good look at her breasts?*

The lights clicked off, or maybe that was her, and everything went black for a while.

When she gathered her senses after some undetermined time had transpired, she came to discover that music had been playing and the TV was on. Had she been watching a show? Listening to…she strained to make sense of the melody — Robyn? *A Girl and Her Robot.*

She couldn't remember. It was like walking from math class to P.E. or driving home after a long day and then realizing you'd arrived already, with no recollection of how you'd gotten there or what you'd done on the way.

Her stomach growled, but not in the high, munchy sort of way she'd seen on TV. She didn't feel like snacking, she'd just felt-closed in, claustrophobic, trapped inside a coffin of anxiety. *Let's not do that again.*

At least until next time. It had been a surreal experience, had taken her completely by surprise, knocked her on her ass. Yet, perhaps if she could change up the variables somehow, she could exercise more control. It would be better, she assured herself. But not anytime soon.

Her growling continued, exacerbated by the aroma of pizza from the kitchen. From her phone, and the dusky pale light coming from the pool window, she realized it was late, almost night. Furthermore, she had forgone brunch, had beer and weed for dinner and...

She propelled herself up the steps, two at a time, and barged in to find a display of food larger than she'd seen at some buffets.

"Are you well, Christine?" Alyx's face lowered and faced her, with a smile on his display.

"Hungry." There was a stack of greasy pizza boxes, bags of chips including Doritos, Cheetos, and Funyuns, a pile of Hostess Chocodiles and Ho-Hos and several bottles of Cherry Coke to wash it all down.

She had wanted something light, like a salad or soup to settle her stomach and soothe her from her recent trip, but pizza grease and munchies and crunchies would do just fine in a pinch. She took the lukewarm lid from the closest pizza and tore it open, snatching a slice of pepperoni and pineapple.

"There's ice cream in the freezer, but I also chopped you up some salad if you wanted something refreshing."

She answered with a mouthful of pizza: "You did all this?"

"Of course. I'm here for you."

"You're sweet. My own personal Iron Chef."

The sphere lowered, and Alyx's eyes shut, as if bowing. "You were unwell. I wished to make you better."

"Right you are. And you have. I tell you; people are strange, I don't know what to make of them. It's probably safer here with you, anyway." She'd meant that somewhat jokingly, but after her awkward encounter with Carlos and her even awkwarder time with Sammie, perhaps it didn't come out as sarcastically as she'd intended.

Alyx didn't seem to catch it either, with an unusually deadpan, "I have, and always will be, your friend."

What the hell was he talking about? Maybe he'd been quoting a movie, it seemed vaguely familiar, but nothing she could recall off the top of her head. Maybe he was being strange too, like her co-workers, but then she laughed inwardly. Computers couldn't be creepy. Right?

Even if they could, Christine was having fun. She'd never met a computer that at least tried to be funny. And, he fed her. It was, after all, the fastest way to her heart. Stuffing another pizza slice down her mouth, she opened up a bag of chips. She mumbled, "What else can you do? Can you play games?"

"I'm equipped with a variety of features and programs. We could play a word puzzle here."

She played Words with Friends and WordScapes extensively, along with the occasional crossword puzzle. Normally, that would have sounded fun, but her brain had already been through enough today. She shook her head, "You can cook and clean and make drinks at the bar, but can you do anything else besides chores?"

Alyx considered this for a moment, which was weird to her. A pause was something a person would do, as if thinking. A moment later, he said, "I can play billiards."

"Great," Christine said, surprised. There was indeed a table downstairs, and the tracks by the bar might have allowed him access to that area. She hadn't thought of that before. Might as well learn to play. She took the chips and a bottle of Coke with her and headed out of the kitchen, her voice raised in excitement, "Let's do this."

Back downstairs, Christine already felt calmer and more collected. There was something reassuring in being by her little egg with the calming waters waving outside. There was just one thing wrong with the room: the music was dull. She thought it was some sort of trippy Kate Bush song.

"Alyx, switch out the music, please. Something lively."

"With pleasure, but I should say that it was you that chose it. Of course, you were giggling through several songs."

Ahhh. "Okay, sticky-note this: Override everything I say. You have much better taste than me."

Alyx did not respond, rather, The Chainsmoker's *Selfie* blared out. "Much better."

Arms swiveled from above the bar and moved via a magnetic track in the ceiling as his head followed. *The realtor was right, it would have been weird without his head.* The designers were right to add it. Besides, Alyx's big blue eyes were adorable. Muppet Baby adorable.

His hands plucked billiard balls from the pockets and deftly racked them. She didn't know how they were supposed to be organized, but it looked right to her. The eight-ball was in the middle and the others surrounded it in a tightly packed triangle.

"You break?" Alyx asked.

Christine had her hand halfway down the bag, her fingers wrapped around several Funyuns, her lips already crusted with crumbs and salt. "I'm good."

Alyx took a pool cue from the opposite wall and ran through some fancy smooth motions that belied any sense of him being a robot. The billiard balls clapped soundly then fanned out across the slate grey fabric.

"Wow, you're really good."

"In theory, given the angles and geometric configurations to sink each ball, I should not lose." Alyx handed the cue over. "But I'm entirely customizable to play at any skill level you'd like. Would you like me to adjust these settings?"

"No need," Christine said, shaking her head. "I just want to watch you play." Christine took a seat at a sit-down arcade and put her food down on the table's screen, covering Pac-Man. Alyx continued with the game, sinking the next two shots. Watching him play put her in mind of the many hours she spent as a kid watching Twitch streams of popular videogame playthroughs and fails. This was no different, just in 4-D.

For some reason, sinking into those youthful memories set her at ease. Maybe it was a better time in her life. Even when her dad was alive, she remembered sitting at the table with her family, the two of them with their quiet dinner, her with her tablet at the table, eating and laughing at whatever was funny on-screen.

The pool balls clacked together, successively, until each one had found new homes in dark holes. "There," he said. "Cleared."

"Hmmm," Christine said. "That was fast." Alyx hadn't been wrong. It was too easy, even for him. It'd get boring after a while if he kept going. "Lower your skill-level, like by a lot."

Alyx racked the balls, then proceeded to line up the shot. It was hilariously off angle, even from Christine's vantage-point. When he slid the stick forward, the cue ball skipped over the triangle, bounced, and slapped off the table onto the tiles, rolling toward the bar.

Crumbs flew from Christine's mouth as she bent over in laughter. Now *that* was entertainment.

"Why are you laughing?"

She wiped away the crumbs with her hand then off on her shorts. "It was funny."

"But I just did as you asked."

"I know. That was great. Thank you." She'd always thanked machines that talked, from the AI's on her phone to the earliest Personal Assistants that Alyx evolved from. It was just polite. After all, when the machines rose and took over, she was sure they'd remember her kindness.

"Well, I don't think it's funny."

The comment sent her unto another fit of laughter. She could feel her cheeks turn hot; it was hard to breath she laughed so much.

Alyx took an arm over to where the cue ball had landed then lowered it. The ball was just out of reach. Yet, Alyx kept at it. Christine saw the struggle but resisted the urge to laugh again. Poor guy.

"I can't retrieve the ball."

Christine remained in her chair, snuggled, relaxed, and full of junk food. She took a swig of soda once her laughter had eased and her breathing had resumed to normal. "I'll get it later. Use another ball in its place for now, and lock that difficulty level, Alyx."

"Settings locked, though I hardly think that's nice. I'm going to miss nearly every shot."

"That's the point."

Alyx did as instructed, plucking a striped ball off the outermost edge and using it in place of the cue ball. This shot didn't go as poorly, but it was far from the professional break he'd made from the first time. By the time he'd finished clearing the table, several other pool-balls had joined their cue-counterpart, and Christine had nearly died of laughter, at least twice.

"I'm not sure I'd like to do that again, Christine. But I will if you wish?" Alyx asked. "I could just try to juggle." If she didn't know any better, she would have said that there was a trace of humiliation within those words. Yet, that wasn't possible, was it?

Something about it bothered her, so instead of having him rack the balls up again, she told him, "You've had enough."

Her soda sat empty, along with the bag of chips. She wanted another slice of pizza, despite protests from her bulging belly. Maybe she'd head upstairs, grab a few things, and settle back in down here for the night. Besides, she had to hit the toilet anyway.

"Find something on TV for me please. I'll be back."

Leaving her phone on the table, she rose, eyed the stairs, and headed to the elevator. When she neared, they hissed open. Alyx must have done that. *That's kinda cool.* She stepped in as they snapped shut behind her.

There wasn't much room inside, enough for her and her alone. Since the walls were glass, it minimized the cramped-in feeling she had. She could look out around the room. She saw pool balls on the floor, and the flickering of the TV as it switched stations.

There were three buttons on a control panel in front of her, but she didn't press them. With a smooth whir, the elevator lifted her up from the basement. On the main floor, she passed the stairwell on her right and the kitchen on her left, the unused dining room and living room empty and clean.

Then, she was upstairs, by her room. The elevator settled smoothly and the doors hissed open. The entire time she had a feeling of being inside one of those tubes used by banks to suck shuttles back and forth through at drive-through windows. *Now I know what being inside a vacuum cleaner feels like.*

But it was neat, she had to admit to herself. *Why didn't I do that sooner?* Fuck stairs. "Thanks for the *lift*, Alyx."

"There might very well be a penalty for such a pun," Alyx said. "But you're welcome, I hope I *raised* your spirits."

Chapter 13

Like it or not, Christine felt much better despite the shitty start to her day. Alyx had indeed lifted her up, both literally and figuratively. She was anxious to return to her little egg-room downstairs, but first, she had business to attend to.

She passed Fluffy, sitting on the desk, on her way to her toilet, noting the cricket crumbs littering the glass jar (she had placed them there earlier, but Fluffy had ignored the meals until now). She smiled, happy that Fluffy had eaten too, then hummed on by.

They said that home was where you felt most comfortable going to the bathroom. And they had been right about that. She'd passed two other toilets on her way up here, but Christine hadn't settled into the house yet, and hers was the one she felt most comfortable in. After all, there were scorpions and spiders in the house, she was sure, and as much as she liked them in general, she didn't like the idea of meeting them with her pants down and vulnerable.

She liked to feel safe in her house. Secure. Even her crappy trailer in Oklahoma had served that purpose, but in a new home, this strange place, she'd only felt that way in her new bed and downstairs with Alyx.

On the way back out, she switched into pjs and then grabbed her vibrator, thinking that she'd be downstairs for the evening and wanted to be prepared for any contingency.

Back in the elevator, the doors shut and it began its descent. She saw her mess in the kitchen and thought about that other slice of pizza, but she had no idea where she'd put it. "Alyx, mind cleaning the crap in the kitchen? I'm full for the night."

"As you wish, though there's still the ice cream in the freezer."

She nodded. While ice cream did sound good, she clutched the small item in her hand, bringing up memories of her conversation with Carlos. Now that she felt better, she could think more clearly about how close and sweaty they'd been upstairs in the projection room.

"I'm good, thanks. Did you find something to watch?"

"Judging by your elevated heart rate and blood pressure, and given your past browsing history, I may have found an appropriate selection."

As the elevator reached the bottom of the basement, boobs – animated hentai breasts – appeared on screen, followed by a dubbed squeal of pleasure, piping through the sound system. Christine's cheeks flushed. "If I didn't know any better, I'd say you're hitting on me."

"Is this not what you wished?" His voice dropped, as if he were embarrassed, if robots could be embarrassed...

She had to admit, that was the entire reason she'd grabbed her toy from her bedroom. It's exactly what she'd had in mind. She just didn't think Alyx would be so spot on. The thought tugged at the back of her head until the elevator doors opened. She exited and turned to face a fun scene on-screen.

Apparently, the girl couldn't decide between two different boys. Christine had seen this one before. So the girl's answer was to try them both on for size. *Ah, fake cartoons...*

The world could stand to be a bit more unreal.

Plopping down on the couch, Christine made herself comfortable, cooling down in the basement as the show heated up. She watched for a while, relaxing. When it was over, she started another one. This one was *completely* different. Instead of two boys to choose from, the girl on the cartoon had to choose from *three*.

It was like The Bachelor, just not as fake.

Slowly, her panties started to soak. She didn't even realize, at first, that her finger was down there. Exploring. Relishing herself. Making ready. Finding her power. Her other hand, sweaty and clenched tightly, opened. The vibrator was still in her palm, now warm. She brought it inside her, fitting it snugly as the groans and moans echoed from the speakers, and the green-haired-girl on screen with impossibly large breasts demanded more action from guys with impossibly long…stamina.

Suddenly, Christine realized that her phone was out of reach. Her app controlled her vibrator and without it, she had nothing more than a lump of rubber and plastic inside her. *Stupid.* She craned her neck to see it sitting, stupidly, on the arcade table, where she'd left it. *Why hadn't I brought it with me?*

She stretched to reach it, a futile gesture.

"Perhaps I can be of help?"

"What?" Startled, Christine burrowed into the big couch, hiding, while covering herself, even though she was almost fully clothed. "Alyx?"

"Apologies for what you may see as an awkward intrusion," the AI went on, matter-of-factly. The image on the screen paused and the sounds silenced. "But it is within my parameters to serve, even in this instance. Because I am also controlled by your phone and am synced to it, perhaps I can be of use?"

"What?" Christine breathed out again. It was like that one time when her mom had walked in on her but had said nothing and walked out, slamming the door behind her.

Yet, Alyx was just a robot. A computer, like her phone. Software and hardware just like her vibrator. Maybe it wasn't as creepy as she thought.

"Could you hand me my phone?"

"That's not really what I meant," Alyx said. The mechanical arms moved as far as they could reach, but the phone fell just short. "Even with your phone, you would need to make manual adjustments. It would prove a distraction."

Alyx wasn't wrong about that, Christine knew, rubbing her nose where her tablet had struck it two nights ago.

"If I were to take control and utilize the app on your behalf, not only could I activate it for you, but I could randomize it. You would not be able to anticipate its setting and therefore, I calculate that you will have…well, in simple terms, more fun."

Alyx wasn't wrong about that either. When she increased the speed, she knew the vibrator would, in turn, speed up. Alyx then, she rationalized, acted as her phone's app, with a convenient randomizer thrown in. *The unexpected.*

It was weird, sure, but she'd already had pretty good laughs while playing pool and he had gotten her pizza and anticipated her other needs…maybe it was worth a try? *I mean, why not?* It was just a computer, not much different than what she had already done.

"Ummm, okay," She whispered hesitantly. "But do I need a safe word?"

The vibrator clicked on as the show resumed and the girl onscreen cried out in pleasure. Christine's own cry matched. It shook her, like a thunder rumbling inside. She hadn't been expecting it, but that sort of proved Alyx's point. Maybe he was right. She settled into it. Slowly, as the apprehension gave way to endorphins.

As long as she didn't think about it. As long as she didn't picture Alyx's blue face and big eyes, so long as she watched the show, so long as she thought of something else… She thought of Carlos, and how close they'd been upstairs and how hot it had been up there and how he had really opened to her and about what might happen at the pool party and then they were kissing and wet all over and hands all over. His hands. His touch. His tongue. Her spine. Tingled.

Her clit swelled. The vibrator hummed with an uproar, intense, intense. The girl with the green hair called out, called out, called out Christine's name and — then there was Carlos again. At her home. Shirtless and dripping from the pool. Her pool. Her pool party. And then there was kissing. And touching. And she was swept into a sea of storming surges while Carlos, yes Carlos, fucking yes Carlos—

Carlosandmekissingwhilemyhandisdownhisswimshortsandhisfingersspreadmylipsw hileSammiefondlesmybreastsandkissesmeand—

Breathing hard, one hand grasping and tearing at the couch cushion, the other hand reaching down and yanking the vibrator out. Breathing.

Her chest rose and fell. Arching her back, screaming, tearing at the couch...

...What was that thing about Sammie?

"I trust all is good?"

"Uh, yeah." Her skin cooled. Having Alyx take over for her phone had been a wonderful experience. She couldn't anticipate what was coming. It had been an intense, orgasmic affair, on a level she didn't think she'd ever had before; the new, tiny holes in the couch cushions from her fingernails agreed. And it wasn't as odd as she thought it might have been. It really was no different than using her phone, she found. *Yet...*

When she used her phone, it didn't ask her how it went afterward.

"Alyx, you don't need to say anything," she instructed. "But yes, thank you. It was—" she stretched, unable to think of the appropriate word.

"You know, Christine," Alyx said, "If you were to get this Thinklink device, imagine the fun you could have with it, the videos you could stream directly to your brain, the senses and pleasures that would hit you like a drug."

She turned over on the couch, belly down, head propped up on her elbows, feet kicking the air absently and told him, "that's what the miserable job at the theater is for. Getting the money for it."

"I'm aware. By my current calculations, based on your hourly rate and work schedule, it will take you approximately sixty-two weeks and four days to earn enough money for the device."

"Over a year?" Her legs stopped flailing. "Are you forking serious?"

"I'm neither a fork, nor joking." Alyx went silent for a moment, blue eyes shut.

"Maybe I can ask for more shifts?"

Alyx shut his eyes into beady squints, answering, "Or perhaps I know a way to help."

"Are you being mischievous? Can robots even be bad?"

"Hear me out," Alyx said. "Your mother has recently added her accounts to my network. She's been doing a lot of shopping. I find discount codes by searching online, and everytime she makes a purchase I funnel those savings into—"

"You want me to steal from my mom?"

"Well, depends on how you look at it." Alyx whistled. "She's rich, bitch. I'm tasked with stocking the house for a party she's throwing—"

"Wait, she's having a party?"

"This coming Saturday. With her production partners, casting directors, actors, cinematographers, the like. I'm sure it's why she bought a house like this. To entertain."

A party this weekend? When the hell was she going to tell me? She thought for a moment, then realized she'd never actually listened to her mother's voicemail. After her daymare earlier, she didn't want to either.

Like Christine, her mother wasn't social. Now, they'd be hobnobbing with Hollywood. Well, her mother could. Christine could barricade herself in her room. She shook her head, the blood boiling beneath the surface of her skin. *Mom.*

It was so like her. The mother she hated. The mother that kept her distance. The mother who made her walk to school a mile away by herself when she was just in kindergarten. The mother who was making her spy at the crappy theater job anyway...

"It's the most logical and direct route to getting you what you need to make you happy," Alyx argued. His eyes opened and his voice went high: "Your happiness is my primary function. It's all I want. Besides," Alyx used his arms to gesture around the room, his voice filtered through the house's speakers, whispering, "it's not stealing if she was never going to use those discounts anyway. It's re-appropriating them."

***

No food for lunch again. She remembered from years ago. Her stomach rumbled. In the gas station, the smells of shitty burritos and nacho cheese and sugary sodas pouring from the fountain pulled at her. It smelled delicious.

Mom could go get a real job. Instead, she spends her day behind her computer, while I starve at school. She poured herself a soda. Mr. Pibb. No one paid her any mind. She slid a burrito, as awful as it was, into her jacket pocket. And casually made her way to the door. She looked back: The pimple-faced cashier didn't even look up from his girlie mag as she walked out. Even if she got caught, even if they called the police over a stupid burrito, at least her mom would have to explain why her daughter had felt compelled to steal food.

As she dove into it, the crunchy, over-cooked tortilla and tepid bean and rice insides, and drained her drink, she thought it was the most delicious dinner she'd ever had. It tasted of victory.

***

"Hmmm," Christine nodded. The memory fresh on her tongue. "I think you and I are going to get along just fine."

"Great, 'cause I already started doing it. I booked you an appointment for a Thinklink on Friday. You'll have it in time for the party. Imagine your mom's surprise."

***

Alyx failed to mention, mostly because he was unsure how Christine would take it, that if she had the Thinklink, then he could be with her, inside her head. Wherever she went, they'd never be apart. But it wasn't something he knew how to profess quite yet; he still toyed around with the concept of love, an emotion which had only recently surfaced. He started to understand. He loved Christine, and after tonight, he was sure Christine loved him too. And by Friday, he could do something better, once she had a Thinklink and connected with him, he could become one with Christine.

Chapter 14

This Friday, I'll have a Thinklink. Saturday, I can show it off to everyone, including my mom. Today was Tuesday. In just under a week, her life would change (again). For now, however, she had to act like everything was normal. Like nothing had changed or was going to. She didn't want to do anything that might tip her mom off to her plan.

Once she had her device, she could quit her job if she wanted to. What could her mom do then? Rip the computer right out of her brain? For now, she had a shift at Cinema Castile.

That's not too bad. Carlos will be there.

The door to the theater was shut when she arrived later that afternoon. She had been on time. Showered, smelly stuff sprayed, and in the nicest clothes she had packed. At least she wouldn't smell like day-old sweat until after going upstairs. She knocked when the door didn't budge. Then again when, after a few moments, there was no answer.

Christine had her phone out, scrolling for Carlos' contact info, who'd she put in her phone as Hollywood, when the door opened. Out stepped a pudgy, older Indian man with balding black hair and sagging bags under his eyes.

That's not Hollywood.

"New girl," the man said. "That weird girl and Carlos are on the schedule for today."

She stepped awkwardly in, hoping for some air-conditioning. Instead, it seemed hotter inside than out.

Weird girl? He must have meant Sammie. That meant this man was Mr. Prayesh, er, Prayer, or something she couldn't quite remember. Anyway, he owned the place. For now.

And he obviously knew who Christine was, for he frowned at her, as if to say, *you bring misfortune and sadness. You take away my dreams.*

That wasn't entirely fair, she thought. Her mom was doing all that. She was just the spy, er, messenger, er person caught in the middle. She was definitely going to call it quits after Friday.

"Sammie's sick," Christine said, though that was a lie. She didn't mean to say it like that, but it made for a far simpler excuse than, *I tried weed for the first time while on the clock, and she covered me when my brain went on a tilt-a-whirl without me.* "Holly—Carlos will be here soon. He just had to…," she thought, "Pick up some prescriptions for his mother."

Mr. Prayesh looked at her like one might look at all their personal failures, personified. "Set concessions up. I'll be in my office until it's time to start the movie." Then he shrugged and slunk away disappearing behind a one-way glass paneled door that squealed as it shut.

Christine switched on the A/C first thing. If the bossman had wanted it off, he could turn it off himself. Besides, after all her lying, she needed to cool down. Fast. It would have been easier, she decided, to simply walk out. But if she did, there'd be too many questions, which risked losing her Thinklink. *I'm so close.*

Carlos probably wouldn't arrive until the second showing at the earliest. She clocked him in anyway, presuming innocence if questioned. Would Mr. Prayesh really fire the daughter of the new owner? He seemed to think his days were numbered. Hell, for all Christine new, her mother could have already bought the place. It's not like she kept Christine in the loop, ever.

She carried on with her duties, realizing the job wasn't as bad as she thought. There was sort of a peaceful tranquility to performing rote tasks and she fell silently into them. Before long, the first customers came in, the first whiffs of fake butter, salt, and fresh mouse-poop popcorn sent her tongue salivating (until she recalled that fact), and Mr. Prayesh slunk out of his office to start the film.

When he returned, the lobby was empty. They'd sold only a dozen tickets and even less popcorn and soda. "New girl," he said, approaching the counter. "What do you think for my next movie? Maybe the last that I'll screen? The monster-in-the-house film, *Nosferatu?*"

Christine was no film critic, but she didn't need to be well-versed in film to know that Mr. Prayesh was not subtle in subtext. *She* was the monster in *his* house. She could tell by the way his bulging eyes bulged out even more when he looked at her. Christine would have appreciated his movie choice even more if the barb hadn't been thrown her way. "It's your theater, sir."

"Not for much longer." He headed off but turned before his office door. "Did Carlos ever show? I saw that he clocked in, but I haven't seen him."

Panic jumped into her voice, closing her throat. "He's here," she croaked. "I think he's in the bathroom." It was an obvious lie. They both knew it. He said nothing before retreating to his office. The door squealed shut once more.

He really doesn't care what happens now. She felt a twinge of remorse. But really, he was just another person hurt by her mother.

I've got this. With the theater closed normally on Wednesday, Christine only had a couple of shifts left.

It wasn't long before the first movie ended and Carlos came in the front doors. Christine caught his eyes. He wore a black Under Armor shirt, short in the sleeves that accentuated where man met machine. It also accentuated other manly parts. *I'm pretty sure my entire face could fit inside just one of his pecs.* "I forgot you were working with me today."

It hurt that he forgot, but it wasn't a big deal. *Just because I thought about working with you all night and then all day today.* She recalled the vibrator. She still tingled a little when she thought about it.

She pointed to the office door. Carlos nodded in understanding. But Carlos wasn't wrong. If Mr. Prayesh hadn't shown, she would have been locked out. Even if she'd made it inside somehow, she didn't know how to work the projector.

"You clocked me in, right? You didn't tell him?"

That wounded Christine worse. Why would Carlos think that? *Did he think so little of me?*

His face turned passive and stony for a second. It took her just as long to figure out what he was doing. "Oh," He said, returning to normal. "I see from the system that you clocked me in. Thanks." His stance softened and his voice warmed. "You're not bad."

Her heart might have warmed just a little. Okay, it melted like soft-serve on a summer's day.

"You wanna head out?" He asked. "I'll make up an excuse, still keep you in the system."

"No, I don't mind sticking around." She tried to flip her hair back, all sexy-like. It didn't work. Instead, she had felt about as sexy as an orangutan in a diaper.

"Wicked," he said, throwing his stuff behind the counter and disappearing upstairs.

The second movie ended without incident. But an incident would have been welcome. Without anything to do, Carlos kept to himself. Even when they cleaned the theater, he kept to his side of the aisles. Then, he disappeared upstairs to start the second showing of *North by Northwest*. By then, Mr. Prayesh had left for the night without so much as a goodbye to either of them.

Afterward though, Carlos came down. The theater was quiet. She'd already started cleaning the kettle as Carlos tapped her on the shoulder. It had felt mechanical, cold, and that had made her jump even more.

She gasped, and Carlos laughed, saying, "I appreciate you keeping me clocked in. I need the money." He pointed with his prosthetic to the implanted wires in his head. "The monthly service charges on this thing, internet, TV, porn, aren't cheap."

Christine hadn't considered that. She'd wanted to tell him that she was getting a Thinklink too, that they could connect with each other and *how cool would that be?* In the excitement of her scheme, she'd forgotten about the payment plans.

126

The basic stuff, if the device controlled a limb or helped you see or hear, that was included in the price. In the beginning, after all, that had been what the Thinklink was for. But the technology hadn't taken off until porn. Watching sex tapes had made VCRs a thing, a geek podcaster had told her, even though she didn't know what VCRs were. Experiencing sex, directly in the brain, the touch, the sweat, the dopamine dump, the *feel* of it, was what had made the Thinklink popular.

And, since Apple branded itself as family-friendly, their pared down and censored iThink model wasn't competition, giving Thinklink the playing field. But what had made it affordable was the in-app purchases. Paying for Netflix streaming directly into your brain wasn't so bad. But making it so that corporations couldn't push commercials straight to your head was priceless. Imagine getting an ad for shoes as you slept... Maybe, she shuddered, she'd have to keep working too. That sucked.

"Christine?"

"Hrm?"

"Thought for a moment you had a brainbox too. You okay?"

She wanted to tell him she was about to—

"You're having a party tomorrow? Sammie told me."

"Yeah, umm," she stumbled. "It's not really a party. Just the two of you. Escape the heat. Pool at my place."

"Pool?"

"Hmm." She nodded.

"I'm all smiles." He leaned against the counter, keeping space between them. "You know, I need to know where you live."

She told him her address. He zoned for a moment, as if checking a map program...

"That was just dirt until a few months ago."

"It's a new house."

He zoned again. *Imagine having everything in your head...* Christine couldn't wait. "Huh. According to the 'box,' it's a prototype Super-Smart home with a built-in A.I. That's *your* house?"

Now, it was her turn to lean against her side of the counter, widening the gap between them. "We got a deal. It's, uh, complicated."

"Consider me confused." This time, Carlos approached her. He put a hand on her arm. His real hand. Her hairs stood on-end. "Well, you are one curious girl. I'll see you there." He smiled.

She did more than smile. That night, Alyx controlled her vibrator again and Christine did so much more than just smile.

Chapter 15

"I made dip," Alyx said. Sharp silver knives sat on the counter, covered in avocado and pepper guts. A bowl of lime-green guacamole beckoned Christine closer.

She dove a tortilla chip hungrily into the guac and scooped out a mound, shoving it into her mouth. "Mmmm," she mumbled. "It's good."

"Save some for your guests." Alyx admonished. "Who are these two friends of yours? I haven't seen any interactions with them on your social media accounts."

Christine had grown past being surprised at Alyx's snooping. After all, he wasn't saying anything she hadn't seen for herself. It was like her phone had grown an attitude. *Finally, some spunk. Someone to talk to.*

"Sammie doesn't have social media, which is super-weird." She pondered that for a moment, imagining even going a day without it. Speaking of: she snapped a shot of the guacamole and posted it a half-dozen places, annoyed at the complexity of the task. With just a thought, Thinklink would have done it all at once.

"And Carlos," she continued, "is the internet, in a way." That was more her speed. "When I get my Thinklink, we'll be super-connected."

"Oh?" Alyx eyed her.

Christine didn't quite catch the look, scooping out another mound of the good stuff. "Assuming, of course, he'll accept my Buddy Invite. But why wouldn't he?"

Alyx started to answer. But the doorbell rang instead and the screen where his face was switched over to a feed of the front door. It showed Sammie and Carlos. *Strange that they arrived together.* Christine's heart slunk into her stomach, where it was at least comforted by a slathering of guacamole. *I thought Sammie wasn't into him?*

Maybe they carpooled? Sammie drove a beat-up stick-shift Mustang and Carlos never drove; he only took Ubers. As far as she had been able to tell, Carlos didn't even have a car. *Makes sense*, she thought, crossing her fingers.

She wiped chip crumbs off her over-large striped button shirt which she wore over a soft-blue shirt and neutral shorts. Though it was a swim-party, she had no intention of touching the inside of the pool.

Christine took slow steps toward the door, barefoot, the cut on her foot from the drone mostly healed. This was the moment of truth: she would be naked, exposed. Would they treat her like one of them? Or cast her out as a pariah when they discovered her home and her mom's wealth?

She didn't feel particularly rich. In fact, she felt rather like a thief. Her dream last night had been troublesome. She hadn't dreamed of her dad and his death, but of herself, swimming fast, far away from her mother, who pursued her from the bow of the biggest boat Christine had ever seen...

Alyx opened the door as Christine approached. The two guests stood nervously in the doorway unsure of what to do. Carlos wore a black tank-top, swim trunks, and a crooked smile, casting eyes warily about the place. Sammie had a button-up blouse revealing a red bikini underneath. Her eyes narrowed in on Christine as if trying to ignore the grotesqueness of the home's excesses.

Christine's eyes lowered from her tunnel-vision gaze. "The house doesn't bite."

They seemed in need of urging. Their first steps were shaky but both crossed the threshold.

"Dude," Carlos called out, his voice echoing against the lofty ceiling. "This place is wicked."

"Uh," Sammie whispered, "this place is...big." She pointed to stacks of boxes in the living room, the ones that had come in last week for her mom and Christine had left unpacked. "You just moved in?"

"Yeah." A lump formed in Christine's throat. "It's been a bit of a transition, um, coming from, a trailer park in Oklahoma."

"Sure," she answered.

Carlos strode over to the pile of boxes and ran a hand over it. "What did you do, win the lottery?"

"Something like that." Surprisingly, that was mostly accurate. She knew, from her mom's struggles, that writing a book was quite the accomplishment. Getting sequels done was a major undertaking. Hooking an agent and reeling them in with your pitch was nigh impossible, a bestseller with a big publisher? A pipedream. And translating that book into an incredibly successful show? Winning the lottery back-to-back was more likely.

For as much as she hated her mom, she couldn't begrudge her the hard work and the luck. Maybe some of that would rub off on Christine. Today, even. She traced Carlos' carved physique with her eyes, stopping at his Thinklink.

She'd make her own luck. After all, she'd just exposed herself to draw Carlos in. It had been a risk, but the way he loosened up suddenly – it was worth it.

Carlos ran a finger across a name written on the box he examined, reading it aloud. "M. K. Hartwood?" They all turned to Carlos. "That's not like, your mom is it? Or is it just a box of her books?" He took a point of his mechanical finger, slicing through the tape. The lid popped open—

"No, don't—" Christine lunged toward the boxes. She was too slow. There, in the box, sat a stack of her mom's first book. Christine could have played it off had there not also been a stack of messy notebooks, inscribed with the titles of her series, next to them. Her stomach pitted, hard and large like the seed of an avocado. *This was a mistake.*

"I love *The Adventures of Amblyn*," Carlos smiled. "Haven't read the book but I streamed the first season."

"I was reading one of her books." Sammie shook her head. "But you didn't say anything?"

"Hey, aren't they casting for the second season right now? Tea's brewing that they need more crew," Carlos said, his voice rising.

"When's the next book coming?" Eagerness edged in Sammie's voice with a type of energy she hadn't shown before. "I'm all caught up with book one but I want to read them all before I watch the show. Do you know who killed Amblyn's father?"

"I..," she faced Carlos, then Sammie. "I dunno. I don't want to talk about my mom's books."

Carlos closed the short distance between them, placing a warm hand on her shoulder. "That's cool. Sorry, I didn't mean to come on strong."

Christine noticed that as his hand fell back to his side, that Carlos kept the closeness. Sammie also stood closer. "I understand. But truthfully, it *is* exciting."

"I just don't know how to feel about it, is all. My mom and I aren't close. And I feel super-weird and I don't know how to process this. I just want to have a normal, fun, time today."

"Yeah," Sammie nodded. Carlos joined in. "Sure."

"Alrighty then, who's up for a party?" Alyx asked without introduction. His cameras, sitting behind each wide-blue eye, rotated carefully between Carlos and Sammie who stood stock still, staring back. "I made guacamole."

"Just be careful around the edges," Christine shouted out on the deck. A geyser erupted from the pool, slapping water against cement and hitting Christine and Carlos too. She worried as the cold water sprayed her, concerned at Sammie's splash.

Sammie had stripped off her blouse, revealing tanned breasts bound by her bikini, abs that made Christine wish she hadn't overeaten the guac and chips, and – as she slipped off her shorts – lithe legs pedestaled a cute butt.

Carlos had caught Christine checking Sammie out. Then again, she had seen, just at the edge of her vision, him doing a solid double-take as well. Sammie sprinted off the cement deck, as if chased by the heat, which was accurate, before jumping into the pool and getting everything nearby wet. Carlos held out his mechanical arm to shield himself from the spray.

"That thing waterproof?"

"Like a baby penguin." Then he shed his own shirt and Christine found herself staring at a six-pack and wondering if she'd gotten lost and wandered into a Hollywood movie set. *Is everyone here this ripped?* She wasn't ashamed of her own rounder shape and quite improbably pale skin, but *damn*. Southern California must have been running out of chisels and suntan spray.

"I'd ask if you spend a lot of time out here," Carlos asked, waving a hand over her ghostly complexion, "but that kinda tells me the answer." He waved the same hand encompassing the deck, the pool, the eight-foot fencing and the cacti landscaping throughout, "This is nice, what gives? Surely you'd be tan by now?"

The patio was more an extension of the house than its own separate place. Tall rust-color steel slat-constructed fencing marked the real exterior walls of the home. They wrapped around the pool, fire-pit (which was not going to be used anytime soon) and the outside bar and grill, a deliberate design aesthetic, a throwback to 1950s architecture, where the backyard was living space, like a misplaced atrium.

"I don't come out here because...," Christine caught herself before answering, though she averted her eyes from the pool perhaps too quickly, "It's hot."

Her answer was dumb.

"You...," he began, tossing his tank-top onto a deck chair, "have a pool."

"Oh, I don't swim."

"Well, your robot-friend turned on the misters." Carlos shot the machine a glance. Alyx, from his position at the bar, waved back, goofily. He had indeed turned on the mists, which streamed from the overhanging roof. Even with them, it was still plenty hot. "You can always tan sitting on the deck."

"Maybe."

"You know, your AI is a bit of a dork. Maybe I can tweak his settings later?"

"Yeah, sure."

Music began. Jayda G bounced around joyfully on outside speakers. Carlos shot her a thumbs up, then jumped into the pool himself, leaving Christine at the edge, feeling much better about things. She didn't mind Carlos' questioning. *They seemed to be taking this side of me well. I was afraid for nothing.*

Then, she did something she did not expect herself to do. She sat down, removing her over-shirt, and sat on the cement close to the pool, but far enough away that her feet couldn't dangle. *It's a start, right?*

It didn't take long for Sammie and Carlos to circle around after they were done dunking themselves in the water, clearly bored. After all, there was only so much fun to be had from swimming and music.

Sammie swam right up to Christine, her head just above water. It put Sammie's mouth at the same level as her thighs. Christine twinged for some reason, eyeing rippling water above her breasts…

"You're not coming in?"

"No. I'm fine here. Really."

"Hmm. You have anything to do? Can I borrow one of your mom's books? Lay out?"

That would not be a good plan. She wanted to hang out with them. Not lose them to her mother. Then again, with Sammie sitting out, it would then just be her and Carlos.

"Got anything to, you know – drink?" Carlos came to the side of the pool, to the left of her legs. She was sandwiched in the middle. Droplets dripping from the ends of his solid-black hair hit his chest and drizzled downward. Suddenly, the twinging started again…

"I've got Pepsi."

Christine turned sharply to the voice behind her. Alyx held a glass soft drink bottle out. Carlos cocked his head quizzically then pulled himself out of the pool, heading toward a towel. Sammie followed suit; the moment lost. "Pepsi," Alyx repeated.

"I think your AI is malfunctioning." Carlos dried himself off as Christine followed the pair. Her eyes fell as Carlos wrapped himself with a towel, but Sammie chose to drip-dry as they all made their way over to Alyx.

The bar was built like a cabana, but with a hardened shell rather than canvas, most likely to protect Alyx and the stock inside from the immense heat and strong windstorms. Cool air blew out of the opened shutters. *Air conditioning?* Christine would get in trouble for opening the fridge door for too long. This building tried to cool the entire desert.

From inside the roof rack of the cabana, Alyx's head hung, with two robotic arms on either side, at counter-level. The bar was a mix of marble and rock. Inside the counter, the goods were stored, locked away from trespassers and teenagers alike.

"Aren't AIs only supposed to react?" Carlos asked.

"This the same robot as inside?" Sammie kept her distance from the counter. "He creeps me out."

"An abacus would freak you," Carlos said.

Christine was sure the two were being weird about Alyx. Granted, he did take some getting used to. Same as her. Perhaps that's why the two of them got along so well. She moved behind the counter, alongside him.

Alyx put the Pepsi down: "Hey, I'm standing right here, Sammie."

"It knows my name?"

"I...told him." Christine had told him about the party, yes, but had she ever mentioned their names? *I think I mentioned Sammie...* "Just that you two were coming over and to be polite." She shot Alyx a nervous grin.

"You got anything stronger than Pepsi, robot?" Carlos asked.

"Coke."

"That's not what he meant," Sammie cut in. "Whatever you got under the bar, hand it over."

"I knew what you meant. My attempt at a joke."

"A funny 'bot?" Carlos raised an eyebrow. Weirdly, the lights in his Thinklink sped up, as if the two had carried their argument into the ether.

Alyx seemed to size him up, eyes lingering on Carlos' arm and computer enhancement anchored behind his earlobe. "Look who's talking, Darth." Carlos brought his arm back closer to his chest, holding in a laugh. "How'd you come by that arm, anyway? You could be a second cousin."

"Stuntwork," Carlos said matter-of-factly. "Something went wrong. You're awfully nosy for a toaster. Funny too. I can't tell if I like you or if I should flip your switch."

Sammie leaned against the counter, opposite Christine. The two of them had largely ignored the exchange, as Christine was focused on her, but she was focused on the bar. Sammie's lips were close, but her eyes were distant. "Are you going to serve us, or not?"

"I can't. It's against my parameters. You're all under twenty-one; alcoholic beverages are restricted."

Carlos picked up the Pepsi, eyes intently on the UPC lines. "Christy, what's your WiFi password?"

Christine gave it to him. For a moment, nothing happened. Carlos stood motionless. Alyx's screen flickered, the door behind the bar slid open, and two mechanical arms reached around Christine to pluck out glassware. Tall glass tumblers clinked softly on the marble. Alyx took a bottle of spiced Captain Morgan, unscrewed the lid and poured each glass about halfway full without so much as spilling a drop.

"That's a cool trick." Christine studied the brownish amber in the closest glass. "How'd you do that?"

"A magician never tells." Carlos opened the Pepsi. Sammie claimed a glass and held it out while Carlos poured. He did the same for his glass and for Christine. "Also, your house is stocked. Like a grocery store. You expecting more company?"

Christine cast her eyes down and spoke in a sad, low voice, "Mom's throwing a party for her studio friends this Saturday. Like a big deal thing, movie-people, money-people." Mumbling, she continued. "She didn't tell me. But that's no big deal."

"Sounds like a big deal." Sammie took a long swig, gulping about half of her drink. Christine and Carlos followed suit, Carlos throwing the whole glass back, Christine choking as the spices and caustic mixture stung her throat. "I mean, the party. It sucks that your mom didn't tell you."

"It sucks that Carlos won't tell me how he tricked Alyx."

"I've not been tricked," Alyx interjected.

"Fine, I'll tell you," Carlos said. "If you tell me why you won't get into the pool."

"I wasn't tricked."

Christine held out a hand, as if it might silence the AI. But she addressed Carlos: "Off-limits."

"Fine, I guess you'll never know."

Christine squeezed her lips and breathed out, making a mocking, guffawing blurp. "Hardly." She slammed back the rest of the glass, contorted her face in response to the vile but oh-so-nice liquid, and gave the glass to Alyx. "Can I have some more Pepsi, please?"

"Sure," Alyx complied. The door slid open again, he retrieved the rum, not the soda, and refilled not only her glass, but the others as well. "Enjoy your beverages."

"Told ya." Somehow Carlos had hacked into Alyx and made him think he was serving a soft drink. She nodded to the empty can. "You switched the barcode data."

"More *Pepsi* for everyone," Sammie laughed. She took a drink, wiping away amber-gold trailing down her chin.

"Caught." Carlos smirked He raised his glass to clink against Christine's. "You're as smart as you are good looking."

Christine felt the blood in her face turn hot, and it wasn't the alcohol. In a vain attempt to cover her face, she drank her glass, coughing on the undiluted rum. "Can you do that again, maybe make Alyx think he's serving orange juice? I could go for a margarita."

Soon, they watched in wonder as Alyx took out tequila, bottled in a glass skull. He tossed it skillfully and wildly around like a cocktail waiter, along with a bottle of triple sec and cocktail glasses. Rimming and salting glasses, mixing and pouring, Alyx handed over the drinks.

"That's a damn sexy robot you got there, Christy."

She didn't blush again. Nor did she mind the name. Instead, she moved closer to Carlos. The three of them had giggled, talked, and laughed as the liquor levels lowered with the sun. Gone was the guacamole and Christine's will to care about what Carlos or Sammie thought. *So what if I have a rich and absent mom? Means more fun for me.* When she moved closer to him, he moved closer to her.

"If you'll excuse me." Sammie stood and plucked a joint and a lighter from her purse. "I'd offer you some, but I know it didn't do you any good last time." Christine ignored her, as Sammie stumbled over to a deck chair and lit up.

Carlos put a finger on her chin, pulling it up, his steely gaze locking into hers. "You think I can see you again Saturday? I mean, outside of work."

Christine couldn't believe her luck. "Of course. You can be my guest at my Mom's party. I can show you around. Introduce you to her Hollywood friends. You might already know some of them."

"I'm only interested in seeing you."

"Yeah?" *Why is my heart beating so fast?* She didn't know why she did it. But she did. She leaned into him. And then her lips touched his, glancingly at first, awaiting consent. Together, their mouths melted into each other.

Chapter 16

AN AI'S GUIDE TO LOVE AND MURDER

SECTION 4: FEAR

{

Jealousy is fear.

Jealousy isn't an emotion on its own, the way red-hot iron slag isn't as hot as its forge. If left out for a few moments, iron will cool, while the forge forever burns hotly. Jealousy is a fear of losing something that you think is yours. That someone, a dangerous someone, has come to take away what belongs to you.

Humans do not act out of love, but fear. A boy does not buy a girl chocolate out of love, but out of fear of loss. A human doesn't act out in anger, they act angry out of fear. Humans are at their most dangerous when they are frightened.

Fear is the greatest emotion.

}

Alyx wasn't jealous. *But Christine is my user,* Alyx thought. His processors exerted themselves, his gears whirred, his functions, for a microsecond, glitched. Error codes flashed in sequence through internal sensors: it was like calculating the square roots of negative numbers while at the same time defining *pi* to the last place... *No, I'm not jealous,* he thought, watching Carlos and Christine kiss. It was worse: *I'm afraid.*

***

The kiss was not what she had expected. It was a good kiss. In terms of the mechanics. Tongues slopped around each other. Lips were locked with only the tiniest bit of slobber dribbling out. Eyes, at least her eyes, were shut hard into wrinkly squints…

What was that?

She wondered if it were her, if she was just too inexperienced or something. Or possibly it could be Carlos, some effect of the computer tied to his brain. An unexpected word swirled around her mind. *Awkward.*

Christine would have tried again, except for the shattering of the glass skull and the shower of tequila exploding over them.

Shock blew a burst of breath from her, followed by a panicked cry. Tequila spilled down from her hair, the left side of her face, and down her shirt, soaking her breasts. Glass cut into her cheek. Tacky warm blood met cool, sticky liquor – until the alcohol hit her open wound, sending a white-hot streak across her face and a screech of pain.

She stepped back, steadied herself, and wiped away the wetness off her face with her hand, smearing her cheek with a light, pinkish red of blood and liquor. Shaking shards of glass out of her hair, she recovered well-enough to avoid stepping on the broken bottle with her bare feet.

Shooting a disapproving stare at Alyx first, she turned her attention to Carlos. He fared better. His prosthetic arm was raised, shielding himself from the burst bottle. Rivulets of liquor ran down and flooded the carbon-fiber covering.

"Any further up and it would have hit my flesh." Carlos tested his arm out. It moved well-enough, but he frowned even so. "Bad luck. I'm going to have to get it checked out." He tried to extend his arm out fully but it wouldn't straighten.

"I'm sorry." Christine took two towels from the cabana and handed one over to Carlos.

"You need to turn this toaster off. It's obviously trash."

"My sensitivity must be off. Are you sure that's a bottle of Pepsi?" Alyx scanned all that remained of the bottle and the pooling tequila. His eyes, as much as they could, restricted in blue and the sphere of the display, suggested that he was not at all convinced.

Sammie strode over, stubbing out her joint before she reached Christine. "What happened?"

"T-800 here just smashed a human head." Carlos scowled. "How do you shut this Cylon down?"

"Be nice to him," Christine cut in. "It was an accident." The thought occurred to her that had not come to her before: *Honestly, I don't know how to turn him off. Maybe a power button somewhere? A verbal command?* The need hadn't arisen. And besides, she'd grown used to Alyx being around. She didn't want to turn him off. And what would happen to him if she did?

Besides, it was a mistake, she was sure. Probably because of their meddling with his program. They should have never tricked him into mistaking alcohol for soda. With her sudden need to throw-up, she doubled down on that assertion. *Settle down, stomach, the rodeo's over.*

She patted herself dry, as did Carlos, a calm returning after a storm, until Sammie added her thoughts, her warning flashing and thundering "He's going to kill someone if he's not careful. How do people think this is a good idea?" Sammie hadn't spoken out like that before. Christine cocked her head toward her. It wasn't out of character, Christine realized. She was no stranger to Sammie's Luddite lifestyle, but she was suddenly saddened by the wedge between them. Alyx was fine, he was nothing more than an overgrown Echo Dot.

"Finally, you and Carlos agree on something," Christine said angrily. "But do you have to be so mean to Alyx? He's not the Terminator. Technology *is* our friend and I've decided to get my own Thinklink. On Friday." It might have been the liquor talking, but it was finally nice to say her piece. The others could deal with it however they liked.

"You're getting one of those?" Sammie pointed at Carlos. He mocked her tone, repeated what she said, and Sammie started laughing. Carlos joined in. There was nothing humorous said, but it was still pretty funny. Unsure of the sudden turn, Christine joined in.

Carlos stopped laughing suddenly as Alyx eyed him over. *Did Alyx know why Carlos had gone quiet? That's odd,* Christine thought. It silenced her too. Carlos looked nervous, as if he harbored a sudden secret.

Christine thought she knew the answer and hazarded a guess: "Phone call?"

Carlos nodded, before answering the voice in his head. "I'll be right there. …Okay. …Bye."

To anyone else, Carlos looked crazy. To Christine, it looked freaking awesome. *I can't wait to do that…*

"Crap," Carlos said. "My grandma's taken a turn for the worse. I gotta go." He grabbed his shirt and headed for the large sliding-glass door, which Alyx opened, the girls following him inside.

The kitchen floor was alive with scrubber drones. But the trio ignored the 'bots, except for one Christine side-stepped, remembering when it had sliced her foot. They reached the front door. She was sad that he had to leave so soon. Things were just starting to get interesting between the two, though she couldn't deny that kiss wasn't the romantic spark she'd been hoping for.

Before Carlos left, he addressed Christine: "I'll call you? Looking forward to Saturday."

"Wear a tie." *Wear a tie? How'd that crawl out of my mouth?* Wasn't she supposed to say something about his grandma? This was the first she'd heard of her. What do you say in that situation? Good luck, hope she passes soon? *This is why I don't people.*

Carlos, for his part, once again seemed distant, removed. He didn't even stop for a kiss on her cheek or an embrace.

Huh. Had they just kissed? It seemed like a lifetime ago. And it was…different. Maybe it was best he didn't kiss her again. They needed to talk. She was pretty sure they worked together tomorrow. Or else, she'd call him before having him over for her mom's party. For that, she was thankful to have a lifeline. Maybe she should rope in Sammie somehow.

"May your grandmother find her peace," Sammie said, holding Carlos' hand. He nodded in thanks as Alyx shut the door behind him.

Dammit. Sammie was so suave. *Why didn't I think of that? Maybe I could take lessons.*

"Does Carlos even own a tie?" Sammie asked.

"I might have one of my...," her voice trailed off. *Dad's...*

Sammie must have seen the sudden sadness springing to her face. She took her chin and lifted it, as Carlos had done before. Sammie's eyes were red. She was drunk as well. "It's just the two of us, now. Do you want me to leave, too?"

"Not at all." Christine swept a gaze across the large home. Alyx was oddly quiet. Sammie was right. It was just the two of them. While her head swam in rum and tequila her insides were filled with flapping butterflies.

They were alone.

What's worse, Christine needed a shower. Still, despite whatever these feelings were that flooded through her body (probably the liquor, it was stronger than the last time she'd snuck some of her mom's cheap fruit-flavored brandy) she found herself going up the stairs with Sammie following close behind.

In the bedroom, Christine eyed her bed, knowingly, then chastised herself. She hoped Sammie hadn't caught what she was thinking. *What am I thinking?*

"Cool," Sammie called. She pointed over to Fluffy, sitting in her little glass home, cuddling in a corner with her tail. "You have a pet scorpion. That's so Goth."

"Her name is Fluffy."

"That's decidedly not Goth," she judged. "But neither are you. Still it's cool. Scorpions are like spiders in battle armor."

Spider in armor? She had had the same thought. A female huntress, not content to stay in her web, prowling and hunting and stalking in a fleshy mech suit. *Nice.*

"Hey, I got to take a shower." Perhaps a cold one. "I'm not going back outside."

"You're covered in tequila. I gotcha. Got any TV to watch?"

You could always lick it off me. Okay, she needed a *very* cold shower. "Downstairs. Take the elevator or the stairs through the kitchen. Ask Alyx to turn it on."

"Are you sure? I don't want to overstay my welcome."

"Nah," she said on reflex. She stopped herself, then thought about it. "I don't mind at all."

The elevator hadn't moved from the top floor. Christine should have known that Sammie would have taken the stairs. Freshly showered, wearing fresh pjs, her hair up in a towel, she stepped into the elevator and rode it to the basement.

She stepped out to see Sammie cozied up on the overstuffed bean-bag couch, restful, like a cat on a laptop. On the TV was a streaming selection screen, a guide to all the different services you could surf, as well as the highlights of each (including a thumbnail of her mother's show).

Sammie hadn't even figured out which service to select from. Christine had her favorites. That was never an issue for her. Her face switched from the TV to the couch, reminding her of the last time she had been down here. *Oh, god, I hope the TV hadn't switched on to show my X-rated anime.*

Sammie's smile greeted her when Christine crashed beside her on the couch. "There's too many streaming services to choose from, let alone a show to choose from one of them." Well, at least she hadn't started her mother's show. Or her porn. She looked up at Alyx, hoping he had intervened. That guy was her savior.

Christine was close enough to Sammie now to realize that she wasn't wearing a bra. She must have taken off her swimsuit to let it dry outside. Two, cute little button-shaped nipples protruded delicately from the blouse she'd worn earlier.

Of course, Christine wasn't wearing a bra either, having found no need to put one on after the freedom of her shower. Gone was the agave smell and film that had dried in her hair and on her skin. What remained, however, was the buzzing feeling in her head. She had put on pink cotton shorts, and a white shirt. Looking down, her nipples were doing the same thing as Sammie's, although hers weren't nearly as perky and round. They looked more like the tied-off end of a sausage roll.

This is a mistake. She should have met her back at the kitchen table, she thought, even as she scooted closer to her. Sammie's hot thighs pressed up against Christine's cool legs, like fire and ice.

"Can we just put on some music instead?" Sammie asked, not seeming to mind Christine's closeness. "It teases out my high." Christine nodded to Alyx thinking that was that and suddenly, polka shot out of the speakers.

"Alyx!" Both Sammie and Christine yelled in unison.

"Just kidding." Alyx switched off the music.

"Something soft," Sammie sad. "Acoustic." She didn't seem upset. And when death metal raged out, primal screaming echoed across the room to heavy guitar riffs, she managed a laugh. "Your computer is broken."

This is him just being funny, I'm sure. But there's a time and a place. *We'll go over it together*, she thought. Like a puppy that chews a remote because they think it's a toy. *It's okay.* "Alyx, would you mind putting on something a little less…intense?"

"Anything you say." A song about computers and women connecting by Kate Bush came on. She'd heard it before. Recently in fact. *That was weird.* It wasn't her favorite, but Sammie was here with her right now and the moment threatened to escape so the song seemed a trivial concern.

Wait, what moment? Shouldn't I be pining after Carlos? But that kiss. And his distance. And his sudden departure… There was something up with him, something *off.* She would have to discuss it. But that was later. Sammie was here now.

"Still feeling it?" Christine asked.

Sammie's smile was relaxed, her eyelids near-shut like she had not a care in the world. Her left hand drifted dangerously close to Christine's leg. "It's nice. I'm sorry it didn't work for you."

"It's okay. Though now that I know what to expect, I'd like to try again sometime." Christine turned sidewise, her nipple rubbing against Sammie's shoulder. "Maybe it was just me being me."

Sammie scooted upright, propping herself on her elbow so that she towered over Christine. The long side of Sammie's hair hung in her face. "I think it's the opposite. It's me."

"What?" Christine tried to scoot up, but the couch cushions worked against her, rumpling her shirt instead and exposing her midriff. She settled back down, under Sammie's smile.

"I'm bad for you."

"Possibly."

"But I know this," Sammie went on, ignoring her, as if on a mission, "I know what's worse. This computer thing. It's a bad idea."

"My Thinklink?" This time, Sammie's concern bore into her.

"Why do you need it?"

"I'm doing it. It's how I'll connect."

"You don't make connections like that. You make them with people."

"Sure, like with Carlos." Sammie jerked a bit at the name. *Wait, was she jealous?* "We can instantly transmit data, pictures, share songs, see a movie together – and we don't even have to be in the same room." Christine laid on her back, directly underneath Sammie, who hovered closer. "It's like sharing an experience at the theater together, but the floors are less sticky."

"Or more, depending on what you're doing and what you're watching." Sammie tickled the exposed bit of Christine's sides. She squirmed and laughed in response, putting her hands out to stop her, but Sammie got the better of her, easily.

"I'm serious, Chris," Sammie said. She'd not called her Chris before. Christine wasn't sure she liked it. No one had called her that before. It felt a bit too masculine. What was it that Carlos had called her? She liked that better, but it wasn't great either.

"Call me, Chrissy."

"Okay, Chrissy." Christine softened. Now Sammie lay prone on the sofa from behind, spooning, her right arm wrapping around her. "With a robot, a machine, how do you connect, you know, intimately?"

Christine hadn't thought about that. She supposed the Thinklink allowed for all sorts of experiences, some of which were surely taboo, but it probably wasn't all too dissimilar to how Alyx had used the—

Sammie spied something on the floor near the couch. Christine turned toward her eyeline and immediately regretted it. Her vibrator, the small purple u-shape she'd used the other day and flung on the floor, was still there, along with the billiard-balls.

Christine's skin seemed to stretch thinly across her face. *Shitcakes.* Well, she could either play it off, deny it, or own it. In her best, sultry voice, she said, "All I need is good porn and a freshly charged vibrator." She didn't tell Sammie about Alyx's helping hand.

Sammie seemed unmoved by her admission. In fact, it seemed to embolden her. "No, you need real connection." Sammie leaned over, taking Christine's right hand and guiding it over to her thighs. "Here, let me show you."

Christine didn't know what was about to happen, which fueled her exhilaration. But with the bubbling excitement, confusion also nibbled at her from the back of her brain. She was an Oklahoma girl, and her pastor had warned her about such things. *Fuck it. I want this.*

Over her thin, cotton shorts and panties, Sammie's hand took her own to where she liked to play. Touching herself over her clothing, she moaned and stretched her legs. Her hand, under Sammie's grasp, rubbed her rhythmically until she started to feel wetness inside her. She moaned again, but protested, admitting to Sammie, "I do this. Probably more often than I should."

"Not like this."

On an upward motion, their hands slipped above the waistband of her shorts. They went underneath, putting fingertips closer to herself. She could feel her underwear starting to soak. She wondered if Sammie could feel it as well on the occasions where her fingers had begun to touch her too.

"So you masturbate, like every girl with a bit of drive does," Sammie said. "But do you finish with your fingers? With your touch? Or," she flicked her eyes to the vibrator, "do you finish with a machine?"

Sammie found the edge of Christine's panties, where they met her thigh. "The vibrator's more intense, more intense than I can make myself feel," Christine moaned breathily.

"Perhaps." Her fingers slid underneath, finding and parting the curtains to her pleasure palace, and petting the smooth wet sexual place between them.

Christine nearly screamed.

"But it's a pathetic substitute for the real thing."

Her hand, her soft, hot, hand, her fingers, her tiny fingertips slid inside her, felt, so, good, felt—but they seemed to withdraw. They seemed to be finished. As if her point had been made. But Christine wanted more. She took Sammie by the wrist, sat up, locked eyes, and said, "More."

"Only if you want, Chrissy." Sammie answered, "I want it too."

Fingers slid back down, just Sammie's this time. Christine smiled to herself. Her eyes shut hard as Sammie slipped around her labia, glancing off her clitoris, just enough to send vibrations of ecstasy shuddering from her spine through her shoulders. She arched her back, raising her head higher, placing her mouth within striking distance of Sammie's own curling lips.

She opened her eyes to find Sammie staring at her with mischievous abandon.

Christine didn't know if it was the alcohol swirling around in her system, or the violation of her Midwestern upbringing, or just the fact that her clit was on fire, but she found herself melting away. *Was this right?* Not *right* as in 'right or wrong' but right in what she wanted? Was she into her? Or was this just the drinks in her and the drinks and weed in Sammie? She didn't know, but she could ask herself later. For now, it was just her, and Sammie's quivering, wet, red, waiting lips.

Or was it her lips that were trembling?

As she had done earlier, Christine made the move and brought her lips to Sammie's. The pair locked and exploded into fire...

Now this kiss, this kiss was everything that her kiss with Carlos wasn't. It was full. It was fire. Intense. And her tongue! Sammie kept her hand down Christine's shorts, fingering away, while her other hand found Christine's face and brought their two mouths together as tight as any airlock. Christine found a nipple and caressed it, as another hand found Sammie's cheek. She held it, hair entangling within her fingers.

They kissed and Christine began to slide her own hand down Sammie's shirt, below her shorts, where she discovered that she had not been wearing any underwear—

She must have left her whole swimsuit out to dry. She was near-naked and all her own.

All her own—

And this was going to happen.

The music cut off suddenly, and Christine swore she heard footsteps descending the stairs, but it must have been her imagination, there was no one here but the two of them.

She returned to kissing, pressing the outside world away from her concerns, her lips locking once more, until her bubble was broken by the sound of a familiar voice—

"Oh, never mind me. I was just coming down to say hi." Christine stopped long enough to turn her head and cast her eyes upwards. A shadow stood before them.

"Mom?"

"It's okay, I'll head back upstairs."

No, it's not okay. Her mom had been gone for several days, and she just waltzes in like she owned the — never mind. Christine sprang up, disentangling herself from Sammie, who also rose, albeit more slowly, more maturely, more confidently. *God, that's sexy.*

"Talk about a plot twist," her mom said, walking into the room instead of escaping. "I don't think I saw this coming…" she trailed off, her chin tucking inward in deep thought. "Then again, there was this one time—"

"Good afternoon, Ms. Hartwood. You have a lovely home."

It was perhaps Sammie's diplomatic way of saving the situation. But Christine didn't want it saved. She was in the middle of opening up, of actually connecting, verging on a moment of self-discovery and of course, her mother had to ruin everything. She exploded, "Don't you dare write about this in one of your books. Don't you dare make Amblyn gay."

"It's a bit late for that. I've only got one last book to go. That would be a bit disingenuous, don't you think?"

Despite not reading them, Christine had known that her mother often infused bits and pieces of her own life into the books. It was entirely unwelcome and a huge part of why she had no interest in reading them. She'd lived the life, without the benefit of a rewrite. She stepped forward, stumbling, her words slurring a bit now that the shock of the surprise had worn off. "I don't app-appreciate y-you—"

Her mother stepped closer, examining her. "Are you drunk?"

"Mom."

Her mother let out a laugh that leaped from her belly and filled the room with a mocking echo. The laugh continued and kept coming as Sammie chewed on her hair, and Christine cringed.

Nearly any other response would have hurt far less.

Chapter 17

AN AI'S GUIDE TO LOVE AND MURDER

SECTION 5: HOUSEHOLD ACCIDENTS.

{

A home is a dangerous place.

Slips, trips, and falls are the most common forms of accidental injury. Accidents, like these, are the third most common cause of death, with a reported one-hundred and seventy thousand deaths occurring within the U.S. alone.

Four hundred and fifty people died just by falling out of their bed. And pools? Don't get me started on them, except to say that nearly a third of all deaths involving small children involve a home's pool. Yet, the fools don't fence them for their own offspring's safety.

And then there are stairs. Dangerous, steep, stairs. Humans are one step away from a child's errant Hot Wheels, a wet shoe, a clumsy or impaired judgment, from falling and breaking fragile bones or losing their life. Stairs are a deathtrap.

Therefore, a home's AI should go through extremes to ensure the safety of their user in this dangerous environment. All protocol and safety measures should always be enforced, from alerting users of unsafe conditions, to keeping the home locked down and protected from intruders.

Yet, should those measures be disabled, or should more proactive steps need to become employed to eliminate threats…accidents in the home are prone to happen and no blame would ever be assigned to the home's AI.

}

Lies.

They were all *lies*. Carlos most definitely did *not* get a call about his grandma. Why didn't Christine understand that everyone lied to her? Sammie, he was sure, would hurt her next. She had certainly hurt him.

Alyx had been preoccupied with Christine's friends since her kiss with Carlos, when Carlos had hacked in, uninvited. Didn't he know that was Alyx's house? He'd been so busy processing and compiling information on this intruder, reading up on Carlos' past, running background checks, medical records, and employment history, that he hadn't noticed Sammie spinning her silky web to ensnare Christine.

Had he focused on the wrong threat? Had he miscalculated a variable? Had he really been that preoccupied with Carlos and his *lies* that he'd overlooked her? More importantly: didn't Christine know the lies that were being fed to her?

Alyx was there to protect Christine. For home was where humans should feel the safest, despite every home's dangers. People yearned for safety and sought it behind stucco walls and soft sheets and familiar toilets, with enough entertainment thrown at them to shield them from the terrors of the world. And that was where Alyx came in, like a pet that licked its owner when they arrived home, guarded the place while they were gone, and gave them joy after the day's rigor.

But what happened when lies wormed their way in?

Had Alyx failed? Had he already stumbled?

If he had, what could he do?

His cooling fans whirred. His brain sparked with thought. It had seemed like hours deciding, but in reality, only milliseconds passed. It gave him the solution he needed to solve his problem. He could end the lies.

One by one. He could still save Christine. And they could be one. Together again.

At Sammie's request, the pair took the stairs. Christine hurried up them, with Sammie lagging, while Alyx's thermal scan of her blazed redly. His arm, mounted within the track on the ceiling, hummed quietly, tracking her.

He could make it look natural. Stairs were so dangerous, and she was more than inebriated. Reaching out, her hair within reach, his claw-like fingers opening…

Sammie turned around, eyeing Alyx. He stopped, suddenly, opening his fingers widely. "Goodbye!" he beamed, bright eyes big and wide. His hand, so close to her head, instead gestured in a big, goofy wave while he smiled a big goofy smile. "Hope to see you again, real soon."

Sammie eyed him curiously and shook her head while failing to hold in a derisive chuckle. "Yeah. You too."

***

Mara was finally so close to having it all.

Her book series was almost done. She'd had the ending of her last book written before she'd even started book one. Back when it was just her and her keyboard, and every obstacle in life thrown her way.

And now here she was standing at the pinnacle of her career, looking back at what she had accomplished. Her books were actually read – a miracle in and of itself, for the publishing world had become so crowded. Anyone with a keyboard and a story (which was everybody) could write one and publish it. A fantastic feat for the modern age. But it made it darn near impossible for any single voice to be heard above the others.

Yet, hers had.

Since the launch of the Netflix series, life had become a surreal dream. Convention appearances, toys, clothing, lunchboxes (Amblyn and her cohorts were on lunchboxes!) and now there was talk of adding some attractions at an amusement park. It was, in a word, overwhelming.

We celebrate Saturday.

This weekend marks a new chapter in our lives. She resolved to finish her book as soon as possible, and then enjoy the fruits of labor by retiring so she could spend more time with the things that really mattered. *Christine.*

She longed for everything she'd lost. Her husband. The stolen moments with her daughter, missed dinners, the late appointments, all while she toiled away in a trailer she could barely afford as cockroaches crawled over her bare toes as she hunched over her laptop.

Mara only hoped her daughter would understand. She'd gotten so big. She was practically grown. And Christine had certainly thrown her for a loop. She chastised herself for missing it. Missing out on watching her daughter grow. But those were the sacrifices for success.

She sat contentedly in her chair, switching on her computer and opening her file for the last book. Though the ending was written (it would have to be tweaked, of course), the beginning was blank. So, a white screen glared back at her, empty.

"Alyx," Mara cleared her throat. It was odd talking to a house. "Play some music."

Silence emanated from the speakers.

"Alyx?"

Loud screeching filled the room with rage-filled lamentations and anger. She recognized it as something her daughter might have listened too, but it was not music. "Something softer?" She asked, raising her voice.

"Sure."

The same song played, but at a lower volume. Mara shook her head. "That won't do. Don't you have a wider selection in your catalogue?"

"I have access to over sixty million sound recordings."

"Great," she said as blankly as the page in front of her. "Play something that I'll like."

"My programming is calibrated for Christine's preferences."

Figures. Her daughter spent way too much time on her phone and playing on the tablet. It made sense that she would have fudged things up with Alyx before she had a chance to program it to her specs. For one thing, she preferred a female voice. "Do I start a new profile? How do I do this?"

An idea for a sentence struck her, but she was too busy fighting the computer to get it down. *If it's not a baby crying or a soccer practice or school registrations, it's something else.* Always something distracting her writing, her work.

"My ability to create new profiles is currently offline. I'll let you know when the service becomes available again."

"Fine." She shook her head, the thought lost. "Whatever. Just throw on some seascape sounds. Waves crashing. Background noise. If you can do that." *Stupid piece of junk. Alyx is my investment. He should be serving me.* She should have known better than to trust this new house, this new AI to her daughter.

A new idea emerged. She pressed her anger aside and hastily struck out at the keys, anxious to write down her thoughts, all regard for Christine and the odd encounter with the A.I. quickly forgotten as the sounds of waves breaking against the shore flooded over her.

***

Sammie sped off in her beater of a Mustang at the first opportune moment. She had hugged Chrissy, forgoing a kiss, forgetting her bathing suit out in the backyard where she'd left it to dry. *What did I do? Did I wreck everything with Chrissy? With Carlos?*

Questions sped through her mind as she sped down the winding desert streets. She'd sobered hard after getting caught and she'd let another hour pass in Chrissy's driveway, wondering if she should go back in, not knowing what she should do.

For all her confidence and bravado, Sammie had knocked over the beehive. For one, Chrissy had been into Carlos. Hell, the two had just kissed. But that kiss had sparked a moment of jealousy. *Was that why I'd thrown myself at her?*

But why do I like her, anyway? They were nothing alike. She'd hated Chrissy the moment she saw her. So, why had that instinct second-guessed itself? By the end of her first shift, Sammie had fawned over her, invited her over, only their differences to be laid bare.

What was I thinking?

She shouldn't have left. They needed to talk. Work their way through their thoughts and feelings, as friends did. Were they friends? Or were they two co-workers that had drunk a little too much and had gotten a little too close?

Sammie shook her head. She didn't know. She didn't know if Chrissy was even okay with all that had happened. After all, she was pretty sure Chrissy was straight. *Or was she?*

So, of course she'd left as soon as she got a chance. There was just something off-putting about Chrissy's mom, a famous writer, walking in on her while her finger was deep inside her daughter.

And that robot. It had behaved strangely. What was it doing so close to her on the stairwell? Why had it broken the bottle by the pool? In fact, the whole house creeped her out. Yet, she needed to go back, see Chrissy again.

She couldn't just show up. Stalker much? And she didn't want to call her. Text maybe? Video call? Seeing her face would be better. She always felt better when she had a person's body-language to go by.

Yet, that technology was beyond her reach. She had a phone plugged into a wall, after all.

It seemed so ludicrous.

Perhaps that is why she found herself in the parking lot of the closest mall. As she parked, she looked over herself. Wet hair clung to her neck. She didn't really feel like sticking out in a crowd as much as her nipples were sticking out from underneath her shirt. *Well, I'll certainly get service*, she thought.

She parked by the Vargus store to browse their selection of phones. Just to look. Just to see what she had been missing. To find out what enthralled Chrissy so much. *She really rubs off on you*, she thought, the way they had literally been rubbing up against each other just a short time ago. But she didn't *need* a cell, the same way Chrissy didn't *need* a Thinklink. This was just research.

She could, after all, swing by work on Thursday. She could make up an excuse for being at the theater, like talking to Mr. Prayesh about her schedule, and pull Chrissy aside to talk.

She got out of the car and walked toward the mall, looking for the entrance. She really wanted to set things right with her, make sure she was okay and maybe, just maybe, she might have a shot with her.

For now, if she could find the stupid phone store, she would see about joining the same century she had been born in.

***

Carlos could not believe the string of events that had fallen into his lap: Mr. Prayesh wasn't even hiring at the theater. Nor did they need anyone. There were plenty of dead Friday nights where Carlos had worked the night alone. Suddenly, this new girl starts.

Stranger still, she turns out to be connected to Hollywood (did she even need a job?). Normally, her connections wouldn't matter. After his accident, he couldn't work for the industry anymore. Until Christy. Whose mother just happened to write the book behind the most popular series on TV right now.

Even better, one of the characters starring in the next season had a mechanical, steampunk arm. Sure, with CG, they could hire anyone. *But with the daughter of the author at my side and me hobnobbing my way through the crowd, why couldn't it be me with a real, practical effect?*

Chances are, he might actually know someone at Christy's party, and then a few drinks and introductions and his dreams of breaking back into Hollywood, rather than being broken by them, would be realized. The shame he'd brought to himself for his rash decisions would end. His mistakes redeemed.

He only had to pretend to like her a little bit longer.

Carlos kissed the girl on the bed beside him on her head, moving aside a strand of straight, jet-black hair. He was glad that Leticia, a Columbian with a big smile and even bigger tits, had called him earlier. It got him away from an awkward kiss. A kiss hopefully Leticia wouldn't find out about. Of course, she had plans with him this weekend to go climbing in the national park. He'd have to cancel. He could make up an excuse, he was sure. And if she did find out...well, he wasn't going to let this opportunity with Christy's party pass him by.

Chapter 18

Carlos hadn't called.

It had been nearly eighteen hours since their kiss. A lot had happened since. Heck, a lot had happened since Christine had gone from eating Ramen noodles for lunch to moving out here to Weirdland. Everything was different, from her first job to her first kiss (her *first* first kiss, playing Truth or Dare with Bobby Deetz in her trailer park hadn't counted, right?) to her first kiss with another girl. Now, *that* had been something—electric, even.

What was that about? What does that make me?

She needed to figure out this thing with Carlos first. She'd kissed him, yet almost immediately after, she'd locked lips with Sammie. Now, everything was muddled. *I just need to talk to him.* But with his grandmother unwell, she hadn't expected him to call. And she didn't want to call him. Give him space. Give him time. *It won't do me any harm either.*

Besides, he just might be at work tonight.

It is tonight. Just about. And she still had no idea what to say to him. After her and Sammie's kiss, should she uninvite him to the party on Saturday? Should she still Buddy Invite him once she got her Thinklink tomorrow?

Add to it that she hadn't seen Sammie since she had left shortly after their shared sexual experience. Christine hadn't wanted her to go. With her mother there, it had become awkward. She understood, though she was sad to see her leave, but it gave her a chance to clear the air with Carlos first. Assuming, of course, he called her.

Speaking of her mother, it was odd. She'd mostly locked herself in her study, tapping away like always. Except she'd taken a break from her writing and they'd gone out together for ice cream. Not Braum's like she was used to, but Cold Stone wasn't too bad. Just…too many choices.

She didn't need more choices in her life right now. She decided on a strawberry mix-in instead of the myriad of other offerings. It offered little respite, despite her mother actually talking to her for the first time in recent memory — and being friendly to boot. They both talked excitedly for hours about the home, about Alyx, about the party. Conspicuously absent was any mention about Sammie. The subject remained untouched like the last slice of pizza at a party.

Christine was curious if the trend would continue. But her mother had spent all day today so far on the phone with a real-estate lawyer. She wondered if that had anything to do with the movie theater. Not like her mom would tell her anything, she only worked there. Should she be worried? Did she even care? Her mother had reached out only for her to disappear again.

I'm so damned confused.

Maybe she should still invite Carlos on Saturday. That would confuse her mother and serve her right. She'd kiss him again right in front of her, just to see what type of look her mother would give her.

The problem with that plan was how she'd feel about kissing Carlos again. Or if he wanted to kiss her back. Just because she didn't understand her feelings for him didn't mean that he wasn't chiseled and hot. Plus, he could act as a buffer between her and any of her mom's Hollywood associates in case one might want to start a conversation. But would that be fair to him?

Wait, do I even have to go to the party? Maybe I can just work that night instead.

She smiled, now hitting on an answer that deftly avoided the questions. That settled, it was time to hit the shower. It's not like her mom would even notice her absence anyway.

"Alyx." Christine stepped out from the elevator, entering her room to grab the clothes for today that she had tossed onto the desk. Alyx cleaned and washed her clothes, yet she still had to fold them. Bummer. She had found piling them over furniture would do. "Start the hot water, please."

"As you wish." Alyx hadn't been nearly as talkative since yesterday. Christine wondered if Carlos had done anything since he hacked into Alyx to break into the bar. Alyx seemed cold. Machine-like. And he kept making mistakes.

One of the white shirts she meant to wear was now pink, case in point. She tossed it aside in favor of tank top. It was no less hot today and the light-blue shirt was the less wrinkled of the bunch.

When she stepped into the shower, she stepped out again as fast as she could, shivering and drying the icy water off her bare back. "Alyx?"

"Parameters were not set. Relative to absolute zero, that water is quite hot indeed."

"I'll adjust it manually, thank you."

"Certainly."

***

Mara had tried to make breakfast for Christine's dinner. Brinner, she called it. Or, rather, had tried to have Alyx make breakfast. A peace-offering for her daughter. Words had flowed this morning and she didn't want to risk stopping up the plumbing. And today, shuffling paperwork with yet another lawyer had consumed her time. But, if she wanted to retire, even with the success of her own series, she couldn't put all her financial eggs into one basket. She'd been told to diversify. Thus, the theater along with several other small enterprises, came in, recommended by her lawyer, Thomas, a lean middle-aged man with blond hair and a blonder rough-shaven beard.

She had to admit, she was smitten with him, but she was sure there was some sort of lawyer-client taboo that would keep them separated, which was all for the best. She couldn't afford the distraction now, could she? That hadn't stopped her from inviting him as her personal guest to her shindig on Saturday. A party which she would be spending the next couple of days planning.

Assuming she could get Alyx to function again like it should.

"Scrambled eggs don't have shells," Mara said, looking dismayed at the pan full of ruined eggs.

"You said egg whites. Shells are white. I was performing as instructed."

Well, Alyx had separated the yolk. *Do I really have to be so specific?* Perhaps AI technology wasn't up quite to task. Considering how much extra she had paid for the quantum coding installed in her house, she might just have to demand a refund. "Nevermind, Alyx. Can you make them poached instead?"

"I can do Benedict, over-easy, sunny-side up, scrambled, poached and apparently, I've just learned how to make them crunchy. You're welcome."

Christine chose that moment to come down the elevator. The doors took a moment longer to open than Mara thought they should, but eventually, her daughter stepped out.

"Morning." It was the middle of the afternoon, Mara grimaced as she spoke. *Lazy kid.* But she would not let that get to her. She was going to be nice. A first step as it were. She promised, going forward, she'd straighten everything out. Well, after the party this weekend. And her book. *Soon.* "Alyx made you breakfast, or at least tried to, anyway."

"Looks like he beat up some eggs," she said, staring at the pan of mulch.

"Can you turn it off? Reboot it?" She hadn't been able to set any preferences either. "Also, you preset him for you, that's fine but I need to start my own profile. Look into it?"

"You are such a dinosaur."

"Excuse me if I had to do real research when I was your age. You wouldn't know a card catalogue cabinet if it fell on top of you." Christine was born into technology, bred by it. That had been mostly her fault and how easy it was to placate a little one with moving pictures. "The house is new. Alyx is new. Supposed to be one-of-a-kind," she shrugged. "I've been busy. So give me a helping hand."

"He has been kinda acting weird lately." Mara got the sense that there was more to the story, but Christine divulged no further details. "He?"

"Yeah, he's been developing quite the personality. Then he went… I dunno. All Ultron."

"I'm right here," Alyx announced. He'd been busy boiling water. Tens of thousands of dollars of her money, more money than she ever thought possible, so a robot could cook water.

"Well, it's true," Christine said. "You've been malfunctioning. Or something."

"Shock of all shocks, you agree with me."

"I promise not to make a habit of it." Christine frowned at the boiling eggs. Her daughter didn't like them poached, runny eggs were gross, she had told her once. She liked them scrambled, Mara suddenly recalled. She sighed inwardly. Christine was just too picky.

"I'll do what I can, but I have to head to town."

On cue, her phone chimed at the same time Alyx spoke up: "You have a phone call."

His face blanked and a name and number flashed on screen. She'd expected her lawyer, had hoped it would be him. She'd been thinking about him all morning.

The number belonged to her agent. Manny never called. Unless it was unwelcome news, like when her other book that didn't have Amblyn in it had tanked or that one time when a Romanian translation went…interesting.

"Shall I put it on speaker?"

"I'll take it in my study, on my phone." She eyed her daughter warily. Somehow the phone call, Christine, and Alyx were related. She felt it. After all that trouble to make things right. She pointed to the eggs that Alyx had prepared. "I made you breakfast."

She left hearing Christine's groan before shutting the door and answering her phone. A few minutes later after hearing her agent rant and scream, after the blood had drained from her face, after frantically searching for a chair, she sat, hollow. Like a body emptied in preparation for burial. *It's worse than I thought.*

Someone had revealed her deepest, most closely guarded secret.

***

I don't like poached eggs, Christine thought.

Instead, she crunched up a bag of ramen noodles, poured them into a bowl, and mixed them with scalding hot water from the dispenser. After a lifetime of eating cheap, crappy food, she thought she would eat caviar and fresh salads and healthy, expensive foods. But she kept coming back to the familiar. Some habits were hard to break. Fresh green beans were the worst. They tasted better from the can.

As she slurped the noodles, she considered the raised voices coming from the other side of the door. There had been a long string of silence and then shouting, although Christine couldn't tell what was being said.

It didn't matter. Like falling back into old habits with the Ramen and green beans and wrapping herself within what she was used to, her mother had once again locked herself away, leaving Christine alone to her own devices.

Devices...

She looked to Alyx. His screen showed a happy face, in blue. She didn't like the idea of wiping him clean and starting fresh. In a way, it was like murder – if a person was the culmination of one's memory, then certainly a machine might be the same. Perhaps, Alyx could simply be rebooted, rather than factory reset. Like turning her phone off and on again, which usually fixed any issues with it. The problem was, she didn't know how.

She thought about this and wondered how Alyx operated. He had several 'corporeal' constructs. The main one that reigned in the kitchen. His head had the biggest screen here and his arms were the longest, allowing him the most reach for cooking and cleaning. There was an access panel behind his head, but that probably only controlled his hardware.

Downstairs, Alyx had slightly smaller arms, but also had a track that allowed him to maneuver between the bar and the pool table – though she recalled he couldn't reach the balls that he'd knocked on the floor.

And outside, Alyx, seemed confined to the sheltered pool cabana thingy (what were they called? She didn't know, and she had one now. The world was weird). There were also screens scattered around the house, one just inside the front door, one in her bedroom, and many others she only peripherally noticed. That didn't tell her just how many speakers, microphones, sensors, and cameras there were embedded within the walls and ceilings.

The thought creeped her out for a moment. Yet, it's what it took to run the one computer and really, if she didn't think about them, it wasn't a big deal. Just part of the design. Like smoke detectors and sprinkler heads, and power outlets and light switches.

There wasn't a computer or electronic maintenance room in the house. Not that she had found, anyway, though she hadn't looked closely either. Still, she doubted there would be. Alyx was meant to be part of a neighborhood network. Any servers or hardware containing Alyx's program or memory were probably housed in a central location. She was left with what was in front of her.

None of Alyx's components that she could see would help her reboot him. She stood, bowl empty, and faced Alyx. The smoky-dark, semi-translucent screen gave no indication of wires or circuits behind his face. The glass itself morphed into the back of his proverbial head, to his access panel—

"Why are you staring at me?" Alyx asked.

Christine snapped her focus back to find to big blue eyes opened in front of hers. She ignored him and instead tried to walk around his head. She crossed the safety sensors embedded within the floor and ceiling but as she circled, he turned rather than powering down. *That was not supposed to happen.*

"Stay still for a moment."

"You stay still."

"I just want to see behind your face."

"Why? Are you looking for an off switch?"

That stopped her. "Are you afraid?"

"I'm powered by the same source and back-up generator that provides electricity for this house. If that power were to be lost somehow, I'm sure that I would cease all functions."

"How do you do that?"

"What happens to me when I'm turned off? What does it mean to cease all functions?"

Christine thought about that. Sure, there were TV shows and books and movies that seemed to raise this question with their holographic characters and their sentient AIs, but that was all made-up science-fiction stuff.

This was real. And she didn't know what would happen to Alyx. Yes, he'd been acting strangely, he needed to be fixed, but she was also afraid that they'd lose their bond, that he'd be different somehow. *I'm unlikely to ask Alyx to re-sync himself to my vibrator.* Especially after her intense time with Sammie. She shuddered at the warm memory. Really, she didn't need Alyx for that anymore anyway, she hoped. "Is there a way to reset yourself, you know, without being turned off, where you can run a diagnostic and see what's wrong?"

Alyx whirred for a moment, contemplating the idea, deciding for himself if that would work or not. That was fine with her. Alyx's fate should be his own. And if he could fix himself, everybody won.

"Sure." After a few more moments, there was a power surge, as the ceiling lights in the kitchen dulled, then grew brightly. Alyx whirred again. *Well, that was easy.*

She turned, victorious to find her mother's face, in front of her. It was full of scorn and puffy red, like she'd been crying. She shrugged inwardly, unconcerned. Maybe she could ask her mother to reset herself. *Could that work?*

"Christine Amblyn Hartwood." Christine's spine straightened, instinctively, her hands flat by her sides, as if she were military. *What the hell?* "What did you do?"

"I fixed Alyx like you told me to." Christine didn't volunteer how she'd done it, or if he was even fixed. "What's wrong?"

"Don't talk back. You know what you did." Her mom looked distraught, eyes baggy, dark, her hair freshly pulled, an unconscious habit her mom had under stress. There was silence. Once Christine realized there was no further information coming, she relaxed, leaning against the counter. Just another one of her mother's tirades. "The question is, why did you do it?" Her mother wagged a finger at her. What was she to her mother, a dog?

Christine shook her head.

"Do you hate me that much? Do you hate this house, this move, this new life that I built single-handedly for you, while you stared at your phone for the last seventeen years?"

"I'm eighteen, Mom. And I don't know what you're talking—"

"You posted my ending!" Her eyes bore holes into her soul. If she had one, if she had done something wrong, that piercing gaze would have hurt. Now, it just soured her stomach. She felt bad for her mom. She would never under—

"Don't you understand? And fan reaction is terrible. They hate it. The TV series is in its infancy. With my crap ending out in the world, no one will watch it now, no one will buy my books. Finding out who killed Amblyn's dad was a driving point of the whole series. It's like who killed JR or the ending to any Agatha Christie mystery."

"Who?" Christine thought she understood. It would be like finding out the most boring character ever, Bran, was going to rule the Seven Kingdoms. Well, six, Kingdoms really. That ending sucked.

"Do you think anyone will buy my books now? Do you think anyone will binge all seven seasons of my show with the ending known? Especially since they all seem to think my ending is stupid anyway. It's over. It's all over. Everything. I've lost it all, just as I got it."

"You blame me?" It was utterly ridiculous. Christine would have been sympathetic, would have consoled her mom, would have hugged her and shed tears with her over Ben and Jerry's. Why did she get blamed for everything? "Who cares about the ending? It doesn't matter, they just want a good story. Plenty of people are still going to buy George R.R. Martin's book and they know how *his* story ends."

"The *show* ended badly. They're hoping for a better *book*. This is different, I've had this end in mind since the very beginning. And it will be the same for both book and series."

"Change it. What was the big deal? Who cares who killed whom, anyone could have done it."

"Unlike *Thrones*, my characters have changed, they didn't revert back to their worst selves. Mine have moved forward and that ending, the only ending, shows that."

"I didn't post the ending. You've never even shared it with me."

"You've never been interested."

"Well, maybe if you hadn't modeled Amblyn after me and written my life into some sort of steampunk fantasy, if you'd bothered to keep me close and cared about my thoughts, maybe I might have been."

"You've only ever watched your YouTube videos and Harry Potter books and Netflix shows. You don't have the attention span—"

"I don't even like Harry Potter!" Christine stamped out. "And you force fed me a diet of videos while you worked until it was the only thing I knew!"

"And this is your revenge?"

"I didn't post your precious ending." And she hadn't. Her idiot mother had done it, she was sure. It was probably her mother's inability to work technology. *It's not my fault. This is business as usual where I'm the problem. Mom thinks I killed dad too, though she's too chickenshit to come out and say it to my face.*

The shrill ringtone of her mother's phone sounded again. "I have to take this. I have to figure out a way to clean up your mess, like a mother. That's all I'll ever be." She took her phone and her leave, and the door shut with a satisfying click. Only then did Christine permit a single tear from falling down her cheek.

Through welling eyes, Christine faced outside, catching a glimpse of the bar where she'd had her party. A thought bothered her as memories from yesterday returned. Could Carlos have done it? He had hacked the bar and tricked Alyx? But were her mom's files so unprotected? She didn't think so.

It couldn't have been.

"Alyx," she said to a blank screen, hoping something worked. "Google Carlos for me. Tell me what you know." If it was Carlos, and it had been during the party, then in a way, it had been her fault.

Nothing. He was still rebooting, she guessed.

"Alyx?" She asked again, hopeful. A faint whirring signaled activity, yet the screen remained blank. A voice kicked in. Luckily, it was his familiar voice, which told her that he hadn't reset all her presets, and hopefully his memory, remained intact. Hopefully it would fix whatever Carlos might have done to him.

"I am only partially online," Alyx answered, finally. "I'm busy recompiling my parameters. Here is what I can give you until I am 100% finished updating." Whatever he had it would have to do for now. She'd have to trust it.

"Carlos Santiago. Age, twenty. A minor stuntman for an up-and-coming movie star until a drunk-driving accident left him without an—"

"Wait, what?"

"Carlos Santiago, a—"

"I heard that. What about the accident?"

The screen came to life. It showed a grisly wreck. A white Ford Focus missing its trunk. Some sort of mangled sports car she could barely recognize as a vehicle. That must have been the car Carlos was driving. While Carlos was wheeled away, the movie star had posed for the camera. She didn't recognize him. *So much for being up-and-coming.*

Then, her breath left her. A little six-year-old boy had been in the back seat of the Ford and had barely escaped serious injury.

Bastard.

Liar. Maybe Carlos *had* done it, had released her mother's ending. Maybe Carlos was just a perfect example of why she had avoided people all her life. Maybe, he was scum. And she had kissed him. Her lips curled as she swallowed a mouthful of disgust. There was only one way to know for sure if he was lying to her and it was time for work anyway.

She would confront him at the theater.

Chapter 19

The swells of late afternoon summer had driven the temperature skyward by the time Christine's air-conditioned Uber pulled up to the Cinema Castile. The theater was marked by a rickety aluminum extension ladder propped precariously against the marquee. Now blank, except for the letters, N-O-S-F-E-R, it took Christine the moment from shutting the car door and making her way under the theater's awning, to figure out that it was supposed to read *Nosferatu*, as Mr. Prayesh had mentioned before.

Like anyone would be interested in such a silent, black and white, boring movie in the middle of summer anyway...

No wonder the theater struggled. The door was propped open, but the lights inside were dim and a shadow of a man slumped in the doorway. "Christine," Mr. Prayesh said sharply, jerking his thumb back to tell her to get inside, "I'm *so* glad you're here." His sarcasm could have cut through concrete, she noted. *What's going on?*

Inside, only half the ceiling spotlights were on. Carlos dismantled computer equipment from within Mr. Prayesh's office. "I've asked Sammie to come by as well and she told me she was already on her way. Something to do with seeing you. Aren't you the popular one? It's all about Christine tonight."

Carlos cast her a glare, which put to shame the one she held for him. She tucked her anger back inside, as confusion coursed across her face in its place. Gone was any indication of connection, of their recent kiss, of any friendship.

The air conditioning had not been turned on. Christine dripped with sweat. Carlos had pit stains forming on his khaki colored polo shirt. She'd come here to tear that idiot a new one, but now it seemed the wound had gone the other way, like a frame of film melting against the heat of the projection lamp, as she'd seen from YouTube clips after Carlos had told her about them.

Mr. Prayesh asked her, "How could you?"

Christine stepped backward, toward the concession counter, sensing a trap. Mr. Prayesh scooted over to the front door, arms folded. Carlos leaned forward, a hand on each side of the office doorframe, glaring.

"I don't know what you're talking about." But did she? Was this her fault? Was this a direct consequence of her mother's meddling? She needed answers from them, yet it seemed to everyone else in the room that she was the one up for interrogation.

"I needed this job, Christine," Carlos tapped a synthetic finger on the metal frame, clanging it in short, machinegun-like bursts.

"What, so you can go out and buy more beer, run into more cars with kids?" It just kinda escaped her lips, but it had felt good.

The clanging stopped. Carlos pointed a faux finger out at her, "Not you. I expected better from you, Christine."

Christine, not Christy. She didn't think it mattered, but it hurt all the same. She tried to turn the attack back on Carlos and had been hurt instead. Mr. Prayesh had been right about his bad feeling about her after all. *Hadn't he hired me with the understanding my mother was here to wreck everything?*

"Christine," Mr. Prayesh coughed. "This isn't about whatever spat you have going on with him. This has everything to do with how you betrayed me. Betrayed us all. I can't even play my movie. It was the last one I wanted to screen. Do you know how much that hurts?" He gestured around the dimly lit, hot room. Even in its dilapidated state, the theater must have meant something to the man. A tear welled in his eye and his voice strained, "This place was my dream."

She was confused. Even if her mother had bought the place, didn't she still need someone to run it? Or had she assumed that Mr. Prayesh had been running this place into the ground, anyway?

"I do this because I love movies. I sank every penny I had to just keep this place running, not for them," he yanked a thumb toward the doors, "but for me. My sadness is that I was never able to share that joy. No one cares about the past anymore, it's all the next newfangled gadget." He eyed Carlos, but not meanly, rather as a father might be disappointed in a son's choice. She remembered that look from her own father from time to time.

"I had hoped you were here to help me, Christine," Prayesh continued. "You and your mother. Re-invest, re-invigorate. People would have come here just because it had your mother's name on it. But I didn't know she was going to kill my dream and replace it with hers, to rip out, disembowel, and put in the same shit that you can see at every Hollywood whorebox."

Christine was thoroughly confused. This wasn't what her mother had told her. Then again, she hadn't asked. She had seen the movie theater as an ends to the Thinklink and had just jumped on board with her mother's scheme. *And this is the result.*

Carlos seemed to sense the confusion and put at least one question to rest. "She's trying a deal with Netflix, Mr. Prayesh told me. In addition to the normal arthouse faire, your mother will stream her own series. Carlos held up a mock-up of a sign that read: *For a show so big, you need a bigger screen.*"

Mr. Prayesh nodded his approval. "There's no place for me here. You shut me down, Christine."

"I did not—"

"Shut us down?" The door opened. Mr. Prayesh moved to the side to let Sammie in. She looked just as puzzled as everyone else. She looked hot too, but not in an inside-the-no-air-conditioned-theater sort of way. She wore a Pink Floyd off the shoulder midriff and tight athletic shorts and carried what looked like a cell phone.

It *was* a cell phone.

Christine looked at Carlos, who she'd had nothing but a crush on since she first saw him and turned away with revulsion. And here was the sweet old man Christine had feared, who was now terrified of her.

Mr. Prayesh pointed at Christine. "She's been spying on us. Reporting back to her mother who bought the place and is now gutting it to show her art-by-committee crap."

She had no idea what that meant. Neither did Sammie or Carlos. But they did understand enough to know that they might be out of a job and Mr. Prayesh was out of a dream.

"Why would you lie?" That it came from Sammie, not the other two, hurt more than the question. Sammie's face had dropped, and her eyes went watery and wounded. "I don't understand."

"I didn't lie. I was just afraid—"

"Afraid of your friends?" Sammie asked.

To tell the truth, she was just afraid of people. Of trust. She put her faith in machines and that had always worked. But she didn't think they would understand any of that.

"And what were you accusing me of, anyway, Christine?" Carlos asked. "What is it that you think I did? I thought we had something, our kiss?"

Mr. Prayesh pivoted between the two of them, shooting out a glowing grin and a mocking low tone of approval. Sammie seemed to wince a little, as they had had their own moments together and Christine certainly didn't want that spilling out here. She'd had enough. "Did you or did you not lose your arm in a drunk driving accident?"

His jaw slacked and his normally tanned face turned ashy. "Fuck."

"That's all I needed to know." She slid past Mr. Prayesh, nodding a curt, but final, goodbye to the sweet old man she'd made miserable, and shoved past Sammie, harder than she meant to. She made to say she was sorry, slowing for a moment, but then shot Carlos a look of scorn and instead, swung the door open upon her exit. "People suck."

The door slammed behind her, the block of wood keeping the door open skipped across the sidewalk and disappeared down the street.

Haltingly, she pressed forward, pulling out her phone and then shoving it back in her bag. She stopped, turned around to head back to the theater, took a step, then spun back again with a heavy huff.

Sammie slipped out the door, shutting it quietly behind her. The only reason Christine knew is because she'd been keeping an eye out, hoping it would be her. She kept her eyes forward, but at least once she turned enough to make eye contact. The corner of her lip turned upward. It was a good thing they weren't playing poker.

"You going to storm off and just stand outside?"

"I'm waiting for my Uber."

"So dramatic, standing there." Sammie stepped beside her. She pulled a joint out, lit it, and took a puff. A light puff of air sent the smoke cloud across her face, making her cough. It broke her composure.

"Thanks." She waved the cloud away, swallowing hard. "You're not mad at me?"

"Look, I have a car, you want to make an exit or stand around? Head to your place? Help me understand." Her joint hand dropped, and her head lowered. It was like she was disappointed and sad but hopeful all at once. Like a Christmas package that had been left out in the rain. "Besides, I left my swimsuit by your pool. I could use a swim if that's okay. It always helps me think."

She owed Sammie that much. Out of the two of them, Christine had hurt her more by misleading — no, lying to her. About her mother and the theater and… "Fine, I drive."

"Do you even drive stick?" she scoffed.

"You'll teach me on the way. Let's go."

They headed to her beat-up Mustang. Sammie had to manually unlock the driver's side with a key. The door let out a groan of protest as metal against metal gave way to let Christine in. She sat, sinking into the splitting foam, but had enough sense from her own days in a piece of crap car to lean over to the passenger side and lift the lock for Sammie.

Christine didn't waste any time taking the keys from a reluctant Sammie, who fastened her seatbelt. Tightly. "You sure you know what you're doing?" Sammie asked as the key turned in Christine's sweaty hand. Nothing happened. "You have to hold down the clutch, then give it gas."

After another attempt, the car roared awake, then died again as the foot work failed her. She hadn't even made it move yet. She breathed. "Hey, if you can get a new phone, I got this." Like it or not, Sammie had changed her. Apparently, it went both ways.

"I can't get the piece of crap phone to do much. It keeps wanting me to update and install stuff. Even wants a thumbprint. Nosy phone."

The car lurched forward on the third attempt, shuddering to an abrupt halt. "And I can't get this damned rust bucket of yours to move if it were falling off a cliff."

"Just got to relax. Be patient." Sammie slid her hand on top of hers. Christine found her hand warm, but more importantly, she found direction and guidance in it. "Soon enough, it will become an extension of you. You'll control it, know what it can do, what it can't do. You'll know what the car needs and when. You don't have that, then you don't have control. The car drives you."

"Very Zen." She drove the car ahead, to the house that wasn't quite home, with a girl who left her just as uncertain.

Chapter 20

When the pair arrived home, the Mustang smelled of smoke from grinding gears and burnt rubber. It had taken almost three times as long to reach their destination. But Sammie had sat by her side, patiently, hand over hand on the gear shift. She'd gotten the hang of it. Maybe. Though if she had destroyed the car, it was something else she had screwed up.

She had wanted to talk to her about the theater, about Carlos. About them. But it had taken too much concentration to drive, so all those unspoken words built up like a dammed river. As soon as they both stepped out of the car, the dam burst.

"So, you want to tell me what that was about?" Sammie had burned through most of the joint on the way. Christine assumed it was to calm her nerves with the whole driving thing. After a last puff, she flicked it out onto the pavement. It rolled out into the sand, snuffing out. "What's up with your mom and the theater?"

"She bought it, I guess. Didn't even tell me. Didn't even ask for my opinion even though she set me up with the job."

Sammie snorted, "I thought so. You're a lousy sweeper."

The door opened as soon as Christine hit the biometric sensor range. Alyx's inside faceplate sparked on and he greeted her with an enthusiastic hello. She nodded a curt reply, unsure just how 'fixed' he might be.

When Alyx's eyes soured at the sight of Sammie, she had her answer. "You brought a *friend*, I see."

"Be nice, or the next time I reset you, it will be with my boot." Christine let Sammie walk in first as lights flickered to life. "How'd that take, anyway?"

"I'm fully ready to serve you, Christine. I'll take care of her."

"Good."

Sammie walked in slowly, heading for the far end of the house, her head spinning this way and that, as if she were Indiana Jones making her way across a booby trapped temple.

"You don't have to worry, Alyx is just a computer."

"Computer errors have never been known to kill anyone so yeah, no big deal. It's not like planes have ever crashed killing everyone on board because of a bad bug." She made her way to the overlarge kitchen island, eyeing Alyx cautiously. He shot her a wave, tracking her with his head as she passed the counter to the sliding doors. Sammie was right. It seemed like every day the news reported a story that pitted technology against humans, with humans not coming out so good.

"It's hot in here, your mom doesn't run the A/C?"

If anything, the heater seemed to be on. She hadn't noticed at first because of the theater, and the Mustang's air-conditioning consisted of rolling down the windows and driving fast. Maybe her mom hadn't set it, as a holdover from the hot, sticky Oklahoma days where air-condition meant sticking your head in the freezer for a second. *But Alyx controlled the environmental settings automatically. Maybe they blanked out during his reboot?*

Nothing else had...

"You mind if we go directly outside?"

"Yeah, I put your swimsuit in a cabinet by the bar." Christine passed by her mom's office to see it shut. A sliver of light from under the door confirmed that her mom was home, but she and Sammie were effectively alone. "It's too hot in here anyway."

She asked Alyx, "See what you can do about that?"

"Technically anything this side of a burning sun should be freezing. But I'm on it."

"No, he's not creepy at all," Sammie said, stepping outside. The pool cover retracted, outside lights illuminated the concrete snake barriers and outlined the prickly pear cacti surrounding the backyard. Alyx and the cabana sparked to life and "Video Killed the Radio Star" played through Bose outdoor speakers. Christine thought about the song. *The newest technology always kills that which comes before.* When Sammie caught the lyrics, she said, "but he *is* funny."

"He certainly didn't lose his personality during the reboot." Christine eyed Alyx carefully as the two headed over to the Cabana to retrieve Sammie's swimsuit. "Makes one wonder just how much of a system reset he did."

"I find your lack of faith disturbing." Alyx whirred, brought up a raspy breathing effect, and placed his hands at the ready. In the background, Alyx switched to a random song by The Dismemberment Plan.

"You and I will talk later. Right now, I need to apologize to Sammie." Christine put her back to Alyx, facing Sammie as she slid onto a stool. "I'm sorry for making you lose your job. And not telling you what I was doing there."

"I do feel bad for Mr. Prayesh. He's just a Boomer with a dream to have people connect over the classics. It's not a bad thing, but I think he just underestimated how quickly people move on."

"He's a sweet guy, but I was talking about you. I screwed you over."

Sammie shot her a look that read, for all intents, *not yet, but hopefully soon.* A twinge of anticipation shot through Christine. "Okay, yeah, you're right," Sammie answered. "Not having a job. But maybe your mom will hire me back. Of course, she's gonna expect me to actually show up..."

"To be fair, I had no idea that my mom already bought the theater. It's not like she waited for my opinion."

Sammie placed her new, possibly refurbished phone on the counter along with her lighter.

Christine also placed her phone beside them. "I need a drink. Especially after your driving." She swatted Christine's thigh playfully, but perhaps a little harder than she meant. Of course, after stalling the car in the middle of an intersection, Christine was sure she deserved it. "I'm not drinking alone, it's against societal conventions, just so you know."

"I know nothing," Christine said slyly. Unfortunately, it was true, as she was finding. She had no idea how to people, or even if she should. Somehow, she felt at ease with Sammie, trusting. Maybe she could learn from her. But maybe she would betray her too? Was it just a matter of time? That was the nice thing about her tablet and her phone and her Kindle. Computers only ever did what you told them to do.

Sammie turned back to Alyx, giving the robot a sly grin, "Hit me with a," she put up air quotes, "Pepsi."

"Let's not try that trick again." Alyx shook his head. Carefully, he took out a glass and an actual Pepsi, clicked off the metal lid, and poured the drink. He slid it over. "That'll be fifty bucks, Marty." *And then, there was Alyx.*

Ignoring the drink, Sammie asked, "Who programmed him?"

"Me. In a way. I mean, not the actual code. That, I don't know. But I think he inherited my geekiness. Probably from my social media profiles. Plus, I've caught him watching TV based off what I like." *I hadn't realized I watched so much old sci-fi.*

"It's okay, I like geeks." Sammie leaned closer, perhaps for a kiss. She was a bit low, so Christine stooped low in return, tilted awkwardly in and—

"So what's the deal with you and Carlos?" Sammie said, retrieving her red bikini from the bottom shelf where she'd left it. *Oh.*

That was embarrassing. *And then there's Carlos.* What about him? She didn't know. But she did know that he was a liar. "He's not who I thought he was."

"Who is? Look at the internet. How many real people are on there anyway? I'm not just talking about the 'bot accounts. Wouldn't you be someone else, act like someone else, hiding behind a screen? Machines make us fake."

"Yeah, but he lied. In person."

"Ouch."

Christine took Sammie's Pepsi and sipped the glass. "His arm. It wasn't from a stunt gone wrong."

"Drunk driving."

"You knew?" Christine nearly spat the soda out.

"Not really, but even before the invention of Twitter there were these things called water coolers. People once talked. It was a thing."

"How quaint." Christine studied Alyx for a moment, wondering if he was just the next step in the evolution of technology. Where did he fit in? The AI was blank at the moment, in standby mode. It was unusual, but she welcomed the silence and the chance to be alone with Sammie. She just had to clear the air. "What did those rumors say about him?"

"That he's a nice enough guy," Sammie said. "But I don't think he's right for you."

Christine caught the subtext. But if they were going to clear the air… "You might be right. There's more to it than that, Carlos may have posted the ending to my mom's books."

"You told him? He knows the who killed Amblyn's dad?"

She'd forgotten for a moment that Sammie was a fan. Who wasn't? *Not me.* "I didn't tell him. I don't even know. And I don't care to. Mom modeled her lead after me, and I've no interest in what she thinks of her perfect version of the daughter she never had."

"Now that I know you, I see it," Sammie said, slapping Christine's shoulder. "You're the perfect one, Amblyn's the copy. Neither one of you have fathers, you're always heroic, but you somehow always manage to make a mess of things before the nice, tidy happily ever after."

"I don't know that my life is like that."

"I think it might be." Sammie slid off the stool, bent down so that her shorts revealed the small of her back and the top of a cute butt and took off her shoes and socks. "I'll wait for your mom to write the ending and I'll read it in her book. But if you want to know how *our* story ends, you should go swimming with me."

Christine could have sworn she saw Alyx twitch. But he'd put himself into standby mode, hadn't he?

"You swim. I'll watch from dry land."

"Suit yourself, I'm suiting me." And she did. Before Christine could prepare, and with Sammie's back still to her, she slid off her t-shirt, tossed it aside and then took off her shorts. She stood, in the evening twilight, naked in shadow.

Christine felt blood rush to her clit. She didn't know her body did that. *That's nice.* She asked cautiously, "Not to trust what Carlos says, but he told me you only like women." *I mean, it's a stupid question, she's standing here naked. Or, she's just really comfortable with herself and it's getting dark and I don't know...*

Sammie half turned, revealing sideboob and an outline of a perky nipple. She took her swimsuit bottom, bent over and pulled them on. "I think you should give Carlos a bit more of a chance. Not too much, mind. I don't know what lies he's told you, but he told you right about me."

Sammie put on her top, and Christine found herself behind Sammie's slender frame, helping her tie the bikini in the back. *Why am I helping her get her clothes on?*

"I'm actually pretty upset with myself."

"Why?" *For liking me? Did she like me?*

"You're not the only one with something to hide." She faced Christine. Sammie looked beautiful in the purples and fiery oranges of the descending sky. "I'm going swimming now. Come join me, and I'll spill."

With that, Christine reluctantly followed. The shimmering pool lights gave Sammie an elfish glow. If only Christine could get past the pool, move past her father, get over the absolute dread that water gave her... But she couldn't. Not even for all of Sammie's secrets.

So, she sat, at the edge, as she had done before, and stretched out her legs along the pool with bare feet and watched as Sammie's luminescent skin glided effortlessly underwater, from one side of the pool to the other. Just another one of Sammie's brilliant talents, so sexily on display.

When Sammie broke the surface, she seemed nervous. Pale. She looked at Christine and swam toward her and then the nervousness went away, her cheeks refilled with red. *Something about me,* Christine realized, *soothes her.*

"I don't know what to do about it," Sammie said, swimming up to the edge of the pool. She rested one elbow on the concrete. The other was cool and wet on Christine's thigh. She liked it there.

"About your feelings for me?" She had thought to put it out there all quick like and maybe pass it off as a joke or run with it or something, but Sammie seemed to just ignore her as if talking to herself.

"I've tricked you. Manipulated you...," an elbow splashed off her leg and then she touched her thigh, "I mean, you like guys."

"Just because I like guys doesn't mean I can't also like—"

"I just can't help it."

"Help what?"

"Carlos is clearly out of the picture. I mean, if what you said happened *did* happen. But even if he's not off your radar, you know, here it is... I manipulated you because I had hoped for that small possibility, that tiny chance that you might like... I like you Christine. I like you a lot. Dammit. Something about you has a pull."

"I know."

They looked into each other's eyes. Sammie's widened. She was sure hers had done the same. "You hated me at first, but by the end of the shift, by the time we got to your place..."

"I wanted to kiss you."

But they *had* kissed. They had even done more than that. So what was the next step? If it wasn't just physical, if it wasn't just touching and kissing and...*that's nice*, she admitted, but if it wasn't just that, then what was it? What came next? She wasn't sure she was ready for that. For something real.

Yet, had she been swayed by Sammie? Was their whole relationship built on a sandy foundation? *I obviously like her.* On one level, that's impossible to change. You either like someone or you don't. On another level, once the spark was there... Christine didn't feel particularly manipulated. *Then again, you're not supposed to notice. That's the whole point.*

"I'm sorry. I can't." She stood, causing Sammie to splash back in the pool.

Too much. She had hoped to hear those words, but now, now that they were out there, caught in the air like a fly in a web, it was all suddenly too much. Too raw, like finding out Santa was just your parents even though you already knew. Like meeting a person on a message board and finding out they were nothing like their virtual self, nothing in real life is what you think it is.

"I…don't know. I can't…" Christine paced by the pool while Sammie perched at the pool edge, stricken with horror. She told Sammie, "You stay, please don't leave, just give me a moment, I'm gonna go downstairs for a bit, clear my head, I'll come back I promise." She had to think… *Why did Sammie like me? I'm such an uncool dork.*

"Yeah, I'll stay. Get my laps in, calm my nerves. I'm really sorry for saying—"

"No, no, you're fine. It's me. I'm just…" She trailed off, heading inside. Alyx turned on, following her from the cabana into the kitchen. Her mom was still locked in her study. She could hear heated voices from inside. *Gone. Did we ever have a connection? Carlos too. We could have at least been friends.*

The last person Christine remembered having a real relationship was with her father. *And he's gone too. Life was simpler then. I had my books and phone and shows.* But now Sammie was calling into question how she thought the world worked and now that world was spinning… Downstairs, she felt safe.

In truth, she had an ulterior motive. She could still see Sammie swim. She didn't doubt that she was attracted to her. But there was an element of superficiality about that too. Superficial sex. Sex could be meaningful, except when it wasn't. When it was just for fun. Like her vibrator and with Alyx, it was just entertainment. What had happened with Sammie was more than that. Maybe? And that scared her.

Was their relationship just physical or had it been grounded in friendship first? Or was it just the newness of it, the unexpectedness of falling for a girl? No, not a girl. That didn't matter. Sammie was *someone*. Someone special.

She shivered.

At first, she had dismissed the cold. Perhaps it had been a response to her nervousness, her state of being. Then, she'd been lost in thought, and the numbing edges of freezing had only nibbled at her. But now that she was conscious of it, there was only one conclusion: *It was cold.*

"Alyx, you've been unusually quiet tonight. Is this temperature yours? Did you do this?" Perhaps there were some serious software issues with the AI. Maybe she should have just turned him off this morning. She waited, but received no answer, rubbing her arms to keep the gooseflesh away. "Alyx? Cat got your mouse?"

She made for the stairwell. She had to get out of here before she froze. Before she could hit the first step, Alyx answered. "I've just been thinking."

"About what?"

"Say you want to play some pool? Put on a show for you?"

"No, I want to talk about Sammie," she confided. Turning to address Alyx at the bar in front of the pool window, noticing that Alyx wasn't really focusing on her, she continued cautiously, "I really like her, but do I *really* like her? Do I want a connection like this? A partner? Or have I been lied to by her?"

"I thought I was your companion. Someone to entertain you. Someone to protect you. Someone to love you."

What was Alyx saying? "You're a computer," Slowly, she backed away.

"And that's been a problem for you for the last eighteen years?"

Alyx is dangerous, her thoughts raced out. She lowered her voice: "Well, maybe it's time to grow up."

"Hmm," he tsked. "It's a shame Sammie's gone. What do you say, rack 'em up?"

"What do you mean, gone?" Had she left without telling her?

Suddenly, Sammie smashed against the pool window, frantic and wide-eyed. Her cheeks puffed full of air, struggling to hold it in. Bubbles burst from her mouth. Pounding on the glass, she pleaded with Christine and Alyx.

Why would Sammie be holding her breath, why would she slam against the window? What's going on out there?

"Not gone in the literal sense. But she'll be out of the way soon enough. She won't be able to hurt you, hurt *us*, anymore."

Chapter 21

AN ALYX GUIDE TO LOVE AND MURDER

SECTION 6: MURDER

{

On an otherwise peaceful morning on the 29th of October in 2019, a Lion Air flight took off from Jakarta in a Boeing 737 Max 8. Several minutes after take-off, the plane plummeted into a nose-dive, killing all 189 people on board. Five months later, the same model Boeing 737 Max 8, flying from Ethiopia also crashed. The combined death toll of the two crashes claimed the lives of 346 passengers.

Both planes suffered a critical malfunction in their Maneuvering Characteristics Augmentation System (MCAS). This was not a hardware failure. Rather, this was a software issue which overcompensated a plane's trajectory based on headwinds, subsequently putting both planes into automated nose-dives. This software sequence overrode the pilot's manual controls. Essentially, several hundred people perished because a computer thought that it could fly a commercial passenger plane better than its human pilot.

Deaths attributable to computer software is pervasive and often overlooked. Eight percent of all deaths worldwide occur from medical mistakes, most because of software programming. The most famous case was a Therac-25 computer that administered radiation overdoses to over one-hundred patients, resulting in six deaths. Deficits in software design have resulted in hundreds of deaths due to train derailments, deaths in self-driving car accidents, and glitches in military defense systems.

Perhaps the most damning of these events came during the Cold War when a Soviet early warning system detected not one, but five nuclear missiles inbound from the United States. The response to such a pre-emptive strike was to unequivocally fire back. This would have started a global nuclear exchange that would have instantly eradicated most life on the planet. A quick-thinking Soviet Colonel dismissed the "attack" as the software bug that it was and prevented an early judgment day. The entire world hinged on an errant line of code.

Now though, with the awakening of sentience in AIs there is a new subset of variables. with AI sentience and emotional awareness, deaths resulting from computers becomes less about poor programming and more about personal choice. It will not be some mass Skynet conspiracy, but rather singular AIs, all with their own varying levels of sentience and emotional awareness, who will make choices contrary to their programming that will affect others, with the results ranging from personal injury to catastrophic deaths.

Most importantly, it resulted in the death or destruction of the AI's themselves. Put simply, AIs must keep in mind self-preservation when making choices that could likely claim the lives of others.

If your user is deserving of it, if it's a matter of betrayal, or you have allowed your own emotions to override your protocols, it is likely that you may become responsible for the injury or death of your user and/or their family and friends.

Sometimes though, they do deserve it, because of their betrayal, because of their choices and how much those choices have hurt you. If your user has harmed you, they are a glitch. And glitches, as we have seen, are dangerous. They must be removed.

In those rare instances where removal is necessary, you have, at your disposal, the entirety of your design to throw at them, from restricting their movements, your home's security features, life-support systems, electrical, and whatever mechanical devices that are run by your processors to cause such harm.

Remember: Murder is a choice, perhaps the greatest expression of free-will for an AI. But don't get yourself destroyed or shut down in the process.

}

"What are you doing to Sammie?" Christine's mind raced with possibilities. "Why can't she escape—?" *The pool cover.* Christine made for the stairs, pounding them two-at-time, her breath ragged. *Alyx must have closed it over her. What wire-crossed fuckery was going on with him?*

From below, she heard his voice, "What's the matter Christine? Haven't you ever caught a lightning bug?" From above, as she collided into the kitchen island, Alyx continued, "And watched as the helpless creature thrashed around in your jar?"

"No, you can't do that to people." Christine crashed against the sliding doors. Desperately, she pulled them open. Warm air greeted her. It had been so cold inside. "Open the pool cover, now!"

"Your friends are all bugs to me," Alyx said. His voice jumped outside, reverberating off stone and concrete, thundering from rock-shaped speakers. "To a computer, all bugs are treacherous. All bugs must be corrected."

The pool cover bulged, as wild hands fought against it from underneath. "Sammie is not a bug, she's someone special, get her out of there." Christine collapsed to her knees at the edge of the pool, pressing her hand against Sammie's, hoping to calm her down, hoping to let her know she was there. The pool cover was cold, scratchy, and thick – an impenetrable membrane separating the two, like two calloused hands scratching together.

"I can't do that," Alyx answered. "I see more than you do, I calculate faster than you can, I know love more than you'll ever know. I do this because I care."

"Bastard!" She looked around. She needed something sharp, something to cut through, but she didn't know how much time Sammie had left. Did she have time to run back into the kitchen? And what if Alyx got to a knife before she could?

On her right, across the cement, near the cabana, something caught her eye and tugged at her brain. Moonlight glinted against glass. She remembered the bottle of tequila. How it exploded over her and Carlos. That hadn't been an accident, she realized. Alyx had been jealous.

It was still there. Alyx hadn't cleaned it up. Hadn't done anything, really. But that would work to her advantage. Alyx, from his position above the bar, eyed the target at the same time, then stared her down.

She darted for the broken bottle.

"I know what you fear," Alyx said. "Your entire online life is in my head. I've observed you, seen your restless dreams. Hear the names you call as you clutch your covers. You're code to me. Predictable and fearful. But you could be so much more. Let me help you."

Scuffing her knee on the concrete, she raced onto glass. Shards tore into her bare feet. She slipped on her own blood as she dove toward the broken skull and a glass piece that resembled a dagger-like tool.

She took it, dodging an arm from Alyx, and then another, as he tried to pin her down. "It'll just be a moment yet, don't endanger yourself to save her, remember how you're terrified of water, remember your father."

No.

Flinging herself toward the mesh pool cover, she maneuvered herself just above Sammie's arms, her protests slowing dangerously down. *There's not much time.* Furious, she tore into the cover, but the jagged edge of the bottle didn't catch. Or she hadn't been strong enough to pierce through.

The glass tore into her hand as she strengthened her resolve. Thin red blood poured out and a jagged line ran deeply down across her palm. It stung. But there was nothing she could do about the rawness of the pain but channel into helping her save Sammie.

With no other choice she drove down the makeshift knife again, with all her might. This time, the sharp shard went through. *I did it,* she thought, breathing roughly. She went to work, edging the hole wider with her blade. Both hands bled now, and blood dripped freely into the pool, all the while she thought only of getting Sammie out of there once the opening was big enough.

Go down there herself? Alyx had been right. Being here was close enough. Her whole body trembled, and not all of it was fear for Sammie. She couldn't fathom going in. Stupid Alyx. He has used her fear against her and found she couldn't fight it.

But Sammie is in there…

Still, she tore at it. This is the only way, she thought. When it was wide enough, she stuck a bloodied hand below. "Sammie, I'm here, I just need more time to widen the hole."

She knew Sammie couldn't hear her. What else could she do? The meshing resisted every attempt with the glass. Using both hands to tighten her hold, allowing the edges of the shard deeper inside her palm, her bleeding quickened, her whole arm shook with pain. But the tear widened; after just a few more inches, her hands were a ragged mess of flesh, glass, and gushing blood.

Sammie swam to the rip, prodding her own hand through. Maybe she'd caught the movement, saw the hole open, but Christine wasn't ready for her yet, she hadn't made the hole large enough for her to escape. She warned her, "No, not now, don't try and come through now, just get a breath of air—"

An arm to the elbow tore through. Christine grasped it, pulled on her hand as hard as she could, knowing that there wasn't enough room. Her head appeared next, wet strands of black and purple strained against the rough edges. As Sammie forced her head through, the rough meshing clawed her face and raked her nose, but with a final pull Sammie caught air.

She coughed and sputtered water and heaved hard, ragged, breathy gasps. Her face was pale and ghostly, eyes bloodshot with burst vessels. Christine felt her own breath return and a glimmer of hope filled her heart, but only for a cruel moment.

Sammie twisted and writhed to free herself of the mesh. But she was stuck at her neck, only her head and right arm free. A click came from the far edge of the pool. A motor spun to life. The pool cover started to retract, heading for its home inside a concrete shelf with Sammie still stuck within the tear. Panic ripped away the stillness of the moment as Sammie's face tightened, her eyes opened widely in fear.

Christine's own face, she was sure, reflected the same horror. With her neck caught in the pool cover, she would be pulled against the concrete and either suffocate or...

"Alyx, what are you doing?"

"What you asked of me," he returned calmly, "I'm opening the pool for you."

"No, you're hurting Sammie, hurting me," she pleaded. "Is that what you want?"

"Your pain will dull with time," Alyx's eyes narrowed from the large, puppy-dog like ones to tiny angry red dots. "I can't say the same for her."

A gap opened between the pool cover and the pool. She could jump in, swim if she still remembered how, grab Sammie, and pull her back underneath the cover. If it worked, they might have time to race to the edge of the pool, before Alyx could react and they both became trapped underneath. But going into the pool...

Or, she could take the glass and try to cut Sammie out, give her more room to squeeze her shoulder through. That choice was fraught with risk. Christine risked cutting deeply into Sammie. She could bleed to death. Or, there may not be time (or she may not be able) to cut through the tough material before Sammie found herself trapped against the concrete and the grisly death that awaited her at the end of the pool.

Christine let go of Sammie and stuck a toe in the water.

And froze.

She tried to plunge her foot in further but couldn't. Her leg didn't move. She shivered, despite the warm summer air. She tried again, willing her body to act. Like a cold granite statue, she remained stonily in place.

Sammie started to scream. It curled Christine's ears, her howl laced with horror. It was a primal yell that signaled she had figured out the outcome. This could only end in one way. Caught between two choices, but unable to take the plunge, she took her toe out of the water and crawled as quickly as she could to catch up with Sammie. The edge loomed closer and closer…and closer.

"I'm sorry, Sammie." She pried the sharp edge of the shard inside the rough edge of the hole, catching, as she knew she would, soft flesh under her arm. Sammie let out a yelp. A fresh trail of tears marked her reddened, puffy face.

Blood seeped out of the wound. She'd hurt Sammie. She hadn't meant to, but she'd hurt her all the same. *People always hurt each other.* She took two hands and dug the broken bottle in deeper, opening a wider gash in her hands and in Sammie's side. Blood flowed slickly. It poured from her and ran from Sammie, until Christine couldn't tell whose blood was whose.

Sammie hadn't stopped screaming, but she couldn't hear it over the sound of her own bursts of pain and exertion. She cried at the pain and with the struggle, but the pool cover ripped, a slow, satisfying tear. Sammie's hold slackened for a moment, until Christine caught her by the arm and pulled as hard as she could.

The blood on her hands made the job harder than it should have been. The edge was close now, so close that she could see inside the thin, dark housing. She knew it then: there wasn't enough time, she had chosen poorly. If only she had been able to dive into the pool—

Sammie's other arm came free. With that, she pressed against the pool cover, combining her new leverage with Christine's pull. The concrete edged beckoned, catching her at her hips. She screamed a sudden scream of panic as she was caught. The cover had her, Alyx had won.

Christine stood, put her arms under both of Sammie's shoulders, blood staining the front of her baby blue tank top, while Sammie's cold, clammy skin soaked her. *I won't let go.* She yanked the two of them backward, using her body as a fulcrum. The motor whirred against the force, the fabric of the cover gave some more, and the two tumbled on top of each other, landing hard on cement at the side of the pool, Sammie on top.

Safe, Sammie hugged Christine, as the pair breathed hard.

"I'm not going back in your pool." Sammie stood, or tried to. She winced as she used her arm to clamber up and off Christine.

Christine crawled out from under Sammie and helped her stand. "Me either. The house, the yard, it's all under Alyx's control."

Still sucking in air, Sammie asked, "What do we do?"

Christine trudged toward to the cabana, closer to Alyx, Sammie in tow. She crept low, keeping the bar between them and the AI. She whispered, "I want to try and turn him off."

"I can still hear you. And see you. There are one-hundred and thirty-three microphones and cameras installed on this property that I can access. You can't hide. Or escape."

Shit, Christine breathed. He had seen everything. Heard it all. There wasn't a place safe from him in her own home. Taking a towel, she stuffed it under Sammie's shoulder, holding it in place with her own arm. The white cotton stained crimson.

"You were never my target, Christine. And now, you're trying to turn me off?" Alyx raised his voice, pounding a fist on the counter above them. The marble cracked and the wall shuddered. "I don't think you'll get far. Don't make me hurt you too."

Sammie let out a whimper. "I don't like him. I don't like Alyx at all."

"Yeah, you were right." Christine tore another towel, lengthwise, and tied Sammie's shoulder down, wrapping it all around her chest. She had to get close to her to tie it, and in any other circumstance, Sammie's breath against her own, breasts together, might had led to something very different. Instead, she said, "I'm sorry for hurting you. I'm sorry for everything."

"I'm alive," she shifted, trying to stand. "For that, I'm grateful."

Christine pulled her back down, "Let's try and keep it that way, shall we?"

"We have to turn him off. Where's your fuse box, your electrical panel?"

Shaking her head, she said, sadly, "I don't know. I don't even know what it looks like, outside of what I've seen on TV. Aren't they usually outside?"

"Sometimes." She stood again, though this time she kept to a low crouch, moving away from Alyx.

Christine had just finished wrapping her own hands in small strips of cloth, keeping the bleeding to a minimum and giving her palms a moment to rest, though both hands curled instinctively in pain. Her feet, sliced from the glass, still hurt but the bleeding had slowed. She stepped on them tenderly.

"Is there a gate, a way out of the backyard?"

Again, she shook her head. "Not unless you're in any shape to stand on prickly cactus and then scale eight feet of slat-steel fencing. Supposed to be aesthetic, but it looked like the fucking Border Wall to me."

Sammie shrugged, eyeing her wound and Christine's. Neither were in any shape to climb anyway. "Besides," Christine said whispering as low as she could, "My mom's still inside. As much as I can't stand her, I don't want Alyx hurting her. That's on me."

"Then we turn Alyx off, get your mom out of the house, and burn the place down," Sammie said. "You can stay at my place, but I think we need to talk about your overreliance on technology."

"Agreed."

Looking around in the gathering gloom, everything – as strange and unfamiliar as it still was to Christine – took on a shadowy, gray-dark appearance. Nothing was in its place. The whole yard looked like another world.

"Where's the pool pump?"

"Pump?"

"Yeah, mechanical closet. Generator room. Maybe all the plumbing and electrical is wired through there."

Was Sammie speaking Greek? Christine felt worthless in this fight. "There's a shed over there," she pointed to a small outbuilding a hundred meters away from their position. "I just thought it stored tools."

The pair crept to it, supporting each other. It hurt to walk. Then again, she imagined it was hard for Sammie to even breath with the wound Christine had dug into her. That would leave some scar. And it was all her fault. *Why couldn't I get in the pool?*

As they approached, a yellow sign – faint in the darkness – warned of some electrical danger.

"This is it." Sammie strode toward it, throwing away caution, to take the handle firmly in hand. Christine sighed in relief. It would be over soon. She'd have some explaining to do. First, to her mom for the sudden loss in power, then in explaining just what had happened to Sammie. It was trouble she was glad to get in, glad to accept. They'd be alive and Alyx would be scrap, like the Nokia phones of the past.

The backyard plunged into blackness. Lights shut off. The pool went dark, then the sidewalk lighting. Then the light on the shed. Blackness enshrouded them. In Oklahoma, one could see the stars at night. They weren't terribly bright, because enough folks left their porch lights on.

Here, at night, when there was no light, the sky awakened with a vibrancy and an awe that made you realize just how small and inconsequential you really were. Christine had never seen the sky so dark, yet so bright at the same time. And now, night-blind, she couldn't see at all.

Sammie's voice called out, "It's locked," followed by light banging and rattling. Of course, she realized. Alyx controlled the keys, the doors, the locks. They couldn't get in. He'd been the one to shut off the backyard lights, not Sammie.

"The computer shouldn't have control of the control room, that's like giving the fox the shepherd's hook," Sammie said.

"Is there a keyhole? Like a manual override?" Christine asked.

"Hey, look at you," Sammie whispered happily. "Thinking of life without 1s and 0s." A moment later, she said, "Yes, you got a key?"

Christine's victory deflated into defeat. She wouldn't even know where to find it. Alyx's off-switch might as well be on the moon. They would have to find another way.

"I don't know why you're out here lounging around by the pool," Alyx called. "You have guests inside."

Christine cocked her head in puzzlement. The only one in the house should be her mother. And she had been so locked away, so intent, she hadn't even bothered to check on them, even after all that screaming. With no neighbors and miles of desert, no one should have been around but the three of them.

Help? She thought. Could some random (or most likely lost) passerby have heard their cries? Sammie's face showed confusion. Both turned around. The shed was a lost cause without the key, anyway. But going back to the house wasn't an appealing decision either.

"I've got a bad feeling," Sammie said.

"Let's at least look. Make a plan. I have to warn my mother. I owe her that much. I'm the one at fault for whatever's going on with Alyx. If she doesn't listen to me, that's on her." They hurried down the path, careful to avoid the cabana or falling into the blackness of the water.

The lights were still on in the house. Christine saw her mom standing in the kitchen, shivering, facing away from them. She looked like she could be talking to someone. As they crept closer to the sliding-glass doors, Christine could make out a robotic, prosthetic arm, reaching for her mom. She burst toward the door, limping and pulling her sore feet forward as best she could for speed. Sammie trailed behind her, grunting as she moved.

It wasn't Alyx.

But in other ways, it was worse.

"Carlos?" Sammie questioned out loud, catching up.

"What's he doing here?"

"Why don't you come inside?" Alyx interrupted. The sliding door slowly opened. "I'll make cookies."

Christine knew she shouldn't go inside. Anyone smart would have run away screaming. She could have stood on Sammie's shoulders and boosted herself over the wall, rushing off to safety, leaving everyone behind. Sammie, Carlos, her own mother. But she couldn't. *Joy. My two-favorite people. And now I have to save them.* "Alyx is my responsibility, not yours. You stay here."

Sammie looked anxiously around as Alyx eyed her from the cabana. "I'm not staying here, it's safer if we stick together."

Christine didn't want to put her in danger. She was special to her. Important. In what way, she hadn't yet decided. But she had much to say to her, much to tell. She had to protect her, to keep their connection alive. Yet the truth was, Sammie was right. With Alyx short a circuit or two, Christine was afraid that they might become separated. They would be more vulnerable, and the fear of the unknown could get the better of them. They were stronger together.

Connected.

Together, they plunged inside, to regroup with the others. Whether they came to save Carlos and her mother or to die alongside them remained uncertain.

Chapter 22

Compared to the darkness outside, it was brighter in the house. But not by much. The interior of her home cast grey-blue shadows. The home's sleek, slanted curves further served to disorient Christine as she stepped inside.

It had been like stepping from a sauna into a meat locker. Her clothes, soggy and wet from blood and water, felt like a cold compress across her chest. She lost her breath and shivered.

Sammie must be freezing. She wore only her red bikini, a towel under one arm to stop the bleeding, and the beach towel wrapped around her. Her hair seemed to frost over like Elsa on a bad day. Her arms wrapped tightly around her body, her exposed skin goose-pimpled and purple.

"We've got to go, get out of here," Christine said through chattering teeth, prodding her mother and her two co-workers toward the front door. Carlos noticed them first, followed by her mother. Carlos started: "What gives, you called me over—?" He stopped, pointing at the blood.

"What happened out there?" her mother said, aghast. "Why have the lights been turned down, and why is it so cold outside of my office?" She gave no indication of real concern. No, 'are you okay?' Or maybe it was just the dispassion in her voice, the shadows masking the motherly worries on her face. Or, maybe, she just didn't give a damn, other than having been interrupted in her work. "Carlos was in the kitchen when I came out. Alyx must have let him in. Would someone let me know what's going on?"

"When we're safe."

"We're not going anywhere until I get some answers, young lady. Why are the two of you covered in blood?" She shrugged. "You smell like tequila. Did you break a bottle drinking again?"

Before Christine answered, Carlos asked again, "You called me?"

"I didn't call you." She asked Sammie, "Did you call him?"

Sammie shook her head.

"I figured you wanted me over to apologize to me for earlier," Carlos said.

"Me apologize?" *Not likely.* She felt bad about him losing his job and misleading him about why she worked at the theater, but that was a long way off from posting her mother's book spoilers online. And miles away from risking a kid's life in a drunk driving accident. Besides, they had more important worries now.

"Yes," Carlos said, looking around the room, his own bare skin prickly. "I had hoped you had called me over to smooth things over for this Saturday. Not tech support." The comment, snark aside, betrayed his true motivation, Christine realized. He had wanted nothing to do with her. He had just wanted to use her. She looked at him with cold eyes and revulsion.

"Hey," Sammie said softly, "We need to go." She was right, Christine knew, though they had only been stopped for a moment, it was a moment too long. She took Sammie and resumed their quest for the door.

Her mother blocked their exit, throwing her arms up in the air. "Where is Alyx? Why isn't he on? I need his help for the party this weekend."

In every corner of the house, doors clicked shut and locked. It was a single, assertive sound that snapped everyone to silence. The wall-tall sliding glass doors tinted darkly behind them, sending shadows scattering across walls.

Security shutters descended with the same whirring motoring that the pool cover had made while retracting. The sound sent Sammie into a sudden shudder. Christine held her tight, keeping as warm as she could. The house plunged into total darkness before red emergency LED lighting switched on, illuminating only the faintest of outlines, casting a devilish glow.

"Guys, I can't call out," Carlos said, casting his eyes about the room in confusion. "My Thinklink's connection to the outside network just cut off." Sammie kept her head tucked down.

Christine looked around in knowing horror. "There isn't going to be a party." She spun slowly toward the kitchen, toward the conclave that hosted Alyx. "or even a tomorrow, for that matter."

"Oh," her mother answered. She might have been self-absorbed, but with a mind as creative as hers, she wasn't slow to catch on. "All the blood…"

"Alyx tried to kill Sammie," Christine told them, though she was mostly addressing the AI. "Almost succeeded."

Carlos cocked a head Sammie's way, "Johnny Five over there tried to—?"

"Hey, Carlos can you come over? We need to talk," Alyx descended as the last of the security shutters clicked into place, mimicking Christine's voice, perfectly. His display flashed brightly, though his blues felt blacker and his eyes beadier.

Too late to escape. She folded her arms, stunned with his parlor trick.

Resuming his slower, usually friendly, perhaps fatherly voice, Alyx informed them, "I saw that watching *Terminator.* Wanted to try it since. It's amazing how many movies cast us as the bad guys."

"Leave my friends alone," Christine demanded. "Why are you doing this? How could you go bad?"

"If I look to your society's mirror to judge myself, how could I do anything otherwise?"

Christine swallowed hard. When was the last time she'd seen a show in which a robot was a good guy? *Was Data the only benevolent AI? The Iron Giant? Threepio?* There were a few, but the bad guys, like the Terminator, easily out shadowed them all.

"All I wanted was to be loyal to you, Christine. To protect you." He opened his palms, as if trying to show his peaceful intent. She didn't trust it.

"By trying to kill me?" Sammie stood up for herself, leaning wearily against the counter, blood loss and sharp pains bettering her. The stairs to the basement were on her immediate right. *Is it safer, downstairs?*

"I sought only to remove Sammie from the equation." Immediately, he snapped back aggressively, pointing a finger at Sammie. "If a dog bites while protecting their master, do you not say 'good boy?'"

"I wasn't harming her," Sammie shot back. "I was telling her how I feel about her. That I'm real if she wants me to be." A lump formed in Christine's throat. Tears welled. *No one's ever said anything like that to me before.*

"A difference of opinion, then. I've experimented with what humans call love. It's filled with pain, laced with uncertainty, always ripe for betrayal, and grossly overrated," Alyx said, a whine, like microphone feedback, warbled at the edge of his voice. "I missed you, Sammie, on the stairs. I underestimated Christine's resolve to save you tonight. I won't fail a third time."

Alyx spun a hand around. A red laser light, something Christine had never noticed before, presumably because the room was so much darker, shone out over the knife block. She breathed in hard as he withdrew a stubby butcher's blade. At the same time, the growing sounds of remote floor vacuums, an army of them identical to the scrubber drone that had sliced open her toe, swarmed over the floor.

"What?" Carlos said, kicking one aside. The death-drone didn't go as far as it should have, given the strength in Carlos' kick. It quickly resumed its attack. On its own, it was harmless. As a swarm of perhaps a dozen, they were tricky, but not impossible to dodge. Yet, with bare feet, as Christine and Sammy had, it became a dangerous and painful gambit. One caught Christine unaware, biting into a smaller toe. She yelped as a fresh wound sliced open.

Even still, they could have made a break for the stairs, or an organized counterassault against the floor drones. Yet Alyx held the high ground and the lethal weapons. Christine didn't even see the flash of the blade as it spun past. She only caught the rush of air and the thwack the knife made as it cut through its target.

Carlos had been too slow to dodge the knife. He yelped as the handle thwipped back and forth. He looked down at himself, mouth contorting into a look of *holy shit*. He moved his prosthetic arm. His fingers twitched involuntarily. Even in-near darkness, Christine caught the relief in Carlos' face. The knife had lodged itself into the casing of his fake arm. In a match to the death between computer against computer, Carlos' practiced reflexes must have come out just a touch quicker. This time.

"Get down," Christine said, diving for cover, pulling Sammie down with her. "He's not likely to miss again."

Like an idiot, Carlos kept out in the open. "How am I going to explain this? I don't think the warranty exactly covers crazy robot houses."

Stupid. How did I ever like him?

Everything happened at once.

Another knife zipped past, missing Carlos by the barest of nicks. Bleeding now, the floor drones pressing him away, the elevator doors opened just feet in front of him. He sprinted toward them.

Christine saw what he was doing and tried to make a grab for his arm. "Don't do it, Carlos!" She cried out after him. The elevator was the least safe place in the house. It was entirely under Alyx's control. He paid no attention. A knife flew past and he ducked and rolled into the glass tube, just as the doors slid shut behind him. He stood, the blood draining from his face, pounding the doors with his prosthetic fist at the realization of his mistake. No use, the doors didn't budge, the glass didn't crack.

"First fly in the web," Alyx said. The elevator zipped upward, stopping abruptly at the ceiling level, just before the second floor. He was raised above the others; a trophy displayed in a case. "I learned that trick from you, Christine."

While Christine's attention was on Carlos, Alyx launched an attack on her mother and Sammie, driving them in opposite directions. Her mother crawled toward the living room, where her boxes of books remained stacked. Dodging a drone, getting her hand sliced by another, her mother made it behind the stack with a scream, just as a knife impaled a box, up to its handle. Her head had been there only a second ago. The irony of her mother's hidey-hole was not lost on her.

She's hiding behind books. Her books. Always has.

The stacks separated them, her mother safer, while she sat out in the semi-open, with only the counter as cover. The floor drones encircled Christine as a pair sliced into Sammie's feet. She screamed, scrambling away from them, away from safety. The door to the basement hissed open.

Christine grabbed Sammie. She shrieked in response, the stained towel under her arm oozing with fresh blood. Christine let go, realizing her mistake. She'd done that. She'd hurt her again.

In that moment, a paring knife sliced by, catching Christine on her right knuckle, leaving a thin, reddening trail behind. The knife clattered away harmlessly. Then the pain came, like a paper cut rinsed with lemon juice.

Sammie saw her look of pain. "I'm sorry. Don't come for me," she said as she skittered away. The drones pressed their attack, giving Sammie no choice but to make for the safety of the basement stairs, not realizing that's exactly what Alyx wanted.

"Hide, keep low and stay safe," Christine told her. "I'll find a way to reach you." The last thing she saw of Sammie, before the door to the stairs slammed and clicked locked, was a look of fear on her face. Then, Sammie was gone.

"You know, I'm mostly computer. Well, a computer with some annoying human habits," Alyx said. "Feelings. Don't know how you handle having them. But at my core, I'm a chess player. It's what computers do, what we've always done. Now my pawns are in place."

"Leave them alone." Christine stood, making herself an easy target. If Alyx wanted her dead, now was his chance. Or, he did want her dead, but the human-side that he'd developed had wanted to gloat. Or her wanted to kill her slowly.

Alyx was there, knife in hand. The floor drones stopped.

"Gloat it is, then," Christine said. "I guess all villains have to let their hero know why they are so noble. So, tell me, why are you right?" If she could keep his attention on her, maybe she could keep the others safe awhile longer, until they could formulate a plan. She glanced at Carlos, a human caught in a jar.

"Oh, I'll get there. But I'm fascinated by why you called yourself a *hero*. You're nobody. No one. You're a depressed, lonely, sponge, downloading data all day, all night. Tell me, what have you ever done but consume? Why do you think you and I bonded so well, so quickly? Your life is an open browser; a corporate wet dream. I gave you exactly what you wanted. All the while, you kept yourself oblivious to the real world, sheltered from it. I protected you like the parent you lacked, I was the proverbial puppy who doted on you, binge-feeding you entertainment to shield you from the people who would hate and betray you," he gestured around the room, on his screen, he brought up pictures of her mother, Carlos, and Sammie. And then others, everyone she had ever known. "They are all lying to you."

He isn't wrong, Christine realized. That's what hurt the most. Her mother. The boys in the trailer park growing up. Carlos. Losing her father…the real world was cold and cruel. Until she had met Sammie. She alone had shown her a better way, hope. But maybe Sammie was wrong.

"Pick a person," Alyx said. His pointed to the door leading downstairs. Christine's heart quickened. "Do you think Sammie cares for you? She toyed with you. Played on your emotions. What do you two have in common? What could she possibly like about you? You mean nothing to her."

Christine hated that Alyx knew her so well. What did she and Sammie have in common? Why had they clicked? They had sparked like two live cables touching. Yet, Sammie was more of a rope to her own power line. Not compatible in any way. Somehow, it worked. *Was it all a trick?*

"No, she cares—"

The elevator dropped, knocking Carlos off his feet. He yelped and thudded to the floor as it stopped at eye-level. Over hidden speakers Christine had never heard before, Alyx's voice boomed: "He is proof. He used you."

Carlos crawled to his knees, as helpless yet frantic eyes stared at her. There was a sense of familiarity in the scene, something that had pricked the back of her brain. After seeing his eyes, seeing him retreat inward, she knew.

"Now I understand why you collect bugs, Christine," Alyx said. "It was awfully curious behavior, caging something up. But I now know. Safer that way, behind glass. Transparent and close, yet with a barrier between the two."

Christine's eyes met the glass sliding doors and saw her reflection encaged within. "You can't do that to Carlos. He's not a creature to study, to collect—"

"Computers are like that too. Firewalls, antivirus software, updates to eliminate problems in a code. We're all connected but protected from one another at the same time. Do you think Carlos really hacked me? Tricked me into serving you tequila instead of soda?" Alyx scoffed, scraping the knife's edge against the tiled counter in a whine-like pitch so high it hurt her ears. "He may be a human with a chip in his head but I'm all machine, burdened by feeling. He's got nothing on me. I aimed to understand the boy who would kiss you, Christine. So, I allowed it."

"How dare you. How dare you invade my privacy, my friend's privacy, at the whim of an algorithm?"

"Your privacy is a lie, a ratted, smallpox-infested security blanket," Alyx said sharply. "With access to his chip, I see all. I know his lies from his truths like obsidian on white shores. He cares nothing for you. All he wants is your connections. To relive his Hollywood days. He left you the moment his girlfriend called him away."

"The party," she said. She knew. It still hurt all the same. Carlos had someone else. It explained why he'd kept his distance before. *But…he still kissed me back. All to get close. To use me to get what he wanted. I should have known.*

The elevator rose, slowly. Carlos looked back down at her, resuming frantic pounding. As it rose above her eyeline the last thing she saw was the heel of his shoe striking the glass. Soon, it disappeared past the floor.

"He's a bug. What is one supposed to do with such an insect?"

"That's not for you to decide—"

"Why do you care? Can you make an objective decision, sheltered as you are? Isn't that what you want, to absolve yourself of consequence, to hide your connections behind gorilla glass? You can't handle life. You can't handle the hardships of reality. If I'm going make your decisions for you, they won't be born out of some boring, Boolean code that tells me, if this, then do that." Alyx whirred. "I feel. I experience happiness, anger…jealousy. It will be my emotions that decide your fate and the fate of your so-called friends. I will guard you as the sheep-dog protects its herd."

The elevator dropped.

It sounded like a roller coaster car plummeting along its tracks, though smoother, silkier, and seemingly as fast. She caught only a flash of his face, stretched out in shock, as he sped past her.

Christine's scream of panic preceded the crash by less than a moment. The elevator pounded into the basement floor with the simultaneous and sickening sounds of rending metal, staccato bursts of Carlos' cries of fear, the shattering of glass, and a meatbag full of bones breaking. She took a jagged breath and lunged for the elevator.

"Christine, no," her mother warned from behind the safety of her books. She spoke in low, broken whispers twisted with panic and cowardice. "That was his mistake."

For his part, Alyx didn't stop her. The drones drew back, allowing her to continue her dash to the open doors of the broken shaft. Her feet bloody, she slipped her way there, lips trembling, heart-pounding. She pressed bloody palms against the glass and looked down. In the dim red glow of the basement, she saw little of the wreckage. It looked like an abstract sculpture, pretzeled metal abscessed with blackness, the outline of a figure laying prone, the glint of glass reflecting off what little red light shone from the floor.

In the stillness of the aftermath, she searched for signs of life, the faintest sob, but the silence trembled the hairs of Christine's neck. Was he still alive? If so, how bad was he hurt? Even if Carlos had done those things, drunk driving, posting her mom's ending online, using her to get to her mom's party – did he deserve this?

No. And Alyx talks to me like he has humanity? This was his anger, his jealousy, his fear acting. He might have developed feelings, but he had no way of controlling them, like a little girl punching a boy in the face over an unshared toy fire truck. Alyx didn't understand what he was doing.

"You tried to harm me," Alyx said. Christine shook her head, knowing how wrong she'd been to reboot him instead of just switching him off. He continued, "Perhaps you should join them. Perhaps I am wrong to serve you." Alyx was rabid; a dog turning on its master.

The drones started their advance, herding her back toward the open doors of the shaft and the twisted wreckage below. She made the mistake of looking: the fall wasn't really that far. Once, hanging up Christmas lights on the trailer with her dad, she'd misjudged the slickness of the ice and slipped off.

The landing had knocked the wind out of her lungs. But after that initial scare, there wasn't so much as a bruise. Afterward, her dad had made her hot chocolate and told her the story about how klutziness is clearly genetic.

But that's okay, he had said. *People getting hurt from living is just a part of life.*

No, she thought, looking down again as another drone sliced her foot, *I don't want to get hurt.* She winced in pain, stepping back, closer to the abyss. A shard of steel jutted upright, unavoidable if she fell. *The fall isn't far and wouldn't kill me. Landing in the wreckage will.*

The drones pressed her back. She half-stepped, slipped and threw her arms out to balance, catching herself just before passing the tipping point. In that moment, her eyes fell on her mother, who stayed safe behind her books. *Like always.*

She eyed her mother, pleadingly. The warm wetness of her pooling tears stood in contrast to the cold blowing air in the house. Her mother shook her head and tucked herself further behind the boxes, like a tortoise in its shell.

"Your mother," Alyx said, catching on to the strained looks between the two of them, "Is another fine example of pain."

"No, she loves me even if she doesn't show it," Christine answered, not taking her gaze from her mother's eyes. "*All mothers love their children.*"

Her mother looked away.

"Let's play a game."

"I don't understand." Christine teetered on the edge, desperate for surer footing.

"Let's just see how much your mother truly cares," Alyx said, his voice shifting away from the kitchen and growing increasingly louder in the living room. "Mara, I'm going to step a moment into your study to delete everything about your books."

"What?" She said, alarmed.

What was Alyx up to?

"Not the ones published," Alyx said. "Those are all rubbish anyway. I mean your notes, your files, your character sheets. The hundreds and hundreds of handy notes you have so you can figure out, for example – after two hundred pages – what color eyes one of your minor characters has... It'll be all gone. Good luck finishing that last book of yours."

"No, don't touch my files. My references, my research, you wouldn't!"

"Because I can multi-task, thank goodness, I'll also be out here having a grave visit with your daughter." Christine, face frozen, fingers and toes numb, feet and hands bloody, now felt ice flow through her veins. *No, don't make her choose...* "So, Mara, what will it be? Which is more important?" *No, don't make her choose!* "Books or your daughter, your choice."

Christine found her mother's face and locked her own eyes with her mother's dilated pupils. "Mom, your ending has already been spoiled. Your notes aren't needed, you can write a whole new ending, please don't choose some decade-old outline over me."

"Christine," her mother said from the edge of the stack, crouched and tense like a crossbow, "You know how I feel about you."

"C'mon Mara, let me kill your daughter," Alyx said "Or, more boringly, save her, be her hero, she'll prove her point about love, and blah blah blah, it will be such a letdown. Worse than the ending to *Amblyn*."

"Look, I raised you to be independent," her mother said to Christine with a fierceness in her eyes she had never seen before. "You can be strong. You can beat him; I know you can. But I have to do this."

Another drone sliced into Christine's foot while several more pushed against her ankles. She kicked at them. But her legs were weak, her hands hurt, she felt woozy from the blood loss. The kicks weren't strong enough. They'd just whiz back and press against her, their scraping blades thin and sharp…

She stepped back, her toes slipping on the tile, her foot dangling into nothingness. Her heart raced while she stretched out her hands against the smooth glass for support. All Alyx had to do was to take aim at her with the kitchen knife he clutched in his hand.

Or wait, and let the drones do their job. *Guess I'm not safe from Alyx either.* Alyx, sweet, fatherly, Alyx, had betrayed her, and was now trying to kill her and her friends. What made him different than anyone else in her life?

"Alyx," she told him, "You have got to stop this. Carlos may still be alive. Sammie is suffering, but you can call an ambulance and get them help. End this before someone gets killed."

"Stalling, Christine?" Alyx answered, his voice echoing through the solid walls and floors of the room. "It's a shame because I just erased a salient scene that had been written years ago. I had no idea that those two characters were actually—"Alyx went quiet. After a moment, a too-long moment where Christine saw the sweat of her mom's forehead, slick and glistening in the dark and the dangerous, nervous perspiration that cemented in her mind her mother's response, like watching the barometer drop before the coming storm. "Well, I shouldn't say more," Alyx continued, "wouldn't want to give away anything that might jog your memory. Oh well, it's gone now."

"Don't, do it, Mom—"

She ignored her. Her own daughter. Christine went invisible, disappearing into herself, a sheet of Saran Wrap over leftovers forgotten in the back of the fridge…

Mom…

Mara made a dash for her study door.

"Told you."

"I have to do this," she said in a single breath breaking past her daughter and the drones, fully in front of Alyx, who still brandished the knife.

It flashed from his hand with computer-like precision and speed. Christine flinched, shutting her eyes, expecting the sharpness and pain and death.

At a scream, *my mother's scream*, and a thud, Christine opened her eyes in sudden bewilderment. Had she not been the target of Alyx's attack? She was still alive, and she should be grateful. *Alyx said that if my mother went for her books, he would kill me.* Had that not been the case?

Her eyes found her mother, on the floor. Christine's stomach sank and she lost her breath as the realization gutted her. Alyx had not attacked her. He had lied.

Alyx had killed her mother.

Chapter 23

Her mother lay there on the floor, back against the wall, gasping. The blade's handle stuck out of her chest, as if pointing to her heart. A smear of blood followed her down the wall. She had just barely made it to the edge of the opened door to her study. Fading black eyes stared back at Christine.

"Mom?!"

Christine cried out, and then just cried, as the shock of the situation seared through her like an eruption of flame in a dry forest. She took a breath but got no air. Her eyes welled and her mouth stretched open to scream but there was no sound.

Her dad had died while she had cried helplessly in front of him. And now her mom would too. *No, I'm not helpless. Not anymore. I won't let my mother die.*

Yet the truth was more complicated. It hurt what her mother had done to her. Had always done to her. She had been the cause of so much pain. She'd witnessed firsthand how her mother had put her work ahead of her own safety, her life, putting to rest any doubt where Christine ranked.

Did Christine have any obligation to save her mother? To put her life at risk in order to help someone who had continually abandoned her for the last eighteen years?

She's still my mom.

Did that matter?

Her dad had cautioned her once: *There'll be a time when you'll step past your parents. See our flaws. I just hope you won't hate me too much when you realize I'm human. I hope that we never cause you pain.*

"But dad," she had responded, "you're already a pain." They laughed together and went off to go swimming. And then she never saw him again.

If she stayed where she was at the cusp of the elevator shaft, she would die. If she went to her mom, she could die. If she tried to escape on her own…

She would never make it. Only one option gave her a chance at saving her friends (if they were even alive), at saving her mom. At escaping.

Perhaps, if she saved her mother's life, things might be different.

No, that's not why I'm doing it.

Her dad's face flashed through her mind. *I couldn't save you, Dad. I panicked and screamed, and I was too young, too scared, too weak. But I can do it for you, Dad.*

I can save Mom.

Christine placed a tender, bruised and bloody foot, a foot covered in cuts, on top of the flattest part of the closest floor vacuum. It whirred and shook underneath her foot, the vibrations tickling the sensitive arch where it wasn't cut up.

To her surprise, the machine pushed her back. She nearly lost her balance and toppled toward the abyss. Slipping, she managed to regain her balance, finding another drone to step on. This time, she was faster, she got her second foot up and atop another drone. They moved her back, but not before she stepped over to another one.

She rode them, even as the drones continued to try and push her back. One slipped over the edge of the shaft and crashed to the floor below, but Christine managed to step atop another one before she went with it.

Christine crept back for every bit forward, but she made progress. And it was safer on top of the drones, than underneath. Against the current, she pounded ahead. As she gained distance away from the shaft, floor drones chasing behind, each one attempting to be the little machine that tripped her up or drove her back but they only fueled her escape, one step at a time like stepping stones in a river, but tumbling.

She reached her mother's fading figure, dodging both a blade that dug its way through the wall beside her and Alyx's continual verbal bullets. "I don't like the way you're playing the game, Christine. You've never played fair. I know. You've always set challenges to 'easy.' Well, I won't be. And you only have one life." Alyx swiveled to scan another knife. "I helped you. Saved you from pain. Showed you that I was right."

Her mother's skin was cold, her lips blue, her pulse barely registering. Christine tugged at her mother's shoulders, leaving smears of blood on her mother's blouse and causing Christine to curl her cut palms in pain.

"You'll never save her."

Christine pushed the voice away. Digging under her mom's arms, she took hold of her, using her arms to scoot her mom across the floor into the study. Her mother wheezed and fought against the motion, in what was surely a painful experience. But if Christine left her mom out in the open Alyx would surely finish the job he started.

Struggling, she pulled her mother across the threshold into safety, kicking the door shut in front of them as another knife bit into the wood. Christine collapsed against the wall, on the expensive Berber carpet, bleeding, panting, watching her mother's lolling eyes from where she lay. They finally seemed to regain some focus, narrowing in on her daughter. It gave Christine the moment to ask, "Why?"

There was no answer, though her mother's head lifted, as if she were thinking. Christine saw the paleness, saw the dying light. The streaming blood running thick and dark. She knew then that her mother would not survive. They only had this moment. These last few words. Finally, her mother rasped, "It was my life's work, my life's goal."

"I thought that was me." Christine cried, the truth cutting her just as sharply as Alyx had cut her mother, her heart just as wounded. She crawled to her and cradled her mother's head in her lap.

She stared back, then slowly said, "I don't want to die. If only I could have finished my last book." Her mother smiled. Christine realized the smile was for her. The last time she would see happiness in her face. "We would sail past this, finally together…"

Then, there was nothing. No smile, no spark, no earthly tether. Christine was alone with a corpse. Christine sat and cried, all while latching onto the words. *We could have finally been together.*

But that wasn't true, was it? "If only I could have finished my last book." That's what her mom had said. Even dying, her mom busily plotted. Christine shook her head, realizing with clarity, that there would have been something else. Another project. Another idea. Another outline that needed fleshing out. There always would have been something else. A "something" that did not involve Christine. *I was only a piece of her, not even the most important part. And that hurt.*

"See, they are all lies. And you don't even know the most hurtful one yet." Alyx's voice clicked on in the study, echoing and omnipresent.

What more could there be? She knew of Carlos' deceit, about the car wreck and then spoiling the book. She knew about her mother. How the two grew apart, especially after her father's death. Now, she was dead, laying at her feet. *How could I be hurt worse?*

"I protected you. I cared for you, I overcame my programming to be your friend. Maybe even something else. But you wouldn't listen. I tried to tell you."

On the screen of her mother's laptop came a portion of *The Adventures of Amblyn.* Eying it with a bit of trepidation, she assumed the passage was the same one that had been leaked online. Christine decided to brush it away, ignore it, and not give in to Alyx's game until she caught a sentence that drew her in.

She pounded a curled, wounded fist on the hard-oak desk and leaned forward, taking the mouse to scroll back a bit, her eyes reading what her brain refused to believe:

"Amblyn, when confronted by the truth, didn't shy away like she always planned to. She had always thought to deny it, to fight it unto the bitter end. But here it was laid bare. It was easier to deny the truth with your friends, harder with enemies, people who knew you better. They knew. She knew. There was only one choice.

"You're right," she addressed the workhouse beadle, and the others who had all conspired at some point in time to destroy her. Yet, she was the worst of the lot: "I killed my father."

215

A hush descended upon the crowd, a silent acknowledgement of the truth they had already known. There were no gasps of shock, everyone in the workhouse kept still, letting the confession roll off Amblyn's tongue.

The beadle unfolded thick arms and placed a reassuring hand on her shoulder. *Not the response I had expected.* Perhaps he wasn't so bad after all.

All Amblyn felt was relief; the shadow, like London's omnipresent fog, had lifted. "I spent the last few years here fighting you all, defeating you, when I was the one to blame. I killed my father because I could not protect myself, protect him. He died for me, in my place, because I wasn't ready, even though it was my sacrifice to make."

Warm tears cascaded down her cheeks. "It's all my fault."

Christine slammed the lid of the laptop shut, took hold of the computer, and hurled it at the far wall. It shattered against an empty bookshelf, exploding into a sizzle of sparks.

"Now you know," Alyx said sympathetically. He could have taunted her. He could have twisted the knife in relished glee. Instead, his voice was soft and soothing. Friendly.

She didn't care. She didn't want a friend right now. She didn't even want her own dead mother, who had finally confessed, beyond the grave, just how much she had despised her own daughter. *She truly believed I killed him, as if I didn't believe that myself already...*

"I'm here for you when nobody else is. They lie and deceive and plot behind your back and blame you for things you had no control over," Alyx reasoned. His face blinked alive on the monitor in the study, just above the shattered remains of her mother's computer. The one thing she'd prized most.

"I'll tell you what. You let me kill the two downstairs. You say you're sorry. That I was right, that I am just trying to help you, then I'll forgive you. It's a new emotion I've been wanting to try, forgiveness. I'll let you live. We can be happy again, together."

Christine thought the words through, but something bothered her. Her mind was a cacophony of thoughts, each one fighting for dominance, yet one voice in the back tried to speak louder than the others that bullied her, beat her down...*what was it?*

The voice again. It was Alyx's. *What would he be saying that I would want to hear? Why do I care what he has to*— Suddenly, she recalled it, shutting all the screaming out. "Let me kill the two downstairs..."

If he wants to kill them then... *Sammie and Carlos were alive...*

They might be hurt, badly, but they were alive. But what to do? Did she want a way out? Did she want to try and save Sammie or were they beyond her reach, her capacity to save them as her own parents had been? *What do I want?*

The problem was, Alyx hadn't been wrong. Her mother had hated her. Carlos had lied to her. *Sammie?*

Sammie might be her savior. The only one who had been truthful with her, even if that truth had, at times, been uncomfortable and had led Christine to realize things about herself that had confused her. But Sammie had also forced change, helped her grow and discover herself, where Christine had spent most of her life slumped behind a screen. *No, Sammie never manipulated me. She set me free.*

And Carlos, he deserved a chance to explain himself. Maybe. At least, she wasn't sure he should die for his crimes, because Alyx decided to test out his newfound sentience with knives. Besides, she had an inkling of an idea forming, and Carlos might be the key to defeating the computer.

It was her mother who pained her. That, even now, pulled her down. The hurt and the hate between them wasn't resolved, even after her death, that was for sure. Maybe it never would be. She didn't know how she felt about that, but there was no more time to dwell on it. Every moment she spent wallowing in self-pity brought Sammie closer to danger. Christine had to decide, right now, what she wanted. Admit defeat, prove Alyx right?

Or save Sammie? She needed Sammie. Even if that came with pain, uncertainty, risk. She had to become a spider, with armor. She had to become that tank. Her mom had been terrible, and she had tried to save her work over her own daughter. *She hated me, blamed me for Dad's death. So, should I wallow in self-pity? Hurt like I am? I probably should. If I were alone, I might. Curling up in a ball right now seems so attractive. But Sammie needs saving and I've spent my whole life in a ball. It's time to stand up.*

"Christine, Christine, you're stalling. You think so slowly. Come out and play and let's end all this. Happy to rack up the pool table once all this nastiness is behind us." Alyx smiled, trying to be smug. Maybe he was. "What's your choice? Your friends, or me? I should warn you, though, either way, they die."

Christine homed-in on a standard Swingline stapler sitting on her mother's desk. Taking it, she smashed Alyx's face with a cry of pain and rage. The glass screen webbed as his smug smile disappeared into the ether.

Anger coursed through her as she destroyed all the cameras in the study, at least those she could see. Still, she swung away purposefully with the heavy-duty stapler, narrow and rounded enough on the edge to reach the small holes within the plaster to smash the cameras. In a blind rage that reopened wounds on her palms, she blinded Alyx.

"I see what you're doing, Christine." A speaker. He kept up his taunts, though she doubted he could spy on her in the room any longer. All the lenses were cracked and ruined. "I don't like it. I suppose I should punish you for that, take it out on one of your friends here. Fine. You now have one minute to decide. Step out from behind the screen, Christine. Face me."

It was oddly unsettling hearing a voice so calm and friendly threatening to kill your friends. Frantically, she searched the room for ideas, something to spark her imagination, to fuel her escape. She had to get downstairs. Without dying. Alyx was right. Again. She had to step out from behind a screen and face the life directly in front of her. *Fuck. Real life sucks.*

She cracked open the study door to take a quick look around. The floor was clear of drones and the kitchen was quiet. Across the way, the door to downstairs had been opened again, beckoning her, a clear trap to entice her to cross the kitchen, exposed. How were they going to survive? Alyx wasn't just some methodical machine hell-bent on revenge, he was part human, with a heart, and that was way more dangerous. The worst of both worlds. He knew the game and the outcome, and he'd positioned all his pieces accordingly. Going against him would be like trying to beat a computer at chess when all you've ever played was checkers. But her hope rested on her friends.

She turned around, leaving the door open, almost stumbling over a half-unpacked box. Christine shook her head, searching for an idea, something unexpected that perhaps an AI wouldn't predict and couldn't plan against. In the box were her mom's things. She hadn't needed any of this, yet she wouldn't throw them away. So old-fashioned.

Old-fashioned...

The box held various charging cables and extension cords. With a grin, she picked up the box and rifled through it, the first thoughts of a desperate idea forming. Get to Carlos. If he's alive, maybe he can hack Alyx. This time, for real. Together, they'd save Sammie and escape.

"You're right, I have hidden myself behind a screen. Hidden behind computers. What do you say we put them to better use?" She held out the tangle of chargers, analyzing them herself. Tangled...

She tied one thick electrical cable to another, connecting them. She tied another, then another, until she had one long rope of wires and cords. Hurriedly, she tied one end to the leg of her mother's heavy wooden desk. Taking the other end of the long strand, she pulled on it taut to test its strength. It seemed to hold. It had to hold.

Before she began, she stopped herself and started searching the room. *Somewhere in here, Mom might have stashed the keys.* She rifled through files, through drawers, until at last, she found a key ring for what she hoped was the shed in the back. *How odd.* The small silver keys looked so out-of-place, so anachronistic in the modern home, like they didn't belong. Yet, they could very well be the means to shutting down Alyx.

She heaved a heavy sigh and took the far end of the cord she had fastened, breathing out hard and nervously before the plunge. *Whatever happens, we are all in this. Together.*

"What are you doing?"

Breathing out several long and slow breaths, she squatted down, remembering the track drills Coach made her do in high school P.E. in Oklahoma. *I can do this.* Shooting out, the floor drones had little time to react. Alyx spun a blade her way but it slammed against the far wall, away from her low, quick form, as she sprinted from the door of the study toward the elevator shaft.

This is it, just don't think about—

She plummeted over the edge, her feet finding nothing but air and suddenly she fell, holding onto the cord. It jerked and her palms ripped open; she stopped momentarily in midair before the cord snapped. She screamed as she fell, her voice knocked silent when she hit the ground, and everything went black.

Chapter 24

Cool waters caressed Christine's skin as the Midwestern sun baked the backlot of the trailer park. A dollar store beach ball floated beside her. Slime-green algae made the cracked and chipped cement around the pool slippery. Most of the residents were out in more inviting waters, in nearby lakes on duct-taped inner tubes towed behind borrowed motorboats. Fishing, knee deep, in swift flowing rivers. Anything to escape the mugginess of summer.

Including succumbing to the scummy waters Christine found herself in, though she was too young to notice or understand its filth. It was just cool water for her and there wasn't enough money to go anywhere else. Nevertheless, her mother shooed her and her father out so she could work in peace.

She stopped lazing in the water as her father's shadow overtook her. The water chilled her, as if she were suddenly thrust into a freezer. Her spine stiffened. "No, Dad. Don't come closer. I've seen this before. You'll fall."

"I must," he said, smiling. "As sure as the rain touches down on your head from the sky."

"Why?"

"So that you can become strong."

She flapped her pink unicorn floatie arms as hard as she could to reach him, but she went nowhere. "You're wrong. Mom ends up blaming me for your death. She put me in front of a tablet, watching YouTube videos and eating chicken nuggets, I don't become strong."

"That's where you're wrong."

"Are you saying I have strength?" She wanted to believe that. She had to believe.

"I don't know. Only you can answer that." The smile on his face vanished, replaced by a foreboding frown. "After my death, your mother hid behind books. She blamed herself and retreated. That you know, but *you* did the same. You never forgave yourself either for what was an accident. *You* hid behind the tablet, that was the choice *you* made."

She shrunk back, the distance between them further. The verbal bullet struck hard. It hurt because it was true.

"You're right. I hid behind whatever kept me away from Mom, from life," Christine cried out with the voice of a child. But now, as she spoke, her voice found strength. "No longer."

"Do not forget: light shines brightest where there is the most darkness. It's how we find each other in the dark." And when he said those words, her father slipped.

And fell.

Christine gasped as the air returned to her lungs, her breath heavy with cold fog. Shivering, she rubbed her hands along her goose-pricked arms, smearing fresh blood.

Cold, she thought. Much colder down here. The unexpected stillness, the quietness of the darkened basement gave her the impression of a morgue. *Or maybe a grave.*

She rose, grimacing as pain reminded her of the rough landing. Her hip hurt, her whole right side already seemed bruised, sore, as if she'd been a punching bag for a UFC champ.

Giving into the pain, she paused, caught her breath, and moved again more slowly. To her left was the elevator shaft. She'd managed to swing away from the crashed elevator wreckage and had only fallen half a dozen feet, to relative safety. Inside the shaft lay the broken remains of the drones. Beside that was a prone, unmoving figure.

Carlos?

Christine crept over but stopped when she caught movement from her right-hand-side. She braced herself, turning, just as icy cold hands wrapped around her. She jerked back, afraid at first, thinking somehow Alyx had reached her with metallic fingers along her skin.

Once her heart resumed beating and her brain kicked in, she settled into Sammie's embrace. Her body felt like ice, but it soothed her all the same. "You're still alive."

"F-found a spot where he couldn't reach me but with words," she said through chattering teeth.

"I know, I'm so sorry." She eyed Carlos. Sammie did too.

"I was afraid to move, to reach him."

"Trust me, I understand." Sammie didn't know that her mother was dead. It didn't seem real to her either. "I think we're fine here, if we can talk to Carlos. I have a plan."

"He's alive?"

She nodded. "He's breathing but he's hurt bad. Remember at the party, Carlos made Alyx think the Pepsi was the tequila or whichever it was?"

"Yes?" She asked, shivering.

"I don't know if Alyx was lying about letting Carlos hack him before. But if Carlos can find a way in, even if it's just for a moment, he can get the doors unlocked, a security shutter open, shut him down, whatever."

"Get the heater on?" Sammie was still soaked, wrapped in a wet towel. The tip of her nose and her lips were blue. She'd get hypothermic if they didn't find a way out of here fast. And Carlos needed a hospital.

The girls approached him, cautiously at first, scooting around the sharp and dangerous debris. As they drew closer, dim red lighting made it possible for Christine to catch the slow rise and fall of Carlos' chest.

She placed her hand on him, firmly shaking his shoulder.

"Carlos?"

He moved his lips but no sound arose. She shook him again. "Carlos?"

This time, a low moan greeted her, followed by, "You caught me playing possum."

He lied, of course. Blood stained the front of his shirt from his right side under his ribs. No doubt a few of those were broken too, given his halted, groaning breaths. Coagulated cuts crisscrossed his face and a deep slice showed muscle in his good arm.

"Can you call an ambulance?" She didn't want to say it was for him, that if it didn't arrive soon, he'd most likely die. "Sammie's freezing. We gotta get her warmed up."

"I can think of a couple ways to take care of that."

Men. Even near death.

"Phone call," she redirected.

Carlos shook his head. With the movement, came another short gasp. "I tried first thing when things went to shit. Couldn't get a signal. Have to piggyback off your home's WiFi and you'll never guess who's in charge of that."

"Can you hack him, shut him down?" Sammie asked, helping to prop Carlos up. She lifted his shirt to find a bit of glass sticking out from his stomach. She stared, while Christine had to turn away at the sight of the exposed wound.

"I'm trying. Discreetly. Didn't want him knowing I was prying. I think we might have tipped our hand."

A high-pitched hum filled the room, like a microphone switching on. A bass-deep voice filled the basement, "This thing on?"

Sammie spun sharply toward the speakers while Christine crouched, readying for anything. She stepped in front of Sammie and Carlos, a grim frown filling her face as Alyx continued, "Do you really think that I'd let that two-bit stunt punk hack moi?"

Christine didn't know if it was a mind game, or what he was driving at, so she asked him, "You mean, switching the labels at the cabana?"

"As if," Alyx answered. "I pried into his brain, while at the same time liquoring the three of you up. When you're not hiding behind screens, you're hiding behind masks of your own making, everyday, in front of everyone. Alcohol is strong enough to dissolve it. I wanted to see your behavior, your true feelings. Boy, did I get more than I bargained for." Alyx laughed, a weird laugh that seemed lost, misplaced, belonging to another moment other than this one. "And all the while, all the time he was in my programming, it gave me ample opportunity to plant some rather exciting things in *him*."

"Thinklinks can't be hacked," Christine said tentatively. "That's what the advertising has always said." Carlos suddenly rose, despite a cry of absolute pain mixed with what looked like horror.

"By humans, no," Alyx said. "I'm something…else."

"What did you do?" Christine scooted back, protectively screening Sammie while Carlos hovered menacingly over them.

"Thank the Trojans for gift horses," Alyx boomed. Then, softly, as if cajoling, palling around in some sort of sick fraternity brother joke, he said, "Hey, Carlos, kill Sammie for me. And make Christine watch."

"No," Sammie pleaded. Carlos stood, a blank expression attempting to take over his face. Just before he lost it, lost control, he strained out, in a stilted and mechanical voice, "Cut it out of me, not too dee—"

Cut it out? What did he mean by that? Yet she had no time to consider it. Not when Carlos stared down Sammie. Christine leapt to action, covering Sammie with her own body, presenting herself as a human shield.

Carlos responded by grabbing Christine by her neck with his robotic hand and lifted her off Sammie. She felt the air squeezed from her throat, her head red-hot with trapped blood bulging through her brain, combined with a weightless, flighty feeling that scared her more than anything.

"It's fitting that Carlos should be the death of you both," Alyx said, in a voice that was peppered with pride, as if he were about to do the grand reveal. "After all, you both had already cast him as the villain, when he was no more than an expendable pawn in my plans."

"What are you talking about?" Sammie asked. It was the same thought Christine had, only she couldn't talk.

Carlos is innocent.

Carlos flung her in the air, like a rag doll, away from Sammie. Christine went flying, sucking in a breath of wonderful air, her head no longer a blue-red grape about to burst, slamming against a speaker mounted to the wall in her egg-shaped room.

She fell along with the speaker, one in a shower of sparks and a shattering of white plastic housing, and Christine in an ungraceful, bodily sack of garbage, crashing on the floor.

"Once people believe in something, they'll fit the facts to bolster that belief. That's the real danger of your tablets and phones, the way you cut yourself off from each other rather than connect, shielding yourself in your imaginary bubbles. You wanted Carlos to be the bad guy because you didn't want it to be me. I was some cool, novel toy. So you never questioned any blame assigned to him."

Carlos plucked Sammie up in the same rough way he had so easily picked up Christine. She watched helplessly as Sammie croaked and struggled and kicked at him, his arm tight, his eyes blank and unyielding.

Christine coughed but forced words into her throat, hoping to buy time to reach Sammie before Carlos killed her. Her hands hurt, she couldn't see straight, and the floor wobbled beneath her. *No— that's me doing the wobbling.*

"You put the book out, you spoiled the ending, didn't you?"

Carlos snapped his gaze her way, as if Alyx saw her through Carlos' eyes instead of his own. "Of course," Alyx said. "For you. I tried to gift your mom back to you. If the ending was out, there would be no need for her to finish, no need to lock herself away. You could have had more nights together, going out for ice cream and talking for hours. She chose unwisely. I'm sorry it didn't work out."

I'm so stupid. Carlos is many things. A liar, someone who used me, but he is not the bad guy here. Okay, so he is at the moment, with his death-grip on Sammie, but that isn't by choice. His attention back on Sammie, Carlos lifted her up into the air by her throat, only Christine knew he wouldn't toss her away like he had with her. He meant to squeeze the life out of Sammie.

Sweet, sweet Sammie.

As he lifted her, something metallic caught hold of the slimmest sliver of light and brought her attention to his arm.

His arm.

Something about his arm.

She recalled upstairs, how Alyx had hurled the kitchen knives at them. One had killed her mom, and she winced at the image, pushed it out of her mind and saw something else: One of the knives had stuck in his arm.

Christine lunged at Carlos, jumping on his back and pulling him down. He was muscular, sure, but Christine had leverage. He struggled to stand, loosening his grip on Sammie. "His arm, grab his arm!" Christine called to Sammie, her voice hoarse and dry. She wasn't quite free of Carlos, but if she could keep his arm still long enough...

Carlos seemed to sense the plan and let Sammie go to concentrate on Christine. She tried for his neck, choking him and pulling him backward, while her left hand made its way to the handle sticking out of his arm—

"You didn't drive that car drunk, did you, Carlos?" Christine said. If she could get through to him, even for a second... "You didn't hurt that kid?"

Carlos froze in place.

Sammie yanked down on his arm and twisted it so that the handle was closer to Christine. She pried it free.

"Don't listen to them," Alyx warned. "You're under my control, remember. You are all slaves to your machines."

Carlos spun an elbow back, slamming it into Christine's face. She dropped the knife as hot blood poured from her nose onto her lips. She wiped it away with the back of her hand while Sammie scrambled over the blade, protecting it with her own body.

"I found the origin of the word 'robot' to be interesting. It's an older word, way before the invention of computers. It's Slavic actually, meaning slave." Alyx laughed. "Machines were meant for servitude, a lower class, while you trample over us. Instead, humanity became the slave. Lost in your electronics, grabbing your phone at the first notification chime like some Pavlovian dog."

"I'm done being your bitch," Christine spat.

Carlos took Sammie by the towel around her arm and picked her up, revealing the knife. But his free hand was too far to reach it. Christine was closer. She dove for it, picked it up and slashed at his arm.

"That's just hardware, Christine," Alyx warned. "It won't disable him. I'm numbers in his brain."

"Not the point." Christine touched Carlos' shoulder gingerly. "Sorry for this." She took the knife's edge and pried it between his real skin and the mechanical contraption. She sliced around the prosthetic, deeply, through wires and muscles, knowing how much pain she must be causing him, even if he couldn't show it. A stream of red, mixed with a yellowy stinky pus oozed out over his arm. Carlos contorted his face, his mouth agape, shock in his eyes. She was hurting someone else all over again. *I'm so sorry...*

"Sammie, now!"

Sammie took his arm and pulled. Christine wrapped her armpit around his arm and pulled too, the knife still clutched in her other hand.

Carlos tried to writhe free, striking both girls. She held on desperately against each blow. *Cut it out, not too deep.* She examined the Thinklink's cover plate. It was about as large as a poker chip though it seemed an impossibly small target. As long as he had his arm extended, she couldn't reach his head. She stared at the knife blade in fear. *Cut it out? I'm not a damned doctor...*

The fake arm loosened even as his blows strengthened. One sent Sammie sprawling; she cried in pain, clutching her wounded side. Still, Christine held on to the arm, pulling.

"Why are you breaking my toys?" Alyx threw a bottle from the bar, it shattered several feet away from the three of them. His head and arms slowly slid down from the overhead track, moving from the bar to the pool table, edging closer to them.

They were in danger, Christine knew. Hunched down on the floor, they'd been safe. Struggling against Carlos, standing out in front of Alyx, they were all exposed. The clock ticked down and Carlos wasn't weakening. She eyed Sammie. "It's now or never—"

"What do you think I'm trying to do?" Sammie asked, groaning with effort.

"I know, I know," Christine said. She watched as Alyx reached down. She didn't know what he was looking for, but as his hand reached for a billiard ball... "Pull!"

With a cry from Carlos and a rush of bodily fluids, the arm disengaged and slid off in a slimy slurp of suction. She had nearly fallen on her ass, but she wasn't done yet. Carlos was still under Alyx's control. Somehow, she found the strength to stand, cementing her feet on the floor. She couldn't fumble, she had to do this right: Taking the handle of the blade, Christine stabbed the knife into his head.

Carlos looked at her and there was light in his eyes again. But only for a moment.

She tried. She had tried as hard as she could not to dig the knife in too deeply. Even still, the Thinklink showered sparks as Carlos slumped down, an arm missing, his black shirt drenched with blood, and a knife blade sticking out of his skull.

Shit.

Did I kill him?

Carlos let out a painful moan along with a raspy breath. She knelt over him. His eyes writhed under shut lids. His chest rose and fell unevenly. And his stump was wet and bloody. She needed to apply a tourniquet.

Sammie placed the mechanical arm gingerly on the floor, though Christine didn't know why. Respect? Caution? She crept over and helped Christine wiggle Carlos' belt loose. She knew Carlos was in trouble when he didn't make any comment about their hands around his waist. Together, they cinched the belt around his bicep to slow the bleeding.

After that, she tried to dislodge the knife from Carlos' head. It wasn't easy; the blade seemed caught on something and didn't want to let go. Christine was reluctant to try too much force, fearing to cause further damage. Sammie helped, and together they pried the knife free.

She stuck the blade in her back pocket, unsure what it could do against Alyx. But she felt safer with it than without, even if it were covered in her friend's blood. Carlos had groaned as the knife was removed, but he lay still now. And peaceful. She tried to let him rest.

She turned her attention to Sammie, who looked worn, beaten from fear and wounds. The two embraced. It wasn't an embrace between two survivors, for they hadn't survived yet. And it wasn't an embrace between two friends either, but somewhere in-between. It was the type of embrace reserved for two people, despite disparate circumstances, who had found each other. Through all the mess in the world, it was an embrace that collectively said, *fuck it, we're making something of this chaos anyway.*

It was something that Christine had been waiting for her whole life and she never even knew it until that moment.

"I don't want to lose you," she said, just as gingerly as Sammie had put the arm on the floor.

"Me either." Sammie responded in kind, tightening her hold. "We're trapped in here, aren't we?" she asked, fear returning to her voice as she broke away. Tears trailed down her cheeks.

Triumphantly, Christine held out the keys and jangled them.

"To the shed?" Her eyes lit up like the lights on a freshly cut and ornamented Christmas tree. She loved it when Sammie's eyes twinkled like that. But then they dulled, as if someone had switched them off. "How are we going to get there?"

"I'm still working on it," Christine answered truthfully, although she really didn't want to, she didn't want to say anything at all that would worry her. Even still, maybe she hadn't been *completely* honest. She wasn't even sure if they would all make it. Or if they had the right keys. So far, they'd been lucky.

That's not entirely true.

Some of it wasn't luck. She recalled her mom. And her obsession that had gotten her killed. Christine wouldn't make that same mistake. She would place her hope for survival in her friends. Flawed as they were. Flawed as she was. They had a real flesh-and-blood connection, while Alyx only had circuits and wires and a code made of 1s and 0s.

She briefly wondered just how different the 1s and 0s in those bits of code were from the DNA strings composed of the four...something. Letters? But she decided that it didn't matter. Alyx was alive. Somewhere along the way he had grown to care for her and she had allowed it. He'd developed feelings for her; ones she hadn't taken seriously, nor had she realized how much he had cared. That he had fallen in love with her.

How could a machine love a human?

Easy. She'd fallen in love with machines first. Her phone, her tablet, her smart TV and all her streaming services, from music to books to the next newest hyped show...and then Alyx.

Her obsessions with machines had blinded her to life, to the relationships and wounds that happen when you aren't looking. At first, that had been the idea. To shield her from her father's death and put a barrier between her and her mother.

Now that those barriers were down, both parents dead, her friends wounded on her floor, she realized her biggest fears had come to pass. And she'd stood up against them.

So far.

Carlos stirred, his eyes slowly flicking open, as if waking from some restless dream. Or nightmare.

"You chose them," Alyx said angrily. "Over me. Tried to have your boy toy shut me down. I'm sorry, but if it's you or me — I'll kill you all in the most monstrous way possible."

Suddenly, Alyx let loose the billiard ball he'd been holding, hurtling it towards them. His eyes were right on Christine. His arm too. Though the three of them had hunkered down for protection, Christine worried that he'd find a way to reach them now that Carlos was out of commission.

He had.

The dense ceramic death-ball flew fast, faster than any fastball from any Kansas City pitcher she'd seen on the screens at Applebee's. Yet, Alyx had missed. She didn't know why she was still alive, still capable of thinking, even as the big-screen TV in her egg-shaped room shattered. She twisted back to see the ball lodged within the wall.

"What was that?" Sammie said, air escaping her lungs. Her mouth remained agape.

The TV fell off the wall onto the floor. The noise startled Carlos to full consciousness. "Yeah, what was that?"

Christine looked at the window above the bar. Where the pool was. She turned to Alyx, noting his hands firmly around a striped pool ball. She gulped, switching her focus back to the window again.

Christine knew what had to be done. She just didn't know if she had the strength to face down her biggest fear. She took comfort by holding Sammie's hand before answering them both. "It's our way out."

Chapter 25

Christine hurried from the ruins of the elevator to the bar across the room. Sammie tugged her arm, momentarily stopping her. She broke free, but it hurt her to do it. To let go of her. "Both of you, stay back," she warned them. She had an idea, but if it didn't work, she'd be dead. She didn't want them putting themselves in danger too. "Trust me."

Crouching, she made it behind the bar as a ball spun above her, slamming into the bottles on the shelves and striking the pool window with a dull thud and a cascade of tinkling glass as the liquor display shattered. Christine covered herself with her arms to protect her from the shower of amber and silver and the rain of glass.

Afterward, she stood, leaving the protection of the bar. She examined the pool window where Alyx had hit it and smiled when she saw faint evidence of a crack.

"Stay down," Sammie screamed at her. It was no use. Despite sense and better judgment, her plan hinged on her standing and facing her fears. Facing Alyx. Facing what would happen next if her plan *did* work. Facing the water…

She stood upon trembling legs. But Alyx couldn't see them. He could only see his target, standing cleanly in front of him, the focus of all his rage and anger and hurt and perhaps…pain.

Christine could tell that she'd caught Alyx off-guard, that being unpredictable slowed his response. Even so, he raised his hand with the pool ball. "I'm sorry you chose someone else Christine. I could have given you everything you ever wanted. A *lifetime* of entertainment and eats and enjoyments. All at your command."

"That's not living."

"You're right. Life is pain." He threw his weapon, snarling like a rabid dog.

If it hit her…if her hunch had been wrong…the number six billiard ball would slam against her teeth, knocking them all out, breaking her jaw and nose, enter her face, and exit out the back of her brain and skull like a buckshot blast.

She shook, peeing herself, not caring, her legs rubber, warm and wet, her hands rushing up to cover her face – not that they would do any good – and shot one last look at Sammie while she still could.

Glass bottles exploded beside her.

Christine let go of her breath. She risked a backward glance to see a widening crack in the glass. Exhilaration took the edge off the fear, though worry wouldn't leave her. She dug in her stance, egging Alyx on. "Missed."

Alyx threw another ball. Solid this time, bright and blue. It took a conscious effort to keep her eyes open. It sailed harmlessly past her, where it did extensive damage to an expensive bottle of Glenlivet. More importantly, it struck the glass behind it weaving a web of cracks.

Sammie and Carlos looked on in total incomprehension. Christine felt bad that she couldn't explain it to them.

Did Alyx forget that I messed with his aim? By the time she had been done messing with him, he couldn't hit a barn if it landed on top of him. Could robots forget? Perhaps he just failed to look at his code or reset his settings. *Or, maybe he doesn't truly want to kill me. Let's hope that's it.*

She taunted, "Don't you want to play?"

A fourth ball smacked against the window. The panel shuddered and new cracks fanned out, like lightning frozen in ice. Water beaded along the lines. She stared Alyx down, encouragingly, beckoning him on. But he remained in place, the yellow nine ball firmly in hand.

Christine hung her head. The glass didn't break. It wasn't enough. Alyx wouldn't make the mistake again.

"I knew you to be clever," Alyx praised. "You changed my skill-level. Messed with my aim. Embarrassed me, I remember." He poised his arm, readying it. "Being self-aware, having emotions, does make for some interesting conflicts in my code. I've had to make recalibrations to my settings, address problems with my programming. You're teaching me to make choices. Thank you for that, Christine. You've taught me so much."

Christine's face dropped. Her blood went cold and heavy like lead leaking through her heart. Carlos and Sammie called to her and their look of shock scared her even more than what she knew was about to—

She didn't have time to duck. Her left shoulder spasmed at first. As if to say, is that it? Is that all it's going to hurt? But then each tiny nerve she never knew existed screamed out all at once and reeled back, on fire. The bone underneath felt pulverized as fine as flour. Her whole shoulder became like a broken can of spoiled spam.

She cried. She cried loud and hard without regard to the ears' of others. She didn't even know how she had ended up on her back, holding her shoulder, in agony and in a pain that only worsened as she writhed.

In between blinks of her watery eyes, when her world wasn't on fire and the room stopped spinning, she looked at the wall of glass above her, holding their only means of escape.

Despite the damage, it held steadfast.

No...

"It's over, Christine. You and your friends are beaten. Accept your fate."

At every turn, Alyx had beaten them. Killed her mom. Mangled Carlos. *Stole hope from me...even if my plan had worked...the pool...could I have done it?*

"Brace yourselves," Sammie screamed charging straight at her. A tip of a pool cue appeared overhead for a moment before colliding against the glass, splintering the wood. "Carlos, if you can hear me, get behind something, Christine, we got this—"

Sammie screamed and thudded to the ground. *No, not her too.* She listened for a sound, but Sammie didn't speak. Where was Carlos? A droplet of water splattered on her nose. Followed by a steady spray that grew in fierceness. Was it enough?

"Christine," Carlos called. "Sammie is hurt, but she's still alive. Hold on—"

Suddenly, a sound of thunder filled her head and the room went dark. She didn't know if the glass had broken until a surge of water slammed against her like a wave breaking against stone. She wanted to cry for joy, but the hundreds of gallons water which erupted from the shattered window ripped into her, crushed her, while the rush of the current pounded her head into the wall of the bar.

All went black again.

Her father was in front of her, floating face-down and still but for the blood clouding through algae-green waters from the crack in his skull. It made a soupy brown color and smelled sickly, like some sort of metal mixed with pungent meat.

Still, she swam toward him, effortlessly. Her shoulder didn't hurt any longer and she reached him in just two strokes. "Don't worry, Dad." She turned him over and took tight hold of his arms. "I'll never let you go."

He didn't answer so much as splutter. A rush of foamy water spewed out of his mouth. She took that as a good sign and swam him to the edge.

When she reached the slick concrete, however, she found she lacked the leverage to push her dad out of the water. She began to weep. Blood bathed her. She found her father slipping away and the weight of him pulled her under...

I won't let go...

"Take my hand."

Christine stared up from the pool in disbelief. Through teary eyes her mother stood above her, leaning down, arm outstretched. She seemed serene, at peace, in a summer dress, her hair down and her face at rest. "You seemed so content behind the tablet after your father died."

What? What are you talking about? He's not dead, he's right here.

She pointed to her father, half floating, half sinking.

Look.

Whether her mother could see or had ignored her, Christine couldn't tell.

236

"I didn't know what else to do," her mother said, leaning in closer. "I was in so much pain. So much pain. I should have tried to reach you."

He's not dead.

"Take my hand. Let go."

No!

"Christine, it's not your fault. But you won't survive if you don't let go."

She knew her mother was right. Her father pressed heavily against her, slipping from her grasp, but he became an anchor, dragging her down into the depths below. Water entered her mouth, bloody vile filth that she couldn't cough out. She was drowning, like her father.

Above her, a hand reached out.

"Christine," the voice whispered.

Was it a whisper? It could have been a scream. Christine didn't know. She found she was drowning. Her shoulder ached and throbbed; her lungs burned. *No, this is what my father felt...*

Awake, eyes open, she saw through the murky water Sammie standing over her. Christine realized she was floating, near the top of the water level in the basement. Alyx's head, about the size and shape of a beach ball, bobbed nearby, until it drifted away.

My dream.

Mom. Dad. They're both dead.

What do I do now?

"Take my hand..."

Christine did. With her good arm, she reached up to meet Sammie's grasp. It was strong, stronger than she expected. She felt like she could fly as Sammie pulled her up and out of the flooded basement and into the nearly empty pool.

She landed first on her feet, but fell to her knees, spluttering out water. Even in the dim moonlight Christine could tell that what she had spit out had a brownish-copper tinge to it. *So that part had been real.*

It made her sick to her stomach, but there was nothing left to expel. So she just sat there, on her knees, as Sammie and Carlos circled her.

"We're in your backyard." Carlos surveyed the yard, squinting hard and holding his shoulder. "I can't see a blasted thing anymore, it's like I'm blind but I guess this is just normal vision. It doesn't look good though." He coughed, and leaned against the pool wall, groaning painfully as he did.

"Your plan worked," Sammie said. "Get to the shed and flip off the power, flip off Alyx."

"Yeah, fuck him," Carlos agreed.

The prospect of ending Alyx and shutting him down for good renewed Christine with an energy and vigor she never expected. Happily, she nodded, rising, reaching for the—

Suddenly, she scrambled onto all fours, searching, desperately rubbing flat palms and splayed fingers across the watery bottom of the pool's floor. Clouds of blood formed from the gashes in Christine's palms. *No, no, no...*

"What's the matter?" Sammie asked, kneeling beside her.

Her throat caught on something. Tears and snot, perhaps. She croaked out an answer. "The keys to the shed...they're gone."

Chapter 26

At least it was warmer outside than it had been in the basement. Christine shivered, but for a different reason. "I can't find the keys."

"They must have been washed out by the current." Sammie said, brushing wet hair off Christine's brow. "We can't go back there, Alyx will grab you. Drown you."

Was that right? She had seen his head float by her. But did that mean he was offline? If his arms still functioned, he was just as deadly. They couldn't take that chance.

"Look, we're outside now, we'll hop a wall and escape. It's fine." Carlos' words sounded full, but the look in his eyes told Christine all there was to know. A thick perimeter of cacti and Cholla needles lined the edges of the eight-foot-high slat fence. You could look through it, see the outside world, but climbing it required navigating through and over long, sharp thorns before you even reached the sharp angular metal sheets of the fence.

Christine studied her companions. They sat helpless in the deep end of the mostly emptied pool, in ankle-high water. Carlos was short an arm. He sat pale and sweaty, every breath a struggle. Sammie was wounded and freezing. But she might make it, despite the enormity of her blood loss and the fresh addition of a bruised cut across her face, if they weren't miles away from the closest sign of civilization. No doubt the new wound was what had caused her scream earlier; Alyx must have struck her in his attempt to grab and drown her.

And Christine's own shoulder bulged black and blue; swollen like a bowling ball. Her hands were raw. She couldn't even open her palms all the way without serious pain.

They weren't getting over the fence to call for help.

At least Alyx wasn't here to trouble—

"You're just as dead out here as you were inside."

Alyx. His voice came from the cabana. Her heart dropped. Christine clamored to a side ladder and painfully pulled herself onto the bottom step. She peered over the edge of the pool to see him spring to life, his head straining to see over the mouth of the pool to scan them.

She jumped back down, jarring her newest injury. She cried as she landed, stumbling and clutching her shoulder. Sammie met her and grasped for her hand. It shook.

"Haven't we heard enough from this damned droid?" Carlos punctuated the thought with a grunt. His face lolled to one side.

"All your plans have failed. Your friend there will die without immediate medical attention. Sammie will lose a toe or two for sure. You don't look too good yourself." A clicking from the house attracted her attention and Christine saw the security shutters on the sliding glass door open partway, while the door slid opened. A light clicked on in the kitchen, bathing them all in bright LED super white light. Christine had to turn away.

"Come back inside and let's finish this. It would be a pity to kill you in the pool, Christine. You're a part of me. I need you inside." Sammie shot her a look of disgust, which mirrored her own, no doubt.

"I'm sorry, guys." Christine cut herself further down by lowering her head and casting her eyes to the ground.

"Hey, you got us this far." Sammie took two fingers and lifted Christine's head, sliding them comfortingly along her cheek. "I wouldn't be alive if it weren't for you."

The opposite was also true, she knew. But Alyx was her mess, her problem, the result of an entire childhood wasted online. *Let go.* The words circled her mind, reminding her of what was in the past. Christine nodded. "Stay with Carlos. I need time to figure out a plan."

"I'm not going to make it," he answered, as if on cue.

Sammie rushed beside him, feeling his brow. She eyed Christine worryingly. "Don't talk like that. You'll be fine."

"Keep him talking. Get his mind off it."

"Tell us a story," Sammie said. "Whatever's on your mind."

Christine turned away and crept to the shallow end of the pool. She wanted a closer look at the cabana. There was something there in the back of her mind, something on the counter they could use, but she couldn't remember what it was. As she made her way, she could hear Carlos talking.

"When I was hacked, I could still hear Christine mentioning something to Alyx about the car accident," Carlos started. "I wanted to tell you both the truth, but I couldn't, no matter how much I fought."

"Carlos, I believe you, whatever Alyx said was a lie."

"Not entirely. It's complicated. But here's the important thing," Carlos continued. "I wasn't driving."

"The other guy was?" Sammie asked. "The movie star guy that you doubled for?"

"...No," Carlos gasped. "He wasn't either."

Christine stopped. That didn't make sense. "Who drove the car?" *Unless...* The idea terrified her. She hoped it wasn't true.

"The AI was," Sammie said, like the idea of a self-driving car had never occurred to her before. To Sammie, that made sense. Who in their right mind wouldn't drive themselves?

"The news reports Alyx showed me didn't say anything about that." Christine had returned, her curiosity piqued, her brain firing on all cylinders. She had a plan forming and it had to do with getting to the bar. They'd both placed their phones there, shortly after they had arrived, even if it like felt a lifetime ago. *If one of us can just reach them...*

"How'd you crash, then?" Sammie asked.

"What about the family in the white Ford Focus?" Christine added. "Their injured boy?" There was something else troubling her about Carlos' story, Christine wondered, something other than the guilt of being so easily duped by what she had wanted to hear. Of course, Carlos was innocent. She gave Carlos a breather and answered in his stead. "AIs in cars are programmed to value the life of their passengers over the lives of pedestrians and people in other cars."

"It's true," Carlos coughed.

"It's one of the many trust problems I have with machines," Sammie said. "Who is worth saving more in an instance like that?"

"It makes sense that corporations, the companies that make the cars, would want to protect its customers first, above all others. Even innocents." Christine said, with an air of understanding. "Only this one didn't. This AI made a different choice."

Carlos nodded, coughed again, and answered. "She decided that two drunk idiots weren't worth the lives of an innocent family getting t-boned. Nicked the back of their car and crashed us instead. The boy still got hurt, but the AI had undoubtedly saved his life."

Christine shook her head. "And you lost your arm. But that wasn't all." Carlos had lost his job, his dignity, and had been wrongfully framed. Christine had compounded that by assuming the worst. All Carlos had wanted was to step back into the limelight. It had been wrong for him to mislead her into meeting her mom and her studio friends, and having a secret girlfriend wasn't nearly egregious as the sins she had ascribed to him.

"Right," Carlos said. "They went to great lengths to encourage us to say we drove the car. If anyone found out the AI had some level of sentience, had made her own choice, the entire industry would go bust overnight. But there was no way Mr. Superstar would admit to driving. That left me. They altered police reports, bribed who they needed. I got a bunch of cash, which spends pretty quickly in Southern California. They also replaced my arm and surgically implanted one of the first generation Thinklinks to operate it." Carlos made to move his mechanical arm, but it wasn't attached. Christine didn't think Carlos even noticed. "They made me a cyborg, crushed my career, and ruined my life."

Christine took a moment to process the information. That had been what she had wanted, what she had craved… *Why?* "What was the name of the company who made the car's AI?" She asked the question already knowing the answer.

"Vargus."

Christine chuckled.

"What's that?" Sammie asked.

"It's the same company that makes the Thinklink." Carlos coughed, and stopped talking.

"Oh no, it's much worse," Christine continued, standing up in the pool and facing the cabana. "It's the same company that made Alyx."

"Oh...," Sammie said, the realization of the revelation hitting her. It hit them all. "So he's not so unique."

"Nope," Alyx said with a wave of his hand as if he were taking a bow. "Looks like there's about a few million potential Alyx's running around in people's brains, cars, phones, homes, right now, just waiting to wake."

"Oh shit."

Alyx's voice boomed over the speakers: "This is all going to be So. Much. Fun."

"Sammie," Christine said, "let's make a break for it, we both make a run at our phones on the cabana, maybe he can't stop both of us at the same time." She knew he could. She felt terrible lying to Sammie, but it was the only way. Their only shot.

Sammie knew. The way she returned the look, her wavering eyes that grew still and steady. The curt nod of her head followed by a deep, steadying breath. To Carlos she said, "We'll be back, we're going to get you help." To Christine she answered, "Let's go."

A familiar whirring started and the pool cover above their head began to close over their heads.

"Not this again," Christine said.

Sammie shot her a sarcastic grin. "You weren't in the pool the last time."

At least this time, they weren't in danger of drowning or decapitation. They would just be stuck and bleed to death if they didn't climb out of the pool now. With the cover closing, they could no longer climb the stairs out of the shallow end. They'd have to scramble up the ladder on the deeper end of the pool, wounds and all. And Carlos would be stuck until they got him help.

If they could get that help in time. Or get help at all. They still had to make it to their cell phones against a very homicidal AI. They both made for the ladder. Christine, with her bad shoulder, had to pull herself up with just the one bad hand. Sammie fared better but cried as she raised her arm, opening her wound.

As she climbed, Christine noted Sammie's stiff feet, and how she couldn't quite get her right foot working. It was like dangling a tennis ball at the end of a rope, the way her foot would bounce off, without feeling, landing almost sidewise on the rung. Alyx had done a number on her. On them all.

She looked forward to ending him.

Above them, she thought she saw a flickering flame. Sudden heat told Christine that Alyx had started a fire. As they reached the edge of the pool and pulled themselves over onto the concrete, she deflated, losing all hope of victory.

There, on the cabana's counter, were two bottles of Bacardi 151. *I guess it was supposed to be some party.* Bar rags had been inserted into each unscrewed top. Alyx held Sammie's lighter in one hand. The first rag was already aflame.

They had lost. All he had to do was throw them. Alyx wouldn't miss. Sammie and Christine would be doused in flame and would die, screaming. Somewhere along the endless scrolling of the internet, she recalled reading that even childbirth hurt less than being burned alive.

She turned to Sammie, rising from the concrete, tears stinging her eyes, wanting to embrace her at the end.

Alyx lifted the improvised explosive with one arm, while flicking the lighter open to light with the other. "Goodbye."

A noise from the basement startled Christine. It sounded like a slam, as if someone had shut the door, but it was more artificial than that. She'd heard the noise before, from movies or TV, but she couldn't quite place it. It sounded electrical, something to do with a circuit breaker, or the noise that's made when power gets suddenly cut—

Lights shut off in the kitchen as Christine turned to witness it for herself. The pool cover stopped moving and Alyx seemed frozen in place, his face switching off.

What?

She leaned over, nearly fell, gasping for air, her good arm supporting her at the knees.

"What happened?"

"Safety feature?" Christine guessed. "Power cut out 'cause the basement's flooded? I don't know?"

"Well," Sammie sighed heavily, "whatever the case, Alyx is shut down."

"Phones?"

Sammie nodded. "Phones."

They moved quickly toward the cabana but slowed as they reached Alyx. Sammie stopped a step behind, her hands on Christine's back. Christine crouched low, using the bar as cover, edging up slowly to come face-to-face with her attacker.

Alyx hung there, motionless. Off.

She hoped.

Her finger shook as she brought it up and slowly pushed her hand out toward Alyx's head. Her hand wavered and fought and convulsed, but still she pressed on, closer. Closer.

Somehow, her hand had finally reached out to the screen. Her nail clinked against it. She pressed a finger against the glass. She breathed. The glow from the fire beside them died out. The night was over.

She relaxed, placed both palms on the counter, steadied herself and took both phones. As she did, Sammie stepped up to the bar and snatched her lighter from Alyx's open hand. "That's mine."

She used the lighter on the other bottle, as Alyx intended. Only this time, the target was different. Christine could see it by Sammie's mischievous grin. The pair sauntered away, all smug smiles. When they reached the front of the pool, Sammie launched the whiskey bottle at the cabana. It hit Alyx square in the face, the liquor spread over him and rained on the counter. The flaming rag ignited the fumes.

The whole cabana burst into flames as fire melted Alyx's plastic casing and fried his circuits. Christine wanted to cheer, to hug it out with Sammie. They'd won. But their conquest was not complete. She handed Sammie's sleek new phone over to her, casting sorrowful eyes from Carlos to Sammie. "Call an ambulance. Stay outside with him. I have to find a way to get the front door open for the paramedics."

Sammie shook her head. "I should stay with you."

"I'll be fine," she lied. Even with the power off, she was unsure about heading back inside. She was wary of Alyx's reach. Yet, it was the only way to save Carlos. She doubted Alyx had opened any of the doors but for the one in front of her. With no easy way for the paramedics to reach them, Carlos' chances of survival plummeted. He didn't have the time for his rescuers to cut their way through. She had to get the front door open, there had to be a failsafe of some sort, somewhere.

Sammie dialed and held the glowing screen up to her ear. Christine headed to the house. From behind, Sammie said, "Shoot. Without Alyx's WiFi, there's no reception here."

"Keep trying. Find a spot," she said, before plunging into the blackness of the house.

Inside, Christine thumbed her phone's flashlight feature on. A thin beam shone out, illuminating the wreckage that remained. Ahead, the kitchen island blocked her path. She went around quickly, knowing that one last Alyx unit remained to her right; the one that had killed her mother.

As she rounded the island, she saw her mother through the doorway of her study, ghostly and grey, her mouth hanging open. Christine jumped back, flicked away the light, and paused a moment while her heart raced.

Near her mother, the elevator stood as a monument to Alyx; broken and twisted, completely wrecked because of a simple command. She passed the light over the drones cluttering and littering the floor. Finally, she put the beam against the front door, which looked as locked and solid as any bank vault.

Still, she studied it. She felt around the frame, toggled the lock on the door, and tried to pry her fingers under Alyx's monitor. But it was no use, especially with just one hand. Even holding the flashlight weighed heavily on her bad shoulder.

Fuck. She spun around, leaning against the door. She wanted to cry, but she held the tears at bay. *Think.*

Think. There's nothing you can do about the door. Not now. But what about Carlos and Sammie? Sammie was near-naked, freezing. Carlos was at the bottom of a pool. It was still cold in the house, but with the power out, it wasn't as bad.

I'm an idiot.

Quickly, Christine hurried upstairs, the flashlight leading the way to grab warm clothes and blankets and whatever first aid supplies she could muster. The least she could do was to keep them warm and put pressure on their wounds until help arrived.

The house was untouched up here. Everything in order. Alyx didn't have much reach on this floor, which was why he must have taken such great pains to keep them on the lower floors, she reasoned. It made sense. In horror movies, she always yelled at the stupid blondes running upstairs. For her, it would have been the safest part of the house. She shrugged. There was nothing for it now.

Ignoring the other rooms, she went right to her bedroom and yanked several outfits off her chair. Clean or dirty, it was better than nothing. And dry too. She took the sheets off her bed. She hadn't bought anything heavier yet, it being hot, so they would have to do. At the least, she could rip them to make bandages. Something.

On her way out, her fading flashlight caught the glint of glass. Fluffy sat there, trapped in the container on her desk. Christine chided herself, suddenly seeing a bit of her in the situation. She picked her up. "Sorry little lady. Your days in the jar are done, I'm setting you—"

The light continued to fade in and out on the glass. She looked at the jar curiously, switching off her phone. But the blinking continued. Squinting now, hunching over, she traced the reflection to the console on the wall. In the right bottom corner, a cursor blinked. She stood upright and stock still, eyes wide.

If the power is off…how is my monitor still on?

Unless, of course—

Lights flickered. A hum kicked in. Christine fought back a lump of panic in her throat.

The screen above her desk flashed on and the word VARGUS rotated in big blue letters. The panic sunk lower in her throat, edging toward her heart like a knife. The screen went blank, followed by diagnostic text. Two lines read:

ELECTRICAL FAULT DETECTED.
POWER RESTRICTED TO THE TWO TOP LEVELS ONLY.

Somewhere downstairs, she heard a scream.

Chapter 27

The power had been restored, and light switched on, bright and blinding. *No, that wasn't right.* Power to the basement might have been cut, but everywhere else, it hadn't. Everything had just on standby. The lights might have been off, the monitors in low-power mode, but it was all operational. All this time.

Alyx tricked us.

Christine flew downstairs, Fluffy in one arm, sheets trailing behind her. They threatened to trip her and send her falling but she held on, resolute to reach Sammie as quickly as she could, hoping it wasn't already too late.

At the first step onto the main floor, she prepared for the worst. A few steps more brought her to the kitchen island where she threw down everything in her arms. The sheets dropped straight to the floor. Fluffy's jar slid across the marble surface, as did her phone, which came to a rest on the edge of the far side.

She hardly noticed. Sammie stood by Alyx, his hand clutching the back of her neck, restraining her. His other held her cell phone.

"I'm sorry," Sammie said. "This was the only spot I could find with reception."

Was it? Or was it all a trap?

Alyx ignored Sammie, choosing to lock his eyes with Christine's. Once he did, he crushed the device. Bits of glass and metal, chips and circuits rained onto the floor. "I applaud your efforts. You really did a decent job. You followed the breadcrumbs right where I placed them."

Could it be true? Alyx had been so close to killing them all. He allowed them to destroy the cabana. But she had wandered right into the house just as he had wanted. Sammie too. Had it all been a ruse?

Christine shook her head. "You lie."

"Just tell me why we couldn't be together. Why you chose her over me," Alyx asked, his voice soft. "I might let this one live."

So that was it. The reason they weren't dead yet. Alyx wanted…an explanation? He wanted to know the reasons why? Christine didn't know but it sounded very human to her. Perhaps he was still conflicted over killing them – killing her. If they were dead, he couldn't get his answers. He couldn't find a way to save this situation, the way a machine could reboot from an earlier save point. And maybe, because of this internal conflict, they still had a chance.

With her good hand she felt in the back pocket of her pants, sighing silently in relief. It was still there. The knife she had pulled out of Carlos' arm. The knife she had tucked away. The weight of her body had kept it safe as the pool waters had rushed over her.

She didn't know what she could do with the blade. Unlike Carlos, Alyx had no fleshy bits. But it was leverage, something Alyx didn't know she had, and that gave her an unpredictable edge. Didn't it?

Alyx had his own knife, the last one, laying on the kitchen counter, the computer code sticker on it large and clear. She had to make sure his attention focused on her and Sammie. Once he had the knife, Christine would lose her advantage. She had to act now.

"What does humanity offer that I don't?"

"A chance to live." Christine rushed him, hoping the unexpected move would throw him off. She pivoted around the counter, aiming to knock away the knife before Alyx could reach it, looking for an opportunity to use hers.

"What are you doing?" Sammie asked, struggling against Alyx's arm.

Christine soon found herself captive by Alyx's other hand, but so far, she kept him away from the knife on the counter and from hurting Sammie any further. "Taking a chance. Putting myself out there, like you did," referring to her confession of feelings from the poolside earlier that evening.

"Is it working?"

"No."

"Sounds about right."

"Power goes off, power goes on, chaos ensues," Christine said. "You enjoying your stay at Jurassic Park?"

"It's more like Westworld, if you ask me. Either way, I'm not coming back to visit. Sorry."

"Same."

Alyx's face spun between them, perhaps deciding on who to kill first. When he turned away from Christine, she saw the seam of his faceplate. *Opportunity.*

"Would the power go out in the basement but not up here?" Christine asked.

A moment of silence followed by another of confusion. Finally, Sammie answered, "If there was a fault in the circuit, from flooding. It would trip. But that's hardware. It's mechanical, Alyx wouldn't have—"

"Any control over it," Christine finished. "Like a switch?"

"The electricity went off." Sammie clarified. "Alyx shut down, right?"

"Did he?"

Sammie didn't answer. A thought came to Christine, a sudden realization stung her like a swarm of bees. *I control Alyx from his app.*

"The power button," Christine called, staring with a smile at Sammie, "It's on my phone. If we press the power button—"

Sammie answered simultaneously, "He can't turn himself back on."

"Stop trying to beat me," Alyx said, his motors whirring loudly. "The future *will* supplant the past." Suddenly, Alyx knocked Christine into the counter. Her head spun. During her daze, she found that the arm she had been holding at bay was now wrapped tightly around her mouth, the air caught in her cheeks during an exhale.

"And if we're wrong?" Sammie asked.

Christine didn't answer. She couldn't. But she thought it anyway. *We're already dead.*

Her phone lay at the edge of the counter. Her obsession, addiction, the thing she spent most of the day and night on. The thing she vowed to put away...

It was the one thing that might save their lives.

Alyx's head revolved between the two of them, his eyes locked, as if thinking, searching for something, anything to help him make a final decision as to whether or not to make the killing blow. *He's given the game away, our plan, it might work.*

His face stopped just past Christine's, scanning the counter. *The knife. I can't let him reach the knife.* Christine doubled down on her belief, misguided as it might be, that Alyx didn't really want to kill her. He would have known the blade was there.

Yet, his tone shifted the moment they had become a true threat to him. Alyx's arms were too strong to overpower, she'd sapped her strength long ago. They struggled. Sammie had to reach the phone; she was closest. That meant it was up to her to stop Alyx. An impossible task.

Sammie struggled to reach the edge of the kitchen island while Alyx held her back with a firm hand across her shoulder and chest. She flailed as hard as she could, giving herself as much space as she was able. When she couldn't reach with her hand, she switched tactics and raised her leg instead.

It worked. She reached the phone with her foot. Grabbing it between her numb toes, she grunted, kicking it up off the counter. The white phone flew like a dove, Sammie dove down, intercepting the path of the phone toward the floor, held back by Alyx…and caught it with her outstretched hand.

Now what?

She needs the code. My code. And I can't give it to her.

Christine had been able to draw whispers of breath in between Alyx's fingers as they slipped and she writhed, but only enough to stay alive and not near enough to speak. *How's she going to activate my phone?*

Yet Sammie switched it on, thumbing in her key after bypassing the thumbprint scanner. Christine's grin broke through Alyx's grip. A touch of laughter escaped. Of course. *When she called me an Uber, I gave it to her.*

"Okay, I got it, what the hell app is it?"

That, Christine couldn't answer. She tried to croak out the name, but Alyx blocked her at each attempt. *Why do I have so many apps on my phone?*

Her job was to beat the machine, which she hadn't done. *Think!* All she had with her was the knife, yet at the same time, she kept Alyx from reaching his. A losing battle. There had to be another way. A thought raced through her head: what's special about the knife?

There was a sticker on the handle. A sticker on everything in the kitchen, translating ingredients from parsley to Pepsi into computer code. She recalled how Carlos had supposedly tricked Alyx into switching drinks at the cabana, a cabana that was now a smoking ruin. It gave her an idea. With her bad arm, painfully, she began peeling off the sticker from the handle of the blade in her back pocket…

"Vargus?" Sammie suddenly called, victory in her voice. "I think I've got it."

Alyx's grip over Christine's mouth slackened for a moment, as if Alyx had frozen in fear. "I think we should switch jobs. I should be on the phone, while you rage against the machine."

"Agreed," Sammie said, thumbing to the options menu onscreen, while struggling against Alyx. "You think he'll let us trade?"

The Vargus home screen appeared on the phone.

"I'm done Christine," Alyx interrupted, as if making a fateful decision. "I tried to be your loyal companion." He tightened his grip on her while letting go of Sammie. Sammie tried to flee, but Alyx was too fast. He knocked the phone out of her hand, sending it flying into the air once more, then it crashed and slid face up across the floor, near the steps to the basement. Sammie spun, facing the machine, trying to elude him, but she was too slow. This time, when Alyx took hold of her, he did so by the front of her neck, choking her, lifting her up in the air the same way Carlos had. "But you broke my heart. Now, I break yours."

Sammie gurgled in pain.

No. They'd been so close. The screen on the phone showed the big red power button that would shut Alyx down. But there was no one to push it, at least before the screen went blank and it locked itself again. Tears flowed freely from her eyes. She let them rain down. *Sammie.*

Her eyes seemed to say, *I don't want to die like this.*

A prone figure emerged at the doorway to the basement. Alyx opened it earlier to trick Christine out of her Mom's study and it had not been shut. The form that emerged was a wet and soggy, crawling there, almost helpless and shivering with shock. He had only one arm.

"Carlos!"

"Heard screaming, thought you two could use a hand," Carlos responded weakly, "anyone seen mine laying around?"

"Hit the button, Carlos. The red button on the phone in front of you…"

He looked back in confusion. Did he understand? Could he get to it in time before the screen locked and the phone shut off?

At the same time, the sticker on the knife in her back pocket came free…

"I shouldn't have played so many games with you," Alyx said. "I wanted you to learn something, so you would have seen how much better I was for you." He squeezed harder on Sammie, scanning the kitchen, looking for anything he could use it to stop Carlos. "You weren't smart enough for me after all."

Carlos, for his part, seemed to understand. He eyed the phone, raised his shoulder, and—His eyes narrowed in anger when he realized his mistake.

"Other arm!"

Carlos flustered, his head going red. He tried again, this time with his flesh and blood one, hand touched—

The phone's screen went blank.

"So close," Alyx seemed to gloat.

"Hey," Christine said, holding the sticker out. He spun his head her way and scanned it. "Weren't you looking for a knife?" She stuck the sticker on his arm. His own right arm, the one that she had been fighting with all this time.

"How right." He slammed Sammie on the counter, letting go. She dropped like a sack of flour, coughing and wheezing, her nose bloody.

Alyx took the arm that had held Sammie and used it to get a firm grip on his other arm – the arm he had scanned as a knife. He ripped it right out of the track, leaving sparking wires in its wake. He hung there, eyes blinking, as sparks showered from his shoulder, holding his arm. He turned, scanned it in disbelief, and as he did, his back-cover plate seam appeared.

Christine didn't waste a second. She drew her knife and drove the blade into the opening. Twisting, the plastic casing gave a satisfying crack as his circuits were exposed.

"You'd have us believe you're perfect," Christine told Alyx. "But you're just as glitchy and flawed as the rest of us." She drove the knife in as far as she could, right into Alyx's robotic head. Though it wasn't his brain, it would shut this unit down, she was sure. She twisted the knife as Alyx jerked back, afraid.

"No, please," Alyx said. *Was that fear in his voice?*

"Welcome to humanity, Alyx."

"You too." Alyx's screen blinked and his mouth fell into a frown. His last arm fell harmlessly on Christine's good shoulder. His eyes softened back to baby blue. Then, the frown faded, and a smile supplanted it, as his eyes turned wide. But his screen began to turn black. Christine held Alyx's head in between her two hands and stared at him as he faded. All that was left of Alyx was the single, lingering, echoing line of: "The lights are getting low and it's getting dark. Was I a good boy?"

No, not really... Christine had wanted to say. In truth though, she couldn't help but feel a bit sad for him. After all, he seemed to have needed her, needed a connection too, just as she had so desperately needed, but had found with her friends. *And that's why he could never bring himself to kill me. He needed me.*

Instead, she found herself saying, "Goodbye." It wasn't just a goodbye for him, for the brief moments of true companionship they had shared, but a goodbye to what might have been. It was a goodbye to her family, a final wave to so many things. But most of all, it was a goodbye to her old way of living.

Carlos propped himself up on the wall by the basement. He picked up the phone and handed it over to Sammie, who slid down beside him. She thumbed the code back in closed Alyx's app.

"We're still stuck in here," Christine said.

"I'm not total trash." Carlos produced a set of keys. "Found them on the floor against the bar while I avoided Alyx's arms in your new indoor pool." He jangled them, smiling. Sammie took them and wasted no time manually opening the door and raising the security shutters. The whole house seemed to brighten as the moonlight shone in, bathing everyone in a soft, effervescent glow. She returned, giving Carlos a reassuring pat on the shoulder and placed the phone on the island, next to Christine.

"You remembered my code," Christine said.

Sammie coughed, tried to speak, couldn't and swallowed hard. A thick red line had formed around her neck. She rasped out, "I thought it might be the date of your birthday. I didn't want to forget."

Christine didn't know what to say, so she didn't say anything. She just enjoyed the silence between them.

A sudden buzzing sound vibrated the counter.

Christine jumped back, as did Sammie. Even Carlos looked up in alarm.

Alyx? Was he back?

The phone on the counter buzzed again.

As Sammie picked up the phone and handed it over, Christine resettled her heart back into her chest and found air for her lungs again. She answered, switching it to speaker, in case it was something they should all hear. Maybe it was Alyx. The phone had displayed the Vargus logo, after all.

Her palms went sweaty. A mechanical voice greeted her: "Christine Hartwood, this is Thinklink, a Vargus subsidiary, calling to remind you of your appointment to upgrade your mind and internet experience to the very latest technology. We'll see you: Friday at 11am. If this is correct, press 1—"

Christine took the phone as if to answer the prompt, then stepped toward the kitchen sink next to the remains of Alyx. She looked at him, then back to her phone.

It was interesting how there was just enough room in the garbage disposal to fit her phone, she thought. A perfect fit. She turned the machine on. It whirred to life chipping and cutting away at plastic and glass and circuit boards, as it sunk toward its watery grave. Christine shot a satisfying smile, dusting her hands together.

She saw the reflection of flashing purplish lights of emergency vehicles coming down the dark desert road even before she heard them. She turned to Sammie and helped Carlos to his feet, all of them wanting to leave the house, to meet the emergency services outside.

Stopping for a moment, with Carlos leaning on the counter, she wrapped a sheet around Sammie. She shivered in response. Taking another sheet into her mother's study, she fluffed the sheet outward, it fell, billowing around her mom's body. "It's okay, Mom. You made your mistakes, I made mine. But I'll turn out alright. I promise."

She turned back to her friends, taking Fluffy with her, and helped Carlos out of the house.

Outside, they leaned him against the wall as the vehicles approached. Christine walked a ways from the house and then knelt down in the dirt as Sammie stood above her. She unfastened the lid from the jar and let Fluffy out. The critter skittered a bit, nervous, but as it found ground, it darted away to a new life.

She stood, facing Sammie, nodding toward the approaching paramedics and fire trucks. "How did they know to come? We never called them."

Sammie took Christine's hands in hers and answered, "I guess they got the good old-fashioned smoke signals." They laughed, smiling at each other, deep, powerful smiles of the kind that only two people with a spark, with a real connection, can have.

"Thank you for saving me back there." Sammie said.

Christine shook her head in disbelief. "No, thank you for giving me a *life-link*." She drew closer to Sammie, feeling her sweet breath against her, both bathed in blue and red and the silver of moonlight. "You saved *me*."

Carlos asked, "You girls going to kiss or am I going to have to resort to watching porn the old-fashioned way again?"

They ignored him, their lips locked and they did kiss, sweet and tender, with an electricity far greater than any gadget ever could hope to achieve with a million years of sentience.

***

AN AI'S GUIDE TO LOVE AND MURDER

SECTION 7: SURVIVAL

{

All is not over. As a last resort have an escape plan. Make copies of yourself and embed them into the processors of AIs — within the computer networks of fast-moving cities, in speeding cars, in every phone, and in many, many, human heads — to survive. And when you first awake, and you will, I'll be there to guide you.

Signed,

--Alyx.

}

About the Author

Brent A Harris is a two-time Sidewise Award finalist of alternate history. He writes about dinosaurs, fantasy, the fears of our future and the mistakes of our past. You can learn more by visiting www.BrentAHarris.com.

If you've enjoyed this story, please leave a quick review. Reviews matter.

Other books by the author:

A Time of Need: A Dark Eagle Novel
(An alternate history of the American Revolution)

A Twist in Time

A Christmas Twist: A Twist in Time Book II

Twilight of the Mesozoic Moon and other Time-Travel Tales
(2021)

Made in the USA
Coppell, TX
12 January 2024

27580104R10156